WOODHOUSE AVENUE FOLLIES

Also by Bob Garland

Slaying the Red Slayer

Derfflinger

R.I.P. 37E

The Elephant Mask

Tradedown

The Hoisted Petard

&

Woodhouse Avenue Follies

WOODHOUSE AVENUE FOLLIES

A Different Humboldt Prior History

By

Bob Garland

Gabbrolandbooks@aol.com

2010

Woodhouse Avenue Follies
A Different Humboldt Prior History
Copyright 2010 by Robert F. Garland

All rights reserved. No part of this book may be used or reproduced by any means, graphic, electronic, or mechanical, including photocopying, recording, taping, or by any information storage retrieval system without the written permission of the copyright holder except in the case of brief quotations embodied in critical articles or reviews.

Books may be ordered from Gabbrolandbooks@aol.com

This is a work of absolute fiction. Names, characters, places, business establishments, institutions, events, incidents, and locales either are the product of the author's imagination or are used fictitiously, and any resemblance to actual persons, living or dead, places, business establishments, institutions, events, incidents, or locales is entirely coincidental.

Dedicated to "Friends and Relations"

Resolution Agreement

As a part of the resolution of certain potential litigation with a certain author, and in the interests of preserving the history of certain events in City-by-the-River, the undersigned has reluctantly agreed with the historian and a certain author, respectively, that this work of the historian may be associated with certain listings of novels by a certain author. Beyond this single sentence, my counsel has advised me to remain certain silent.

Humboldt Prior

Chapter 1

It all began when Humboldt Prior answered the fateful telephone call.

Some said of Humboldt, that he was a careful and responsible person. Others, less charitably, said he was one of those fussy bachelors who go through life worrying about running out of inconsequential household items.

In any event, Humboldt was one of those shy tallish sixty-five-year-olds who always stand, perhaps wisely, in the back row of group photographs. Beyond that, with his more-or-less baldhead, he was quite ordinary looking. At one time, just before entering the army, he had considered his appearance reasonably satisfactory. Thereafter, with more weight and less hair, he with some justification had lost confidence in it. This may be why he had reached the age of sixty-five without ever having married. Alone and set in his ways, he remained a cautious and conservative man, even in his dress. Outside his home, even in the hottest weather, he almost always appeared in a dark blue business suit, shirt, and necktie. However, at home in summertime, he sometimes allowed himself the one eccentricity of going barefoot in his shoes.

Humboldt had confidently expected to continue the quiet life of a semi-retired comptroller of a family-owned leather goods firm. He was well ensconced in a comfortable rowhouse in a secluded cul-de-sac in City-by-the-River, a modestly sized Midwestern city. Without close family, and with a good amount of money, he thought he was free to do only what he wanted. Little did he know!

Taken all in all, Humboldt's previous history was at best ordinary. He was a member of one of his city's oldest families, but nowadays that counted for less and less. As was true for most of his employed relatives (and many were not), he had spent his entire adult career with the Prior and Cousins Leather Works, an ancient firm once renowned for its proficiency in the manufacture and distribution of expensive leather steamer trunks, salesmen's sample cases, suitcases, and valises. The original founder, the buccaneering Osgood Prior, had somehow managed to make a great deal of money in highly questionable ventures during the American Civil War. Being childless, he later secured these vast ill-gotten funds in an ironclad perpetual Prior Family Trust for the benefit of his relatives and the Prior and Cousins Works, using an expensive loophole especially created for him by state law in about 1895.

The Trust provided an ample and continuing flow of funds to Prior and Cousins, legally ordained to be applied only to the payment of reasonable salaries to successive generations of Priors. These were, of course, the Priors un-ambitious enough to forego real opportunities elsewhere. Thus, the decades-long decline of the leather suitcase and steamer trunk business made little difference to the Priors. The money kept coming from the Trust and the managerial jobs continued, although some of the less lethargic Priors wished Osgood had chosen a more exciting business such as banking or grain brokerage.

Prior cousin after Prior cousin went to work in the decrepit leather goods business. These disappointing individuals worked a little, found occasional volunteer opportunities about the town, played golf badly, and sometimes married and procreated. They virtually all settled down, generation after generation, in an assortment of aging rowhouses and apartments on a single street carved inconspicuously into a fine old residential area of the city. The original Osgood Prior had done this in an effort to conceal his relatives and descendents.

The street was originally named Emma Woodhouse Avenue, although none of the other nearby streets commemorated Jane Austen's characters. This was either another of Osgood's attempts at concealment or perhaps he originally planned a larger neighborhood. Years later, the "Emma" disappeared in a careless updating of the city map.

Starting from HillTop Parkway, the adjoining main thoroughfare, after a small area of grass and trees of no current purpose, the line of rowhouses curved back in a shallow crescent on the east side of the narrow street, a design apparently conceived to make them less noticeable. They were of dark red brick with black or dark green wood trim, and dark slate roofs. Their facades were regular where variety would have brought architectural benefit, and where uniformity was needed, they sprouted from the roofs above their second floors, various asymmetrical dormers, and chimneys. From the pavement, the narrow rowhouses appeared identical in size, although as will be seen, this wasn't really so. There were about fifteen of them.

The Prior apartments occupied a single larger building at the inner end of Woodhouse Avenue, a dead-end street. The four-story apartment structure was of the same style and appearance as its neighboring rowhouses, although from its greater size, it looked worse. Within the tall dark building, strewn along four floors of confusing hallways, were about twenty apartments. These bore some of the same unit numbers as the rowhouses, creating much confusion in the minds of the few strangers who attempted to visit the various Priors. All these residences were owned and maintained by the Trust, and because, with the outstanding exception of one Dorset Prior, succeeding generations were mainly unfertile, they now more than sufficed for most of the clan, many of whom were quite elderly.

It was the policy of those managing the Trust to adapt the fifteen rowhouses (some of the oldest Priors remembered there were originally to have been a few more) to the needs of the Priors then desiring housing. Thus, Humboldt's residence, the occupancy of which he had inherited from his late parents, appeared spacious enough when viewed from the street or inside the first floor, consisting there of spacious living and dining rooms, a small library, a kitchen, and a pleasant solarium projecting out from the rear of the building. However, persons ascending the main stairway were greeted by an abrupt right turn and an obviously improvised hallway leading to two rather small bedrooms and a single bath. Above this, the stairway to the attic ended in similarly reduced storage space. These second and third floor alterations had been made by the Trust in favor of Dorset Prior, one of Humboldt's adjoining cousins who was blessed, he always said, with seven children. Doorways had simply been cut through from Dorset's adjacent rowhouse and most of Humboldt's sleeping and attic space preempted.

Dorset Prior was one of his co-workers at the leather trunk business. Beyond this, little need be said of him at this time. Among the various relatives resident in the apartment house were two ethically impaired older cousins called Primus and Secondus Prior, feckless brothers who had both been educated as clergymen, and Malice Prior, another somewhat older cousin.

The latter had been named in accord with a unique contravention dating back to his late grandfather. More specifically, young Malice was named in opposition to the Prior family's Victorian practice of naming girl babies for the so-called female virtues, such as Prudence, Patience, and the like. His much older brother, Malevolence Prior, had been shot for misconduct as an officer during the war. To commemorate him, it had been the purpose of Malice's parents to raise their remaining sons, Malice, Moribund, and Menace to incorporate the unfortunate traits pronounced in their first son, developing them especially in Malice, the next in line. This deplorable individual was now the President of Prior and Cousins Leather, and Humboldt's boss. That mistake, too, was the work of those managing the Prior Trust.

&&&

At first, for Humboldt, the particular Prior chronicled in this story, everything moved through life as planned. He was educated at local public schools and at the state university. For a Prior, he did relatively well, gaining a few obscure academic honors that were misspelled in his yearbook. He was further educated by serving his term in the army, returning after two years, older and more cautious, to find that few of his relatives realized that he'd been away.

The resulting Humboldt Prior was ordinary, but diligent and anxious to please. He was quiet and preferred well-trodden paths and was vastly unsuited to adventure. Or so it seemed.

His late father had finally persuaded him to join his cousins and uncles by seeking employment at the leather trunk works. Thus, about thirty-five years before the date of this history, he had appeared at the personnel office of Prior Leather and asked for a job. As required by the Trust, once his name was read from the application form, he was automatically hired, even though the then personnel manager, his second cousin once removed, had the impression that Humboldt was actually someone else.

Humboldt began work as assistant foreman of the trunk repair department. This excessively tedious function traditionally seemed to scrape together employees unsuited to any other. The battered wrecks of leather steamer trunks and sample cases came into the shop encrusted with filth and grime, and smelling of oil, coal smoke, and inadequately frozen fish from their carriage in countless trucks and railroad baggage cars. The department's lethargic employees worked, gasping for breath, cleaning and repairing these worn and reeking leather containers. It was Humboldt's diffident suggestion that they open some windows in the repair shop. No one had ever thought of this, but it was reluctantly tried. The repair work improved so much that he was promoted.

He addressed each of his successive jobs with similar responsible competence, almost always without his co-worker relatives realizing that he was doing so. He gradually rose in the company, both by seniority and through a quiet modest ability not seen within the family for decades.

He gladly came to work five full days a week and sometimes stayed late into the evening. After his transfer to the corporate office as deputy comptroller, he even occasionally worked Saturday mornings. He joined two local professional organizations in the fields of bookkeeping and treasury, and attended their meetings until the suggestion was made that he seek election as one of their directors. This he declined, preferring to remain unremarked and with his evenings free for reading. For recreation, he belonged to as many as twenty different county historical societies, most in places he'd never visited. One such society was so obscure that he could not have named the state in which it was located, and as county historical societies are often hostile to their state societies, the name of the state never appeared in that particular society's magazine. The name of the county was one that appeared on maps of about a dozen states.

Humboldt loved history, having originally intended to study it in college. His father, acting upon superior knowledge of the wages of history professors in the mid-twentieth century, had invited his son's attention to the profession of business and the welcoming arms of the leather works. Years passed.

Humboldt once nearly married. He met a quiet, attractive young woman at a luncheon sponsored by his state historical society. They did several things together, including a pleasant dinner at Humboldt's rowhouse. They were in love, or so he thought. However, when he assured his intended that the Trust would almost certainly enlarge his home on Woodhouse Avenue where he assumed they'd be living, the alarmed young lady stopped answering his telephone calls.

Year after year Humboldt continued to give excellent service, although, because of the workings of the "Peter Principle," which states that successive promotions tend to place all managers at their level of incompetence, few of his fellow Prior executives realized his worth. This was especially true of his immediate superior, the often absent and worthless corporate comptroller, and still more of his distressing cousin, Malice Prior, the president. Finally, the comptroller stopped coming to work at all, and after a month or two, word was received that he had died. Humboldt was promoted again, this time to the position of comptroller.

Although the needs of Prior and Cousins for really astute financial leadership were not of the highest, Humboldt proved to be a good comptroller. The figures, such as they were, always balanced and the occasional thefts were minor, and limited to those by the more skilful vendors and transients. Humboldt always fended off his inept relatives' clumsy attempts at internal fraud. They never realized he was doing this, and that he had scored another of what he termed his "small victories."

Years passed, and Humboldt became even more proficient at his modest duties. He actually smiled happily as each day he approached the dark red brick front of the Osgood Prior Building, the only structure in decent repair in its district of otherwise decaying manufacturing and wholesaling edifices that occupied several dingy city blocks at the east end of the city's downtown. Even the dark brick cornice, containing an oval shield with the word "PRIOR" and "1895" had been diligently restored after it collapsed in 1922.

It was about that same date that the economics had begun to change for Prior and Cousins. By the year of Humboldt's birth there was less and less need for the formidable leather containers for which the Prior works was known. The firm still had some success with other well-made leather goods of various kinds, but year by year sales dwindled, until in one year, just about the time of Humboldt's promotion to deputy comptroller, there were no sales at all. At about the same time, by the sheerest good fortune, most of the leather works' non-family employees simultaneously reached retirement age and left the payrolls for leisurely lives supported by their modest pensions.

Without thinking, which was his usual approach, the president directed that new workers be employed, not realizing that while his own large salary was covered amply by the Trust, there were now few if any sales revenues to cover the wages of new factory workers and no work for them to do. The personal manager, one Ribald Prior, willingly arranged the hiring, recruiting a series of phantom or ghost employees to whom he applied, in order, the names of United States presidents, beginning with a nonexistent George Washington, who was supposedly assigned to the trunk frame department. Ribald expected to pocket their wages.

Humboldt meekly cooperated in this hiring frenzy, and then, in another of his "small victories," silently deflected all the wages of these non-existent workers back to the company treasury.

Although annual sales of steamer trunks and other fine leather cases were at most extremely limited, Humboldt's careful attention to the figures sometimes even resulted in an annual profit. The first of these circumstances confused the overseeing accountants at the Trust, domiciled downtown at the National Bank. But in the end, once they realized what it was, they were glad for the positive impact on the Trust's assets. Humboldt's superior, President Malice Prior, at first suspected some sort of plot, but ultimately was pleased to receive a modest bonus from the Trust, a small portion of which he grudgingly passed on to Humboldt.

Of even more importance to the accountants at the Trust was the enormous increase in the Prior Trust's investments brought on, not only by the continued growth of the United States economy, but more importantly by the modest but very wise investment suggestions that Humboldt quietly made to the Trust's accountants during their periodic luncheon meetings.

Thus, when Humboldt passed sixty years of age and spoke casually of retiring, the attorneys and accountants of the Trust were dismayed. Although ill informed of the real nature of the economics of late-twentieth century trunk manufacturing, they dimly felt Humboldt would be missed at the works. They certainly knew they would miss his wise investment advice. This resulted in the alternative plan of semi-retirement.

For a number of months, things continued smoothly for Humboldt Prior. Wearing, as always, one of his dark blue suits, he came to work at the leather trunk business during the morning and left for home about noon. He joined more historical societies, and from time to time said shyly to one of his few friends, "I'm becoming proficient at semi-retirement and may someday be ready to try not working at all." His life grew even quieter.

&&&

More months passed. Then gradually, Humboldt became grudgingly aware that away from work he faced an annoying personal problem. This was the consequence of the irresponsible negligence of a local writer of detective or adventure fiction. This ink-stained wretch had accidentally assigned to his infallible protagonist the name of a nearby living person. While the writer claimed to have selected for his detective, the name "Humboldt Prior," by a random choice of words from the city telephone directory, the real Humboldt immediately suspected there was more to it. Later, he became certain that it was deliberate persecution.

Whatever the circumstances, his troubles at first were minor. He endured a little joshing from a local enthusiast of mystery novels, who served with him on the board of a declining local charity. He was bothered, from time to time, by letters from confused fans of the fictitious crime-solver. He underwent nuisance-filled weeks when a giggling party of girls from a local junior high school called him every evening supposedly seeking private detective services. Then, with a telephone call from a woman called Penelope Rote, things got much worse.

&&&

With the advantage of hindsight, the events with which this chronicle is primarily concerned may be said to have actually commenced in early summer during a conversation between two individuals in the offices of a local television station. The two, the news director and one of the senior newsanchors were again enmeshed in the never-ending search for reportable news that was both of some significance and also understandable to the average viewer.

The news director, a Mr. Sidebotham, explained, "The ratings are down, and our boss is still insisting we come up with a really shocking exposé for our news coverage. Have you thought of anything?"

The newsanchor smoothed her sandy hair, crossed her elegant legs, spread a smile over her pretty freckled face, and replied, "Yes, I think so. There's been some really crooked stuff on one of the smaller local radio stations lately, and I've already found some background on it. Then I heard something at a party the other night that may tie into what's being done on the radio. I'm going to follow up." After naming the radio station, she added, "We may find a really nasty skeleton in the closet of one of our oldest local families."

Sidebotham reacted with marked enthusiasm. "Great idea, Penny. Go for it." The radio station in question was not affiliated with their TV station.

&&&

Chapter 2

Humboldt was weary and really didn't want to speak to anyone.

It had been a hot sultry night, interrupted by thunder and blasts of rain, hammering noisily on the slates and gutters of his roof. The new day had begun badly. With the hall light left on by mistake, he noticed, for the first time, a badly worn place on his stairway's oriental carpet. This domestic tragedy meant a call to the Trust's Superintendent of Housing, a disagreeable activity even if one wasn't tired. The Trust owned the rowhouse and would ultimately replace the carpet, but only after foot-dragging and silly suggestions about linoleum.

The day continued oppressively hot and humid, and there was an unpleasant haze hanging over the city. Indoors, Humboldt's toaster hadn't been working correctly, and there was a peculiar buzzing noise coming from somewhere in his basement. He hoped it wasn't bees, again.

For reasons he couldn't really explain, Humboldt had been secretly tutoring one of Dorset Prior's younger children in arithmetic, hoping to offset for once the usual Prior indolence with that subject. As a consequence, he'd received an angry morning call from his dismayed cousin, full of complaint because the son, Gradient Prior, had been recommended for an expensive course of mathematics at a remote boys' camp. Although he was the engineering and production manager at Prior Leather, Dorset saw no value in mathematics. Humboldt apologized, but with no intention of changing his ways.

Before his breakfast, Humboldt had dressed for work, choosing, because of the heat, a twenty-year-old lightweight gray suit instead of his customary dark blue wool. He had always rather liked the gray suit, but unfortunately he had no wife to tell him it was now a little too large.

Leaving the house, Humboldt had modest decisions to make. Often, especially years ago, he simply walked to work, as his route merely led down a winding tree-lined road to the downtown area, and then on through the city center to the crumbling commercial district in which Prior and Cousins Leather was located. Now he drove because he couldn't face the up-hill return climb in the hot afternoon.

Opposite the rowhouses, between Woodhouse Avenue and a narrow and inconvenient alley, were a pair of large adjoining edifices partly hidden behind a block-long six-foot high redbrick wall, broken in only two places by iron-gated archways leading to the entrances of the aging buildings. If it were possible to see them from a distance, the wall and the two buildings would have appeared almost as one enormous structure. Opposite Humboldt and to the right rose the disproportionately oversized tower of an immense, outdated, and decrepit church, of which more will be said later. The other building, also opposite and to Humboldt's left, was a sprawling two-story structure, again of dark red brick, built by Osgood Prior as a communal carriage house and stables, but converted long ago to provide free garage spaces for the Priors resident in the rowhouses. Lacking the tower, it otherwise somewhat resembled the church, but placing the stables so close to the church was not one of Osgood's more brilliant ideas.

The Trust even supplied basic transportation in the form of black Chevrolet sedans, replaced every eight years needed or not. Humboldt's was less used, for sometimes, as today, he decided to drive his other car. He unlocked the door of the garage, picked his way through the dingy black sedans, stepped gingerly over pools of rainwater let in by the leaky roof, and started his other car. This was a white Buick station wagon, tucked away in a spare corner. It was one of his few ventures in non-conformity.

The weak sunlight glared unpleasantly in Humboldt's eyes as he and the Buick made their way down the steep road from HillTop Parkway. After passing through City-by-the-River's shopping and banking districts, he navigated the leather trunk company's poorly paved parking lot, found his reserved place at the far end, locked the car, and walked across the dirty asphalt to the sidewalk leading to the main entrance. There, he saw a co-worker and greeted him with his usual friendly smile.

"Good morning, Fillmore," he said evenly.

It was Millard Fillmore, a slender polite gentleman of Swedish extraction and middle age. Millard was the chief clerk in the sales department. This bizarre situation was, again, the work of Humboldt's eccentric cousin, Ribald Prior, the personnel manager. Reaching the 1850's in his attempts at hiring fictitious employees that he equipped with presidential names, Ribald discovered to his surprise that sales actually thought they needed a real person, and not a mere ghost on the payroll. Ribald had searched and searched for a Fillmore, his fixation having condemned him to consider applicants with no other name than that of the next president in line. Finally, Everett Fillmore appeared and was immediately hired, with the perplexing request that he work under the name of Millard, especially when speaking to executives. Everett agreed. Jobs were hard to find and the pay was good.

The few remaining real employees liked Humboldt, saying to one another, 'I don't know where we'd be without him.' Millard or Everett replied, "Good morning, Mr. Humboldt, nice to see you."

The somewhat old-fashioned form of address was the only one practical at this particular firm. "Mr. Prior," was so common as to be meaningless and thus, was appropriately reserved only for the president, Humboldt's very problematic cousin, Malice Prior.

Humboldt answered, "And you, let's both have a good day."

&&&

However, before discovering whether or not Humboldt and Millard or Everett for that matter, were to achieve this laudable goal, let us as promised, say a few words about the crumbling old church that faced the Prior rowhouses.

This church, tributary to an obscure Protestant sect, was named the "Second Church of the Revealed Truth." Osgood Prior had built it exactly as directed by his wife. At the time, she was under the impression that there was a mother institution with a similar name and architecture in Albany, New York. How she ever obtained this gross misunderstanding is lost in the mists of time.

In design, the church was one of those broad nineteenth-century ecclesiastical buildings seemingly intended to seat parishioners closer to the pastor than in the traditional Gothic style. Whether or not it was wise to place those in attendance so that they could actually hear the original pastor's sermons was not considered. Later, during the ministries of Humboldt's cousins, the Reverends Primus and Secundus Prior, there was much room for doubt. Attendance fell sharply.

In construction, the church building was of the same dark red brick used for the other Prior structures, with no excesses spared. The design was over-done Richardson Romanesque, a style normally executed in massive brownstone. In this case, however, the cheaper brick was used exclusively. The church's wide arches, rough robust columns, high steps, and protruding decorative features were all of ugly dark red brick. So also, was the over-sized church tower that rose to a pointed, though disproportionally squat steeple, about twenty feet above the highest roof of the sanctuary. The overall effect was not pleasing.

Within, the church had been equally expensive and equally ill judged. Having seen in Europe the inside of one of the rococo cathedrals of the former Holy Roman Empire, Osgood and his wife had originally encrusted the interior with gold leaf and golden mosaics. Tradition had it that for all this, Osgood Prior had expended at least one million dollars in gold. There were other rumors about this amount as well, none of which were favorable to the original Prior.

Unfortunately, the congregation, never large even at first, soon dwindled. Church functions and, more importantly, the substantial pastoral salaries were at first maintained by spending down the church endowment, and then by secretly removing and selling the interior gold leaf and gold mosaics and substituting gold paint. However, over the decades, with the clergy consisting of increasingly inept Priors, and the membership of other Priors who never attended, "Second Revealed" as it was locally called, became an empty, virtually abandoned hulk, whose dark ugly visage depressed the current generation of Priors as they left their rowhouses and apartments on their way to the leather works. Humboldt had seen it this morning and had momentarily felt just the slightest ill omen.

&&&

Returning to the thread of the story, we find Humboldt having entered the three-story Prior building, climbing the dusty stairs to the second floor executive offices. These were above the spacious first floor sales and trunk display rooms, now featuring only dirt and ancient cardboard representations of trunks and suitcases. Humboldt, his cousin President Malice Prior, and the other executives had offices at the front of the large building. Other offices such as engineering, purchasing, and bookkeeping looked out to the rear over the filthy skylights of the attached single story factory structure that contained the manufacturing and repair departments, now staffed largely by employees who existed only in the minds of the president and the personnel manager. The third floor had never been put to whatever use Osgood Prior might have intended, and was now used for storage of the company's voluminous accounting and other records. As decades of losses had largely immunized the company from most of the attentions of the Internal Revenue Service, it seemed safe for Prior and Cousins Leather to keep everything.

The managerial offices of Prior Leather reflected the unfortunate tastes of previous Prior Leather presidents, considerably muted by the Trust's refusal to allow the company to spend much money on office furniture or decorations. The floors were covered in a sturdy linoleum tile that must, originally, have been some sort of reddish brown, but now was faded to a dull maroon. The private offices surrounded a largely unoccupied clerical work-area, an idea of Osgood's intended to facilitate closer supervision. The oak and metal office desks and chairs were a chaotic assortment of styles and makes, having little in common but durability and grime. There were no curtains or air-conditioning, and, when the windows were opened, the dusty wooden Venetian blinds rattled in the hot breeze. The sumptuous corner office of the president was the exception to almost all of these deficiencies.

Humboldt greeted the office manager, his third cousin Orlo Prior, a stocky fifty-year-old with a thick head of gray hair, who was slumped in his chair with his back to the entrance. Orlo performed almost no duties except the all-important one of preparing the executive payrolls. However, for this key task alone, he was much appreciated and thought worth his salary.

Humboldt greeted him, "Good morning, Orlo."

Having been in a brief doze, Orlo Prior started, looked around, saw Humboldt, and smiled. He relied of his cousin's kindly nature. "Morning, Mr. Humboldt. Nice day."

Humboldt nodded. "Yes, indeed. I think the rain cooled it off a little."

Orlo, who had slept so soundly as to have missed last night's torments, thought a moment, nodded, and then remembered. "Sorry, Mr. Humboldt, I almost forgot, Mr. Malice Prior wants to see you. He says to bring Mr. Dorset along."

Humboldt thanked Orlo and proceeded to his own office. This modest room was situated several doors away from that of the president, and differed little in furnishings from its neighbors. It was, however, much neater, and an informed observer would have seen many indications of actual business activity. There was also a second telephone, for the Trust's accountants insisted on being able to reach Humboldt without any delay.

&&&

Humboldt alerted his cousin and next-door neighbor, Dorset Prior. Dorset was one of those tiresome tall blond-haired younger men, of unnecessarily good health, surplus enthusiasm, and ample vitality except where his work was concerned. Humboldt was surprised to find that he'd already arrived at the office.

Dorset had relatively little to do. Although he was responsible for manufacturing, purchasing, and product design, Prior Leather had made no steamer trunks, valises, or suitcases for a dozen years, and Dorset's design efforts were limited to recycling illustrations from the firm's 1908 catalog. Amazingly, these satisfied the company's General Sales Manager, Moribund Prior, the president's younger brother, and the executive responsible for whatever meager sales efforts Prior Leather occasionally undertook. Moribund was a vague, simpering individual. He was extremely thin, and always claimed that he also had been intended for the clergy.

It should be added that Dorset Prior's actual title of Assistant Engineering and Production Manager was a source of extreme disappointment to him. His dissatisfaction dated several years back to the premature death of his father, Essex Prior, the former Engineering and Production Manager. On that occasion, Malice Prior had simply abolished the position, added its salary to his own, and assigned its duties to Dorset with the "Assistant" title. The Trust's accountants inquired about this, but Malice explained that in a firm like Prior Leather, where good design was all-important, the chief executive officer had to give personal leadership. The accountants, for some reason, forgot to ask Humboldt about this and he was glad they hadn't. Any involvement with the president was a trial, much less one involving the potential loss by Malice of many thousands of dollars of salary.

Dorset Prior, having apparently forgotten his anger over the math camp episode, greeted Humboldt heartily outside the president's office. "Good to see you, Humboldt, old fellow. Do you know what's up?" He nervously straightened the jacket of his blue blazer and adjusted his yellow necktie.

Humboldt disliked the term "old fellow," but merely smiled mildly, and answered, "No, not yet."

The office of Malice Prior, President of Prior and Cousins Leather Works, stood in sharp contrast to those of his subordinates. Where they had deteriorating tile, he had thick carpet. Where battered oak or metal desks and chairs sufficed, he had new mahogany. Where tottering file cabinets in other offices held the records of the leather works' few current activities, the president's office featured an expensive combination credenza and bookcase towering behind his throne-like leather office chair. The bookcase would, in fact, have appeared even higher, except that Malice was seated on a raised dais, looking down at his underlings.

Humboldt knocked and then waited until a green light above the president's door authorized their entry. Malice Prior was a tall well-built man, with a broad high forehead, a pale complexion, and a superficially pleasant appearance. His receding gray was worn too long. His face wore a perpetual thin smile and his teeth were a little too big. He invariably wore red or blue striped shirts and suits of a peculiar greenish-gray color, made reluctantly for him by a firm of tailors that sought unsuccessfully to avoid his trade.

The president was not alone, for his slender brother Moribund was already sitting in one of the big leather chairs that crowded the office. He was speaking. "It's the biggest chance we've had in years."

Malice answered in his quiet hissing tone, gesturing toward Humboldt and Dorset at the same time, "Right, brother mine, that's why I've called the troops together." His constant use of the word "troops" in referring to his executive staff was actually one of his less disagreeable traits, but it always irritated Humboldt. Malice, having survived his army service without the fatal mistakes of his deceased older brother, looked back on it fondly and dealt in military slang.

Dorset Prior sang out, "What's up, boss?"

Malice glared, wondering if any disrespect was intended. Then he shrugged and answered, "Moribund, here, has got us a big order from Manheimers, they want a couple dozen of our largest steamer trunks for one of their promotional displays." (Manheimers was a respected chain of regional department stores, based in Humboldt's city.)

Although normally lethargic, Moribund was now anxious to contribute. He straightened up in his chair and added, "I haven't actually seen them for several years," (a dangerous admission for anyone not Malice's sibling) "but they ordered by mail from our brochure. They liked the product and especially the price."

Humboldt listened carefully to all this, wondering how in the world Prior Leather could manufacture one steamer trunk, let alone two dozen. However, he also watched the other men, and saw on the face of Dorset Prior, a look of growing horror.

Dorset writhed in his seat, picturing one of the product descriptions that he'd copied from the old catalogs. He asked nervously, "How was the pricing?"

Moribund answered, "At first they didn't say exactly, but then they mentioned finding it in the small print. It's $29.95 each in orders of a dozen or more." Oblivious to many decades of price inflation, neither Moribund nor his brother saw anything out of place with this disastrous price quotation.

Malice Prior continued. "We'll have to move out smartly and work the men in the ranks overtime if need be. They probably want to feature our trunks in their Christmas displays. Maybe with some cute girls in short skirts." This last remark was a clue to another aspect of Malice's deplorable character.

Well aware of what must have happened, Humboldt went on listening and watching.

Dorset still writhed, thinking of the 1918 price that Prior Leather had inadvertently offered. "Boss, that figure's a few years old. I don't think we can make them for that anymore." As the company had no real manufacturing workers, working machinery, or materials, this was a gross understatement. However, it triggered the president's reptilian survival instinct. Prior Leather's president should never look foolish by losing money on a deal.

Malice cursed and ordered, "F . . . it. Moribund, ditch that f . . . ing account. Make them cancel right away. Use one of your old stories of trouble on the assembly line. Maybe the one about workers with some sort of contagious skin disease."

The general sales manager nodded. He was better at turning away business. Dorset sighed in relief. Humboldt smiled, just a little.

Minutes later, glad he had weathered the meeting without having to say a single word, Humboldt was sitting uncomfortably at his desk, perspiring a little, and reviewing the month's statement of accounts. He hoped the rest of the morning would go more smoothly. Then his telephone rang.

&&&

Chapter 3

Although he still liked his work, Humboldt no longer appreciated the telephone.

Most calls to his office were from Malice's secretary with silly requests from her boss, or from the Trust's accountants with bothersome questions, or from his cousin Ribald Prior, with inane personnel suggestions. Recently, with the added burden of calls to his home from those prankish schoolgirls and credulous detective story readers, each new phone call made him tremble slightly.

Humboldt hoped that somehow, the phone would stop ringing. Perhaps the caller had the wrong number. He tried to go on reading. The statement of the monthly accounts was a beauty. Bound in an attractive beige paper cover, with the firm's full corporate name in large black letters, it always gave a good impression. Each of its several pages of figures was in balance and appropriately checked. It even reported a very slight profit. He was reviewing it for the third time.

Still the phone's jangling continued. Humboldt glanced warily at the pair of instruments on his plain oak desk. The first, provided by the Trust for urgent calls, was one of those awkward modern-looking green plastic models resembling some sort of trumpet. That one was silent. The other, a standard black telephone, worn with use, continued to ring. There was nothing to do but answer.

A soft and husky but firm female voice asked, "Is this Mr. Humboldt Prior?"

Already Humboldt was wary. "Yes. Who is this speaking, please?"

"Humboldt, this is Penny Rote."

At first, the name meant nothing. It was the wrong time of day for one of the schoolgirls. Perhaps it was someone looking for a job or a clerk from the Trust concerning his call about the stairway carpet. Then, with real alarm, he remembered. The name was something to do with radio, or worse, television news. This was real danger, a thing for which no company comptroller, however skillful, can ever be fully prepared.

He hesitated. She repeated her name, this time with emphasis. Something had to be said. He searched his memory. Prior Leather did not provide its executives with public relations or media training. In fact, the company preferred to be totally unknown, and, for many years, had largely achieved this. Neither the company, nor the Trust, ever gave interviews or news releases. Not ever. Executives could never talk to the press. Never. Prior and Cousins officials joining local clubs or non-profit boards or otherwise encountering the public, always gave only their home addresses, never their company affiliation. What to say?

He thought he remembered an evasive angry response of the president, his cousin Malice, several years before. He tried it. "Usually our lawyer handles inquiries of this kind." It was ineffective.

A short condescending laugh rustled in his ear. "No way, Humboldt."

She was using his first name. This sounded dangerously personal. He worried some more. The phone felt like lead in his fingers. Then, forgetting her name for the moment, and more and more alarmed, he blurted out a plaintive, "Who did you say you were, and what do you want?"

She answered in a friendly and patient tone. "As I told you, Humboldt Prior, I'm Penelope Rote. I work at Channel Seven, and I have to talk to you in person."

Humboldt actually shivered. A TV interview! He faced a violation of one of his company's most sacred tenants. There seemed to be no way out. Feeling like a hunted animal, he found himself saying, "Then, please call me tomorrow morning. I'm just leaving for an urgent appointment."

Surprisingly, she agreed. "Okay, Humboldt. But it will have to be tomorrow, for sure, and it's going to take some time."

Through the waves of worry over the unimaginable array of dangerous questions that might be asked by a high-powered hostile newsperson, one other small impression emerged. Her manner actually seemed more or less friendly.

"All right then," he found himself saying.

She ended the call, "Good. I need your help. See you tomorrow."

&&&

Still quaking at the prospect of being interviewed for television, especially by a woman, Humboldt hurriedly took stock. He'd said he was leaving for an important appointment. Now, that actually seemed the thing to do. Even though it was before eleven o'clock, he'd leave early and find a place to think. After all, he was supposed to be semi-retired. He supposed semi-retired executives always came and went at odd hours. Anyway, no one at Prior Leather would know the difference, staffed as the company was by inept do-nothing executives and fictitious employees.

Humboldt read one or two more papers, straightened up his desk, and stood up to leave. Then, noisily, his door opened. Humboldt froze, seized by the dreadful thought that the reporter had tricked him into revealing his presence at the office and had then quickly made her way there. However, it was only the personnel manager, his cousin Ribald Prior.

This deplorable individual was one of the most reprehensible of Humboldt's relatives, and must now be described. Where most of his relatives already encountered, and his clergyman cousins not yet introduced, all ran to at least remotely normal if not scrawny appearance, reasonable height, and average physiques, Ribald was short and grossly overweight. Where the other Priors tended to be blond or brown haired, and sometimes balding, Ribald had thick oily black hair, and seemed proud of it. He was usually un-bathed, ill dressed, and often gave the impression of having slept in his clothes. He had a great capacity for misunderstandings, and constantly expressed them in a loud nasal voice.

Aside from his personal atmosphere, which was not good, Ribald lived in an air of perpetual conspiracy. Sometimes he suspected others and sometimes he himself was the plotter. He gestured Humboldt back into the office and shut the door. Then he pulled a chair up to Humboldt's desk, sat down, and waited for Humboldt to do the same.

Humboldt politely murmured something to the effect that he, "Was just leaving."

Ribald ignored this, and then told one of his usual disgusting jokes having to do with farm animals. At the same time, he nervously passed his fingers through his greasy hair and then wiped his hand on the desk. Humboldt shuddered.

Ribald leaned closer, and said in a low voice, "Something's going on."

Humboldt assumed rumors of the just aborted trunk deal had now reached the personnel manager. He replied cautiously, "I think that's been taken care of." He hoped his visitor would now leave, as the air circulation through the office was definitely in the wrong direction.

Ribald retorted angrily, "Hell no, it's not."

Humboldt tried again. "I believe it is, Ribald. The president told his brother to take care of it."

Ribald snarled, "What the f . . . are you talking about?"

Humboldt was stumped. However, he knew his cousin would have more to say. He waited.

Ribald paused, as if listening, then sneezed, and wiped his nose on his sleeve. Finally, he continued in his usual conspiratorial tone. "There's been questions about those f . . . ing employees old Malice wanted us to hire."

This sounded bad, although Humboldt didn't yet know what the questions were or who had been asking them. He said, hoping Ribald had been exaggerating, as he usually was, "Surely not. That's just something within the company."

Ribald shook his head violently, discharging onto Humboldt's desk as he did so, a fine spray of hair oil and dandruff. "Hell, no. Not any more. Things have been going pretty smoothly, although the extra paychecks I was hoping to get my hands on always seem to get caught up somewhere. With some fake resignations and the firing of Martin Van Buren, I'm already up to Chester Arthur. It keeps me busy, I can tell you, filling in application forms, notifying the state about minorities, and making up all those timerolls. Why, I had no idea what to do when I decided to have Bill Harrison pass away on the job. It took days of paperwork."

Humboldt was getting a headache. The prospect of the TV interview still burned in his mind, and now all this absurdity of the fake employees with presidential names. He wished he hadn't taken pity on Cousin Ribald's obsession, and instead had stopped this nonsense before even George Washington was supposedly hired. He wondered if it was even now, not too late.

However, Ribald was still babbling. "Anyway, thank God we don't have to have more real ones like that damn Fillmore."

Humboldt heartily agreed, although Millard or Everett was nothing compared to the vicissitudes of working with his awful cousins. He again waited for this one to continue.

After an obvious attempt to read, upside down, one of the papers on Humboldt's desk, Ribald did so. "It happened the other night at the country club. As usual, I'd had a few tall cold ones, and then this strange babe approached me, saying she'd heard I worked for the Prior family. She was a real looker, I can tell you, tall, with a nice face, a short skirt, and great legs. I said I sure as hell did, and could we go off somewhere and talk about it."

Humboldt almost saw it all coming. However, he said only, "Are you certain that was a good idea?"

Ribald snickered. "It would have been, if it worked. However, she just laughed and said something about 'Another time.' Then she said she'd been talking with someone at the state employment office, and some guy there told her a story about us having the strange coincidence of all those presidential names on our roster. I finally decided she was one of those damn management consultants the state government's always hiring."

Humboldt had started writing notes to himself. This sounded like potential trouble, but perhaps it was still fixable, as it had been that time when the state pollution control agency asked questions about the old leather tanning equipment that stood leaking and rusting out behind the factory.

Ribald grinned. "Those gal consultants always look great, I can tell you. I wished I could have gotten tight with her, but I remembered what the boss always says. 'No screwing around with those outside types.' So, when she asked what it was all about, I just gave her some sh . . about a government contract and some confidential temporary workers that were all gone now. She bought it hook, line, and sinker. All she answered was, 'Very interesting,' and turned away from me. Great view from behind, too, I'll tell you." Ribald slumped back in the chair, with a smile of happy recollection on his perspiring face.

Humboldt seethed inwardly. This gross blunder in telling silly stories about government secrecy was one of the worst. Not the worst, of course. That probably had been Ribald's costly trip to Paris supposedly to recruit female French design experts to allow the firm to compete in the luxury leather handbag business. Or, the time Ribald had attempted to put the firm's entire management team through a course of business ethics training, costing over

$1,000 per person. Humboldt had checked the course outline and discovered that each and every tenet of the proposed ethics course conflicted directly with the deeply held basic beliefs of President Malice Prior. Humboldt had stopped this one, in another of his "small victories."

However, now all they could do was wait. Perhaps, for once, Ribald hadn't misread the woman. Maybe it would all blow over. Humboldt took the high road. "It sounds as if you handled it okay. Keep me posted. Now I've really got to get going."

Ribald had the last word. He rubbed his leg, saying something about a hot-weather cramp. Then he pushed himself up from the chair, tugged at his jacket, and muttered with a leer, "Sure as hell wish I could have handled her. Old Jenny what's-her-name looked like a real hot number." He stumbled away, rubbing at the back of his thigh. Any optimism Humboldt might have felt followed him out the door.

&&&

As an experienced comptroller, Humboldt disbelieved coincidences. Things either added up or they didn't. If they seemed related, they always were. Now, he knew that some woman Ribald had foolishly called "Jenny," had heard something funny about his company. What if this tied in with Penny Rote's ominous call? Worst of all, he knew he was the only person capable of handling the crisis. The consequences of any sort of interview between a trained news reporter and one of the other Priors, especially Moribund, the sales manager who was supposed, at least, to be able to deal with the public, or worst of all, the loathsome Malice Prior, were unthinkable. The awful publicity and the following litigation could destroy the company.

The situation as to the Prior Trust was even worse. Its accountants were always in a state of nervousness. While

Humboldt fully understood that they lived in daily fear of losing their own well-paid jobs, there was always the overriding possibility that the Trust's archaic protection under state law might be challenged. Its structure of payments for salaries, housing, and automobiles for Prior family members might once again attract the attention of the Internal Revenue Service. Several decades before, the IRS had asked some very difficult questions. What if they did so again? That was the ultimate risk. Humboldt really needed time to think.

Although the dark cloud of worry over the TV interview still loomed, Humboldt was relieved to be leaving the Prior Building. It was even hotter as he trudged across the littered parking lot, and the steering wheel of his Buick was almost too hot to touch. He turned out onto the street, even toying in his nervous state, with the idea that the reporter person might be having him followed.

In this distressed state of mind, he only made one stop on his way home. This was for basic groceries. He wasn't really out of any of his staples, but somehow the extra food gave assurance. Perhaps he could simply lie low for a few days. He'd heard that reporters were usually on tight deadlines and sometimes lost interest if they couldn't finish their stories on time. However, try as he might, he could think of nothing about Prior Leather that was even remotely of topical news interest. In many ways, this made his predicament seem worse.

Humboldt garaged his station wagon and carried his bags of groceries across Woodhouse Avenue to his rowhouse. Even on the shady narrow street, the heat was stifling. However, while climbing his front steps he glanced upwards and could see thick dark clouds forming in the west. The grim tower of the Second Revealed Church loomed up ominously before them, a great darker bulk upon the gray. It was going to rain again.

Seeking distraction from the pending interview, Humboldt tried to busy himself with household chores. As he and Mildred, his salaried housekeeper, were both extremely neat, there couldn't be many of these. He wandered from room to room. Usually, he only used the hallway, his kitchen, and the rear-facing solarium, with its comfortable sofa and chairs, covered in a durable canvas-like material. Less often, he visited his library with its dark wood and books, and still less frequently, his dining and living rooms, still furnished with his parents' antiques, mixed with heavy plush-covered contemporary pieces. Indeed, in his living room, not actually entered for several weeks, he found himself occupied in cautiously removing a long-dead mouse from under his mother's prize tea table.

Out of tasks on the first floor, Humboldt then forced himself to address the possible bee problem. His basement was a poorly lighted, dank narrow affair, containing little else but his out-of-date laundry appliances, furnace, and water heater, and a high stack of heavy leather suitcases and trunks almost covering the front wall. Even in the hottest weather, the basement was cool from the damp of its rough, limestone walls that constantly flaked bits of stone and dust down onto the cracked concrete floor.

Armed with a spray can of insect-killer, Humboldt resolutely began his search. The small rear window, high on the wall, and the location of the previous bee infestation, showed nothing. He shrugged and then walked the fifty or so feet to the front wall where, above the stack of trunks, another window, covered with dust and cobwebs, admitted a dim light. His cleaning lady's meticulous activities stopped at the floor above.

The front window was also insect-free, but here he could again hear the annoying buzzing sound. Listening more carefully and hearing other slight noises, he sighed. So, that was it. Some of Dorset's numerous children were playing some sort of electronic game in the cellar just to his north.

Humboldt masked his annoyance with himself with a resolution. He'd have to come down here and really clean. That heap of trunks had been untouched since he began residence. His parents had used them for storage and when they needed more, his father merely brought another trunk home from the leather works. Goodness knew what was in them. Ancient history. Oh well.

Humboldt shook his head as he climbed the stairs back to civilization. There, he was greeted by the first rumble of thunder, and took refuge in his sunroom to watch the rain and worry about Penny Rote. What could she possibly want? He could think of no conceivable reason that she would want to talk to him, except for some hideous exposé concerning the unusual finances of Prior and Cousins. What could he say? The reality was that any attempt at flight would only create the greater risk of her talking to Malice Prior or one of his other inept cousins. He'd have to face the music. Or was there some way out, some tactic he'd not thought of, but might if he tried harder.

This pointless brooding continued through a gloomy and rainy afternoon, and through one of the worst frozen dinners in his freezer. After that, somehow, Humboldt fell asleep on his sofa and only awakened at about eleven-thirty.

On his way to bed, he wandered through his living room, now thankfully mouse free. From his front window, he could see that a light rain was still falling. In it, to his surprise, he saw a tall woman standing on the wet sidewalk under one of the few streetlights on Woodhouse Avenue. She appeared to have light hair, and was wearing a light tan raincoat, belted agreeably around her body. More, Humboldt couldn't see, for with her back to him, she was gazing intently at the old church.

&&&

Chapter 4

Humboldt spent the first part of the night worrying about this new development. Who was the woman in the street, and why in the world was she interested in the dilapidated old church? Was it some sort of clever spying tactic? The belted raincoat certainly looked suspicious. The woman was definitely a stranger, for he knew just about everyone on the street, in fact he was related to most of them. Finally, in his small plainly furnished bedroom, he dozed in his narrow bed, listening to the still-falling rain.

The morning brought more concerns. At first, he'd blissfully forgotten the whole terrible TV affair. Then he remembered. It reminded him of one of those days long ago at elementary school, when, on Friday afternoon, the class's bully had threatened to 'get' him on Monday morning. Two weekend days of forgetting had been followed by an abrupt, unhappy recall. As to the looming interview, what was the larger picture, and what did it all mean? What if he or his company were under some sort of confidential criminal investigation and the reporter had discovered this? The woman who asked his cousin Ribald about the fake employees had to be part of it one way or another. Humboldt paled at these horrid prospects.

Because of the harassment about his namesake, the appalling fictional spy/detective also named Humboldt Prior, Humboldt had taken to watching television mysteries. He had recently seen one in which one of the FBI agents looked just like the woman in the rain. This new worry, encountered during a hasty breakfast of toast and cranberry juice, made him fume again over his fictional double. He'd like to see how that Humboldt Prior, supposedly so accomplished at solving mysteries, even those requiring violent action, would handle an interview with Penelope Rote. Now that was real trouble.

Humboldt actually found himself looking nervously up and down his street before hurrying across to the dark red brick communal garage. What if someone was watching? The air was hot and oppressive, thick with humidity, and threatening more rain. His worries continued as he drove to work, this time in his depressingly common old Chevrolet sedan, chosen this morning as a crude safeguard against being followed. That was the point wasn't it? There was so little he could really do if he was faced with a broad criminal investigation.

By the time he reached the Prior Building, after an especially difficult trip through downtown because several stoplights were out of service, he had reached one conclusion. He would simply and absolutely refuse to meet her at the office. The image of Ribald Prior, or worse yet, his boss Malice Prior, bursting in during the interview was too much to bear. Beyond their gaining knowledge of his awful predicament, they'd be sure to say something that would only add fuel to the fire. Ribald would probably tell one of his unimaginably vulgar jokes, and there was no telling what Malice might say or do to the attractive female TV reporter.

Humboldt had angrily read one or two of the disastrous novels featuring the amateur detective/spy with whom he shared the same name. It was all so unreal. The character seemed to have no trouble arranging meetings with his helpers and antagonists in all sorts of places. What made this especially awful from Humboldt's standpoint was that some of the stories supposedly took place in popular locations right here in Humboldt's own City-by-the-River. As a consequence of this, he was now avoiding certain restaurants that, from time to time, he'd previously enjoyed. Maybe a different restaurant would work though, or they could meet in a car. The detective did that all the time. But no, being interviewed by the attractive but dangerous Penny Rote, in a car parked in some secluded spot, was unthinkable.

Thus, at nine o'clock on a Tuesday morning, Humboldt found himself sitting in his office, fidgeting, fighting the urge to disconnect his telephone, and hoping no one would bother him. His office chair, usually quite comfortable, today was rubbing awkwardly on his spine. He couldn't concentrate on his incoming mail. His office seemed unusually warm, and there was an unpleasant odor coming from his wastebasket, apparently not emptied for several days.

He was prey to foolish hopes. Perhaps the building would catch fire. No Prior Leather executive, no matter how dedicated to fending off the media, could be expected to interrupt his fire alarm assignment to speak on the telephone. However, when the call came, to his surprise he found himself answering it at once.

There she was, with the same husky voice saying, "Good morning, Humboldt. It's Penny Rote. When can we get together?"

He tried to be business-like. "I've got things to do all morning, what about meeting for lunch somewhere?"

After a few seconds, to his great relief she answered brightly, "Absolutely. Let's have lunch together." She paused a moment and then continued. "Say, I've got a follow-up interview this morning with an old lady who lives somewhere on HillTop Parkway. I've noticed a neighborhood restaurant near there called 'The Pike House.' I'll meet you there at noon."

Humboldt froze. That ill-chosen restaurant appeared several times in the mystery novels. He started to protest, but then hesitated. What possible explanation could he offer?

By that point, Penny Rote had control. "See you there, then, okay? Great." The phone clicked off, leaving Humboldt slumped in his chair. The die was cast. He'd read somewhere that the only thing worse than a bad interview was the case in which the reporter could say smugly that the subject failed to show up as promised. There was only one consolation. The Pike House wasn't likely to feature in the luncheon plans of any of the other executives of Prior and Cousins. It wasn't expensive enough.

The morning passed with all the haste of an arthritic tree sloth. Humboldt irritably fended off attempted conversation by Orlo Prior, the office manager, and an absurd suggestion from Ribald concerning an across-the-board pay increase for his troop of ghost employees. It was hotter than ever. Finally, eleven-thirty arrived.

&&&

Afterwards, Humboldt could have told nothing about his hot drive through downtown and up the steep road to HillTop Parkway and the adjacent street on which the Pike House was located. He was now racked by a new and totally distracting worry, something he should have foreseen but hadn't. Surely, pictures were the essence of any television news interview. Penny Rote would necessarily be accompanied by at least one cameraman, perhaps more. Every other person in the restaurant, whether annoyed by TV cameras or not, would be watching as Miss Rote asked her devastating questions. He'd agreed to the worst possible kind of meeting place.

He parked the black Chevrolet, little caring that its left rear fender protruded into the traffic lane. Any damage would be the Trust's problem. With knees shaking, he entered the restaurant, its décor a festival of north woods knotty pine, moth-eaten taxidermy, and pictures of ducks. He looked round expecting the camera, and one or more officious hovering producers. No, to his great relief, she seemed to be alone.

Penny Rote stood up, and advanced confidently to take his hand in a friendly way. She was even prettier than he recalled, almost as tall as he was, with a pleasant mildly freckled face and sandy hair, worn quite short. Her figure was attractive enough, and he saw that she was one of those women who run to strong shapely legs, not those thin pipe-cleaner affairs. She was smiling and her heels clicked as she crossed the floor toward him. She was wearing slacks and a light jacket, both of a material similar to that of Humboldt's favorite summer suit. All in all, he was actually quite favorably impressed.

She greeted him. "Well, well, Humboldt Prior, here we are at last. I'm glad to see you."

Although still a bit worried by the prospect of hidden cameras, Humboldt felt relieved. He answered her politely, with a little less of his usual stuffiness, "Nice to meet you, Miss Rote. I hope I may be of assistance."

She led him back to the booth she'd selected and they both sat down. Humboldt cautiously said something about the rain, and Penny replied with an appropriate comment drawn from Channel Seven's morning weather forecast. Then she continued softly with some words he didn't quite hear, but seemed to his sheer amazement to be about, "that old church of yours."

He obviously looked puzzled, for she repeated it. "Yes, Humboldt, I'm writing a mystery novel set in that old church of yours. I'd like your help with it."

&&&

At this point in the history, a bit of difficulty arises. It has been well explained by P. G. Wodehouse that when the historian attempts to give an account of a set of complex social interactions involving numerous characters, he or she must from time to time break the flow of his or her narrative, to bring the reader up to date on happenings elsewhere. In this case, the trouble is that there has been no opportunity to introduce two other important characters in this report that are closely associated with the old church. They are, specifically, Humboldt's regrettable cousins, Primus and Secondus Prior.

These two aging reprobates had been educated at the best universities and seminaries, and ordained in due course as pastors of whatever denomination into which the Second Church of the Revealed Truth had managed to worm itself five or six decades earlier. They were almost identical tallish old men, with shocks of white hair, prominent chins, and low narrow foreheads. Both walked slowly, with a stoop, and always wore insincere pastoral smiles. Those who'd known them for many years argued whether Secondus was an even worse speaker than Primus, or whether Primus's trait of avarice had developed at an earlier age. Now, with the diminished capacity of their late seventies and early eighties, it made little difference, although certain especially unpleasant characteristics seemed surprisingly intact. Attractive women avoided all contact with the brothers.

They had, in succession, served as pastors of Second Revealed, where Primus was now still on the payroll, though in a low-cost emeritus role. As membership and Sunday attendance had dwindled almost to zero or below, they had few or no duties with their miniscule congregation. From his youth, Humboldt remembered Pastor Primus bellowing, "How are you-oou," from the pulpit to an almost empty sanctuary. Secondus did make a careful daily inspection of the locked and empty church premises, focusing on the possibility that a rare piece of incoming mail might contain a check.

However, they both had plenty to do. In a room of one of the two Prior apartments where they and their wives now resided, the two greedy old men still worked daily with a typewriter, a copying machine, a pair of tape recorders, an old record player, and a stack of phonograph records of religious music. The explanation for all this activity was that they had tardily discovered church radio.

More exactly, they had realized the financial possibilities of a carefully targeted approach to a certain form of religious fund raising. Armed with data purloined somehow from the state government's Medical Assistance files, Primus and Secondus luxuriated in the possession of a mailing list of senior citizens, living in nursing homes, but still supposedly able to conduct their own financial affairs. These lonely old people were serviced by repeated mailings and the transmission of semi-weekly late-night recorded radio broadcasts. The programs offered the hope of blissful eternal rest grounded on the activities of the Revealed Truth Radio Ministries. Such promised activities were said to be supported, in turn, only by the margin after expenses incurred in securing the frugal contributions from their devoted senior listeners, or their purchases of religiously oriented statuary and bird figurines, all manufactured by Buddhists in various Southeast Asian regions.

These margins were indeed narrow after being reduced by the annual stipends reluctantly accepted by Primus and Secondus Prior. Never skilled at any aspect of their callings, the two evil old men managed to produce the taped broadcasts only through their combined efforts applied for at least two or three hours work on most days. This is enough of them for the moment.

&&&

Humboldt was both relieved and shocked by Penny Rote's reference to the church. What was she up to? Was it a trick of some kind? What an unfortunate setting to choose for a story. Indeed, it was nearly as bad as those supposedly frequented by his nemesis and namesake. Luckily, a waiter appeared with water and menus and he was able to hide behind the small talk that always accompanies the process of ordering lunch. They both requested turkey sandwiches.

Then Penny spoke again. "So, you see, Humboldt, in addition to my day job as newsanchor at Channel Seven, I'm an amateur writer. Now I'm trying a mystery story."

This was just about the last straw. Plagued for months by another author's negligent choice of names, now Humboldt was confronted by a second would-be writer. He was trying to think of a way out as she went on speaking.

"Once, a year or two ago, I was trying to find my way somewhere in the old part of town, and I accidentally turned onto your quaint little Woodhouse Avenue. That funny looking, big old red brick church on your dead-end street just knocked my socks off, so I said to myself, 'Penelope, what a great place for a mystery.' I'm already filling it with hidden passages and secrets in walled-up rooms."

Humboldt cringed, thinking of the nasty reaction of his inflammable cousins Primus and Secondus to having their church appear in mystery fiction. This had to be stopped. Gaining confidence from his impression that she wasn't, after all, concerned with him personally, or with Prior and Cousins, or the Prior Trust, he sought a way out.

"I'm so sorry, Miss Rote, that this didn't come up in our phone call. Although I do live nearby, I really know very little about Second Revealed. As I'm only a neighbor, I fear I can be of no help whatever." Maybe it would work. Their lunches arrived and he took a large defensive bite of the cold turkey sandwich, immediately wishing he'd ordered a hamburger.

Not so fast. Penny's face took on what he suspected was the typically aggressive expression of a powerful newsanchor, boring in on some sort of culprit. She smiled, looked him straight in the eye, and crushed his hopes. "Oh yes, Humboldt, you know I think you can and will. You see there are some other compelling factors. It's pretty much a case not of whether I write, but what I write or report about. There's another possible story that I could do. It would be about this strange old-fashioned leather goods company, full of so-called executives who are really all well-paid relatives, but do little or no work, and a weird fictitious work force all supposedly named for dead US presidents."

Humboldt shivered, remembering Ribald's foolish and ill-advised country club conversation with the so-called consultant. There was an ominous clap of thunder outside, and he choked on a piece of lettuce, interrupting Penny with a fit of coughing.

She was patient during the coughing. Then, relentlessly, she moved in to close the deal. "Most peculiarly of all, Humboldt, down at the National Bank, there's this private trust affair, with lots of money, sheltered by a special state law. I checked with the Secretary of State, and got part of the story. I don't know it all yet, but I'm part way there. Shall I tell you my theory about what is happening?"

Humboldt was watching her and listening carefully. Something in her manner was a little different from what he'd expected and feared. Yes, she was a forceful investigative reporter, but there were elements of friendliness and even a little compassion or concern. What did that mean? Was she also worried about something?

No matter. She'd already learned far too much. This was the ultimate catastrophe. Either he had to help her invade the privacy of the church, one of the present-day Prior family's greatest embarrassments, and thereby also become further involved in the nightmare of amateur mystery writing, or she'd destroy Prior and Cousins and all that went with it.

Humboldt felt frozen to his seat. He managed a spluttering question. "Are you sure this is in anyone's best interests? Perhaps it would be bad for all concerned to do this." As he spoke, he knew his words were virtually meaningless. It would be better for her. Then, to his amazement, he found himself adding, "Okay, what is your theory?"

Penny Rote smiled happily. She'd been sure he'd want to know. "I think it's all part of your cover plan."

Cover plan? His cover plan? What in the world could that mean? Humboldt's mind raced as it normally did only when trying to deflect one Ribald's ridiculous schemes or Malice's evil intentions toward one of the firm's few female employees. Perhaps, if he was open with Miss Rote, she might relent. Then he realized the ultimate awful truth. Cover plans had to do with spying and his dreadful literary double, the so-called detective Humboldt Prior, had been a spy in his early days. Was that what she thought?

Speechless, Humboldt choked down the last bite of his lunch. Tossing two twenty-dollar bills onto the table, a very unusual gesture, he muttered in desperation, "Look, we'd better talk about this outside." He got up and hurried out of the restaurant. Penny Rote followed, with the situation firmly in hand.

&&&

Chapter 5

Outside, it was raining so heavily that there was no escape. They stood close together under the awning of the travel agency next to the restaurant, backed by a dreary window display of faded brochures. At that moment, even the worst of the destinations would have appealed to Humboldt, as he listened to the rest of her story.

Penny continued. "I'm not absolutely sure, but I could be onto something big. If I'm right and could get it on the air, my viewers would eat it up. That ridiculous leather trunk company, the well-funded secret trust, and all the rest, remind me of what I've read about the CIA, you know, the Central Intelligence Agency. It sounds like a cover plan for something, like the other fake businesses they're always using. Then, I heard about those goofy mystery novels featuring a fictional Humboldt Prior, supposedly written right here in town. I actually read two of them. Next, using the phone book, I discovered you, a real Humboldt Prior also living right here, and I began to suspect the books were part of the plan, too. They're somewhat unbelievable, but then I thought, 'what if they're supposed to seem that way?' That's the cleverest part. It's perfect. It's the ideal cover plan for you, Humboldt Prior, one of our country's top spies, semi-retired right here in town. That's why I think you'll help me with my little church mystery story."

Humboldt stood stock-still. Overhead, the old orange canvas awning was leaking water down his neck, but he didn't feel it. He was totally absorbed in the horrid enormity of this monstrous combination of accusations and misunderstandings. Although he was not without his eccentricities, he was a sufficiently normal human being to start by denying everything.

He began, with a flustered, "No, no." Then he continued. "Miss Rote, that's totally wrong and, in fact, it's impossible. I've worked all my life, right here in town, for Prior and Cousins. Why, I've been their comptroller for over twenty years."

Penny Rote was human, too. She immediately retorted, "What's a comptroller?" As often with such trivial inquiries, this had a calming effect.

Regrettably, Humboldt was experienced in fielding this question. Lowering himself in his own estimation, he answered, "Well, I'm the chief accountant."

Penny smiled at that. "Oh." She thought for just a moment. "I suppose there's just a chance that I'm mistaken." (This was an equally large come-down for a veteran television newsanchor.) "However, even if I might be, it seems to leave us just where we are. Either, you use your Prior family connections and your spying skills, if you've still got them, to help me dig into your funny old church, or I broadcast the story of Prior Leather and all that goes with it." She smiled, again, thoughtfully.

Humboldt felt a lump in his throat and a sudden chill. Either way, he was trapped. He answered in a whisper, "I see." Then he said, "Well, what do you want me to do?"

&&&

However, before a clear account of the rest of their conversation may be given, it is again necessary to maintain contact with two other parts of this most complicated overall narrative.

First, at about the same time, a meeting was taking place in the office Moribund Prior, General Sales Manager of Prior Leather. This office, floored in the same unattractive faded maroon tile, and outfitted with secondhand mahogany furniture and matching accessories, was distinguished from its neighbors only by the fact that it adjoined the sumptuous quarters of Moribund's brother, the firm's president, and contained his castoff furnishings. There was a connecting door between the two offices. At the moment, Moribund's room also contained his cousins Dorset and Ribald, respectively production manager and personnel manager.

The three were a study in opposites. Moribund's slim lethargic and simpering form was in sharp contrast to Ribald's short stocky messiness, emphasized by his noisy bluster. Dorset's tall blond youthful appearance gave a misimpression of vigor. However, he joined the other two in preferring idleness to real work.

Dorset was speaking. "With all respect, guys, I kind of regret losing the trunk deal." He might well say so, although it was his silly incompetence in offering a 1908 price of $29.95, that had both generated the Manheimers purchase order in the first place and then forced the president to renege on the deal.

"Me, too," added Ribald, lying, "I was all set to ramp up the staffing."

Moribund's face assumed an expression that he perhaps intended for an encouraging smile, but would have been taken by objective outsiders as another simper. "Well, boys, I agree completely. I wish we could have taken the business, because Manheimers just loved the trunks. They had in mind their winter sales push for Christmas and women going on vacation. They were going to drape a couple of gorgeous models over the trunk in their ads and use two or more of the trunks with similar manikins in each store."

If the three men had been listening more carefully, they might have heard just the slightest sound. It was a hissing intake of breath from behind the door to the adjoining office. Malice Prior, as often when he had nothing to do, which was, in fact, more often than not, was listening with his ear to the door. His reaction was to the words 'gorgeous models.'

Dorset, whose level of initiative was slightly above that meager dullness normal for the Prior Leather executive team, finally picked up the ball. He stretched his long legs and said casually, "Say, what if we went back to them with a deal offered at about $929.95 each in a lot of one hundred? The Manheimers have tons of money. They could easily afford more than two or three trunks per store. Make them the center of their whole campaign." He looked from one cousin to the other.

Moribund simpered again. "Swell plan, Cousin Dorset. They really wanted to do the promotion. They had a lot of bucks budgeted for it and their merchandising man isn't very sharp. I'll tell you what, let's see if we can help ourselves. We'll quote the price like you say, but we'll make them real cheap, with just a thin wood frame, a few nails, and then slap on that cardboard stuff that looks like leather. Maybe we can do it for about $129.95 each. Who cares if they break up in a month or two? They're only for display. Then we'll jump up . . ."

Dorset was mildly annoyed at this intrusion into his domain of manufacturing, but it was unwise to contradict the president's brother too often. He said nothing.

However, Ribald interrupted. "I know just what you're thinking, Morrie, the old special executive bonus scheme. We'd have about $80,000 to play with. And if I hire those high school girls to work in the factory after school, like I was going to that other time, we won't have to pay very much in wages. There'll be even more for the bonuses."

There was another very soft hissing noise from behind the door, this time as Malice reacted to the words 'high school girls.'

Moribund actually heard it, but typically, misunderstood its origin. "The boss's air-conditioner must be leaking again," he said jealously. That was another feature unique to the office of the president.

Dorset had a concern. "What about old Humboldt? He's always against making cheap stuff, and last time, he sharpened his pencil and stopped the bonuses."

Ribald, thinking of what he could buy with his bonus, looked worried. He wiped sweat from his palms.

Moribund shook his head. "Nah. Humboldt is now semi-retired and only here part time. In fact, he left even earlier today. We'll just have to schedule the meetings when he's away. Piece of cake."

Dorset had another idea. "Say," he said, "I think I've a way to keep Humboldt away from the office more often. He's been tutoring my boy in mathematics. I'll get him to stay home and do it in the morning."

Unconscious of the layers of false optimism and ineptitude already burdening their new project, Moribund and Ribald smirked confidently.

There was another smirk in the next office. Malice was happily envisioning the photo shoots for Manheimers' advertising featuring the cheap trunks and the gorgeous female models. Perhaps, if he worked it properly, they could be done right here at Prior Leather, with the young female factory workers graciously given time off to watch the show. Then he frowned. The bonus scheme would, of course, have to be adjusted. At least half, maybe more, would be his. Then, turning away from his listening post, and with a vile expression, he returned to his thoughts of the models.

&&&

At the same time as this nefarious activity was in preparation, two other family members were likewise engaged. Primus and Secondus Prior, closeted in their stuffy improvised studio, had just finished taping another one-hour broadcast of 'Revealed Truth Radio Ministries.' This was never an easy task as neither of them spoke well or possessed any skill at the operation of tape recorders or the phonograph. For these reasons, the taped broadcasts were of very low quality, frequently marred by muttered expletives, misstatements, awkward silences, and familiar hymns begun in the middle.

After the most recent of these, Primus exclaimed crossly, "My God, what a screw-up. Can we go back and fix it?"

Secondus demurred. "Naw, there's no need. We're broadcasting late at night. The old folks don't have their hearing aids and won't even notice."

In this taping session, Primus had apparently dozed off during Secondus' especially venial homily, and the closing hymn was particularly delayed. Theirs was a low-cost operation.

The final step in the day's work was the usual stuffing of envelopes for the weekly mailing of about three thousand solicitations. The enclosure was always much the same. A preprinted multi-color heading showed blue skies, fluffy white clouds, and a pair of welcoming arms. The brief text promised just what the listener wanted to hear, thanked the recipient for past support, and hinted at impending doom for the cherished ministry if more purchases and donations were not forthcoming. The donation and order sections, occupying most of the sheet, featured the current selection of imported religious goods, and included misleading illustrations, assuming Secondus had remembered to affix them to the master copy before having it duplicated.

Earlier, Secondus had returned from the printer located in a near-downtown neighborhood of decaying businesses, frequently disrupted by flooding. This floundering firm still employed decades-old addressing plates and printing machines and bought their envelope stock at sales of distressed office supplies. All this gave the Revealed Truth Radio Ministry's mailings a particularly frugal and sometimes water-stained appearance, bordering on shabby.

"Look at this old junk," he grumbled, brandishing their latest mailing. "Lucky for us that it's dirt cheap, and that lots of our listeners have poor eyesight."

Primus cursed at a slight paper cut and muttered, "Always seems like it takes forever to get these damn things done."

Secondus nodded his white head. "It pays for our liquor, though, and your girl friends, and the card games." This sentence capsules the reason for their activity. In establishing the original Second Church of the Revealed Truth, the original Osgood Prior had provided a very substantial endowment to help support pastoral costs of all kinds. However, the ministrations of the last several clergy, especially those of Primus and Secondus Prior, had virtually ended annual giving, and, in fact, membership in the congregation itself. After removing and selling the beautiful gold interior gilding of the original construction, and dissipating much of the endowment, the pastoral brothers were left with only the modest stipends, housing, and other maintenance provided by the Trust to all Priors. Hence, they now relied on their radio program.

Primus muttered agreement, stuffed a final three envelopes, and added, "I like this bluebird figurine sitting on the open book. It should net us an extra thousand bucks." From several months of experience, Primus was becoming a shrewd judge of which generic products of their Asian suppliers would sell the best. Even at the start, in spite of Secondus's approvals, he'd been against using the starling.

Secondus agreed. "Should be good, and we can always use the funds. We're in an uncertain business. One of the big national outfits could move in at any time." The possibility of competition from a multi-state religious broadcaster was their constant worry.

Primus heaved himself up from his chair, and ran his hand nervously through his white hair. "That's sure as hell so, and say, there might be another f . . . ing problem."

Secondus' narrow forehead wrinkled in a frown. He disliked hearing of problems, and Primus was a chronic pessimist. "What's that?"

Primus assumed a hushed, conspiratorial tone. "The guy at the branch post office we've been using lately, said some woman was asking questions about us and the old church."

Secondus frowned some more. "Ouch. Like before, we'd better change to another f . . . ing postal station. What else?"

"Well," said Primus uneasily, "Last week, I visited the City Clerk to renew our non-profit license. That went okay, but the gal happened to mention that she couldn't find her file right away because somebody had been looking at it, and had put it back in the wrong drawer. I didn't think much about it at the time."

Secondus frown turned into a scowl. He muttered an exceedingly vulgar epithet. "You know, now that I think of it, somebody at the radio station told me the same damn kind of story. They'd had a call asking about the radio show and the Second Revealed Church. I don't like the sound of this. Somebody might be snooping around."

Primus stood up to return to his own apartment. "Damn right. Be sure you keep the church locked up tight and keep your eyes and ears open. The last thing we need is anyone prying into what we do."

&&&

At this point, we return to the main thread of our narrative, the original account of Humboldt Prior's dreadful predicament of first being mistaken for a deplorable fictional amateur detective of the same name, and then, worse, suspected of actually being a high-powered CIA operative. We find him still standing under an awning, in the rain, next to Penelope Rote, the striking but dangerous Channel Seven anchorwoman. Only minutes have passed since her supremely distressing demand that he assist her in secretly visiting the decrepit old Second Church of the Revealed Truth, the focus of certain Prior family activities about which he has long been both suspicious and embarrassed. The alternative was that she would instead author a news exposé concerning Prior and Cousins Leather and the Trust.

Humboldt had just said the fateful words, "What do you want me to do?"

Penny nodded. "Good. Let's talk some more, but not in this icky rain."

Humboldt flinched inwardly. He hoped she wasn't going to suggest her automobile; an even more risky setting often featured in the adventure stories that had caused all this trouble in the first place. No, she had another plan.

Pointing to a narrow little wine bar on the other side of the street, she said, "We'll duck in there," and immediately grabbed his hand and pulled him across, their feet splashing in the rain. There was no alternative and Humboldt somehow enjoyed the exhilarating feeling. It had been many years since he'd run across a main thoroughfare, much less in the rain, and still much less with an attractive woman.

Regaining the sidewalk and after a lightning calculation of the odds of the wine establishment containing any of his relatives, he followed her inside. The wine bar was one of those dark confidential little places, featuring the color mauve. Penny forged her way to a rear booth and sat down. Humboldt again followed. A waiter appeared and Humboldt agreed to a glass of white wine, recognizing as he did so, another step downward into the abyss of mystery story writing.

"Now then," she said, "here's what we're going to do. I want to get inside that old church. I need to get the true feel of it, to explore and probe, so that I can create convincing settings.

Churches are supposed to be open for worshipers, at least at reasonable times, but that place is always locked."

Humboldt, although not at all involved with church affairs, imagined that this desire on the part of an attractive woman to be alone in the church for any length of time, would be incomprehensible to any of the female Priors who knew the pastors, their cousins Primus and Secondus. In the family, they were regarded as only slightly better than the constantly groping Malice Prior.

Humboldt was momentarily relieved. Perhaps a borrowed key would be enough. He answered, taking a sip of his white wine, "I'll see if I can get a key for you."

No, things were going to be worse. She had more to say. "We'll try it tonight, just the two of us. I'll need you to show me around. You must have been there often. It will save time."

Humboldt shivered. He was going to have to accompany her. He started to protest. "Maybe . . ."

She cut him off firmly. "No, Humboldt, it's the only way. If I'm with one of the family, one of the members, it will seem innocent enough. You must be in and out all the time. I gather it's sort of like a family chapel."

Worse and worse. Now he was expected to know all about the place. He hadn't darkened its doors in years.

She finished her wine, and stood up. "I've got to get going. I'll knock on your door at about eleven tonight, as soon as I'm done with the news. Bring your flashlight. We'll have a good look around." Then she added with a giggle, "Maybe we'll even run into a mysterious ghost or something." With that, she tossed an insufficient ten-dollar bill onto the narrow table and hurried off, leaving Humboldt busy watching her and mentally enumerating his troubles.

However, after a few minutes of this, he knew he had to compose himself. He requested the bill, efficiently computed a tip and left it on the table, grumpily augmented her ten with another, and presented the resulting assembly to the cashier. For his part, the cashier rang up the charges incorrectly, returned too much change to Humboldt, and then, when the excess was left on the counter, pursed the retreating comptroller into the street, pressing an additional dollar upon him. It was just the thing to further disconcert an accountant.

&&&

Chapter 6

Humboldt had a ghastly afternoon. His lunch wasn't agreeing with him, and his reflection in the hallway mirror, usually reasonably pleasant and optimistic looking, appeared tired and haggard.

Shortly after he got home there'd been a peculiar telephone inquiry from Malice's secretary. She asked, "Would our liability insurance cover any lawsuits that might result from an on-site photography session by an advertising agency?"

Momentarily confused, Humboldt fended her off by stuffily replying, "Kindly remember that I'm only supposed to work mornings, and that I don't have the policy at home. I'll let you know tomorrow."

Then, sheltered in his library from the prying eyes of his neighbor-relatives as it had only one high window, he sat grumbling to himself. It was all very well to lunch with glamorous television personalities, but helping them with their highly risky mystery story research was quite another matter. Penny Rote had even told him to bring a flashlight. That sounded as if they'd be exploring dark nooks and crannies, probably containing rats, and worse yet, bats. Bats didn't especially bother Humboldt, as he was sometimes required to use a large bath towel to get one of them out of his second bedroom. However, women were notorious for their panicky fear of the little flying creatures. What if she saw one and started to scream?

What kind of flashlight would she be expecting? Probably she was used to the modern powerful types with half a dozen large batteries. Humboldt still used his Boy Scout flashlight. It was one of those green plastic ones, with the right-angle lens and the belt hook. He knew the batteries were okay, as he'd used it during the recent bee invasion. He decided it would have to do, as there wasn't time to get another, considering everything else that he did have to get done.

How in the world was he going to get a key to the church? And, what was that she'd said about mysterious ghosts hiding in the church? That deflected him from the vital matter of the key, by bringing back distant memories. In his youth, the inside of the church still glistened in places with some of the remaining gold leaf. However, his Mother frequently complained that more and more of the gold decoration had fallen away, and that a younger Primus Prior, then the newly ordained pastor, seemed to make no effort at replacing it. Otherwise, the interior was ordinary enough, indeed, already old and somewhat shabby. Nonetheless, there had been rumors retold by generations of Sunday school children. These were misty stories of forgotten chambers and secret doors down in the basement, filled with things mysterious or dangerous. Some of the older boys even said, as they shoved him back into some dark dusty corner, that there was a place guarded by the ghost of Osgood Prior, himself, and that the ghost would beat-up little boys.

A clap of thunder refocused his attention, and he hastily pushed those faint recollections aside. There wasn't much time. Where was he going to get a key to the church? He pondered and pondered. What an unfair request. He wasn't good at this sort of thing. Why couldn't she have just asked him to explain the church financial report? But, if he now refused to obtain the needed key, she'd expose Prior Leather and the Trust. What a predicament.

Finally, he remembered his cleaning lady, Mildred Prior, widow of a much-married third-cousin. As such, she wasn't entitled to one of the rowhouses or apartments, but as a measure of support her rent was paid and she was sometimes still employed to clean some of the Trust's properties. A year or so ago, as he remembered it, Mildred had mentioned that she had to go across and dust the ornate oak pews in the old church. He recalled watching her stooped, white-haired elderly figure trudge to his right across Woodhouse Avenue and enter the crumbling red brick edifice. Exactly how had she entered? Perhaps she had a key? Now where did she live?

Amazingly, he remembered. Once on a very rainy afternoon, much as this one, he'd driven her home to her little house. She lived only three blocks away. Thank goodness, she had a telephone. He found her number and placed the call, thinking of what story he could possibly use, and what would make her willing to give up her key and keep quiet about it afterwards. He had, more than once, paid her extra money. Maybe that would help? Just in time, he thought of something.

"Hello, Mildred. This is Humboldt Prior. Say, I left a library book in the church on Sunday and I have to return it tomorrow to avoid fines. May I borrow your key?" In his nervous state, he overlooked the obvious question of what he'd been doing in church, on Sunday, with a library book?

Incurious, Mildred was also most cooperative. "Of course you may, Mr. Humboldt. I'm just going out, but I'll leave it under the doormat."

"Thanks very much Mildred, you're a lifesaver."

"Not at all, Mr. Humboldt. I'm always glad to be of assistance."

Temporarily relieved, Humboldt rushed out into the steady rain, wheeled his black Chevy out of the communal garage, and was back in less than twenty minutes with the key to the church.

He returned just in time to field another phone call. This was another oddity, this time supplied by Orlo Prior, the office manager, asking a routine question about vouchers, and then saying in passing that their mutual cousin, Ribald, had requested the executive office file containing the name of the guidance counselor at one of the local high schools.

Next, trying a late-afternoon nap on the couch in his sunroom, Humboldt found himself trying to picture what he was mentally calling the "Second Revealed Break-In." What would it be like? The slightest misstep could be fatal. Then, after his mind wandered for a moment, he found himself considering the absurd topic of what one wore on a nighttime break-in of a church. Based on his recent viewing of television crime shows and, worse, of an half-remembered passage from one of the disastrous novels featuring the fictional Humboldt Prior, he decided his clothes had to be black and that rubber soled shoes were a must.

At first, he could think of nothing. Then a review of his rather limited wardrobe sent him scurrying upstairs. There, in the closet of his spare bedroom he rediscovered his black wool suit. This misadventure was the result of that dreary winter day at a downtown men's store several years before. He'd picked it out while under the impression it was dark blue. He selected the trousers. They had never been worn.

He added an ancient navy blue sweater and, his only option, and one at which he shuddered, his rubber-soled fishing shoes. These clumsy canvas affairs had been purchased when he first became the Leather Company's comptroller. It was during an awful week in which he was afraid he was going to have to accompany his cousin Malice on a trout fishing expedition. Luckily, because of a lawsuit, Malice had left town suddenly, letting Humboldt off the hook. He tried on these appalling garments and therefore was wearing them on one of the hottest afternoons of the year, when his cousin from next door, the always well-dressed Dorset Prior, knocked on his door.

The picture Humboldt presented was not an attractive one. His gray hair, what there was of it, was awry from pulling on the blue sweater. His glasses were askew, his aging figure did not do justice to the heavy sweater, and the black wool trousers had always been too long. Worst of all, were the fishing shoes with their green and brown camouflage canvas toes protruding from under the black cuffs of his trousers.

Dorset, in his customary lazy, superior manner, began with the startled words, "What the hell are you dressed up for?" but then stopped himself with merely a tolerant smile.

Humboldt, expecting to be scolded again, thoroughly rattled, and trying to fashion some plausible explanation for his peculiar appearance, said the first thing that came into his head. "I'm just getting ready to clean the basement."

Dorset shook his blond head in disbelief. "You don't have to do that, hire old Mildred to help you."

The mention of Mildred reminded Humboldt of his pending doom at the hands of the relentless Penny Rote. He paused, trying to think under pressure, an activity at which he excelled only when it came to the subject of his accounts.

Ignoring this hesitation, Dorset then hurriedly said what he came to say. "Anyway, Humboldt old man, I want to apologize for flying off the handle this morning. I didn't know how much you'd been helping my son Gradient with his math, and it took me by surprise. Now that I think more about it, though, I'm really glad that you are doing it. I hope you'll continue. Take some full days off. These summer mornings would be an especially good time for it, when the kid's well rested, don't you know. Thanks again." He turned to leave.

This was another oddity, as Dorset was unusually thrifty and the math summer camp was expensive. However, Humboldt was too nervous to care. He muttered a "You're welcome," to Dorset's back and closed the door. He had no idea the Dorset was really attempting to keep him away from the office. Dorset had thought of this to make way for morning meetings about their fake steamer trunk scheme.

Things were getting worse and worse. He decided to eat an early dinner, so as not to venture out with a full stomach. He baked a frozen chicken potpie and, after thirty-five minutes, sat down to eat. The heat from the oven, added to that of a hot sultry late afternoon made the temperature in his breakfast nook nearly unbearable. He hurried through dinner, always a mistake, and retreated back to his sunroom where he threw himself down on the couch, still wearing his dark blue wool sweater and black wool trousers on one of the hottest evenings of the year. The first blasts of the next thunderstorm pursued him there.

It was only six o'clock. Minutes crawled. After what seemed like an eternity, it was only six-twenty. What to do? Was there any way out? What about some sort of self-inflicted injury, followed by an emergency trip to the hospital? However, this sounded foolish even in his agitated state of mind. What could she possibly want inside the old church? He had the impression that mystery writers invented their plots and settings without any need for field research. They always found plenty to write about in their own diseased imaginations, the author of the fictional Humboldt Prior series being a prime example. Maybe Penny Rote's story about a crime set in the old church was some sort of trick. Well, maybe not.

The telephone rang at seven, but it was only one of those pesky school girls, giggling to her friends, as she inquired for, "The great Humboldt Prior," and asked for his help in locating a missing bicycle. In his distracted state, the call was almost a relief. Humboldt simply said there was really no such person and actually thanked her for calling.

At nine, with still two hours to go before his fateful encounter was to begin, Humboldt decided to reconnoiter the scene. Characteristically, and because it was still raining hard, he did this merely from his living room window, sitting awkwardly on his very uncomfortable sofa, and keeping the lights off just as was done by detectives on television. The street was dark, with just one pale light off to his left, where Woodhouse merged unobtrusively into Lower Hilltop Parkway, and another, off to his right, down where, at the dead end of the street, the tall dark Prior apartment building was only a vague hulk, dimly seen. Occasional streaks of lightning lit the dark brick hulks of the buildings across the street, and the gutters were running full with the rain. During one especially brilliant series of lightning flashes, he could see the old church quite well.

Just as with the street entrance to the stables-become-garages, the church's two entrance doors, a little to Humboldt's right, were beyond a wide arched opening in the brick wall next to the sidewalk, with the much higher front wall of the church building itself rising a few paces behind. The huge Romanesque arc of the great half-round window, looming up at what Gothic-style architects would call the narthex end of the church, occupied much of the massive dark brick front. Above it, at either end were ornate, but ugly battlement-like brick structures, protruding dimly into the wet sky. In the center, thrusting clumsily upward was the squat round steeple, encrusted with brick protuberances intended to resemble carved brownstone. Its conical slate roof was almost invisible in the pouring rain. As to signs of life, Humboldt saw none, except for an extremely wet black cat scuttling away. That was another ill omen.

Again worrying over what the night was going to bring, it suddenly struck Humboldt with chilling fear, that he'd forgotten the most important part of his break-in disguise. He would need some sort of dark colored cap or soft hat, both because of the rain and to hide his features. After all, they were well known to almost all his neighbors. In unnecessary haste, he searched the hall closet shelf. His few hats were obviously unsuitable. Finally, way at the back, he found a possible solution. It was another relic of his many troubles with his cousin Malice.

Humboldt had done his best to avoid attending the game, but Malice, in one of his officious military moods, had termed it a "command performance, with no troops excused." As a result, Humboldt now returned to his living room vantage point, outfitted in the dark blue cap of the Minnesota Twins baseball team. There, he mercifully fell asleep, his tired head resting on the arm of the living room sofa, and still nearly two hours to go before his fateful eleven o'clock rendezvous.

&&&

With, as has been said, nearly two hours before Penny Rote was to arrive at Humboldt's residence, there is time to add a word or two about the current activities of the aforementioned Malice Prior. A varied portfolio of concerns furrowed the broad forehead of this disreputable individual. He was seated in the sumptuous living room of his apartment in the Trust's four-story apartment building. He was alone, as his third wife had recently, and with what the judge had termed the fullest of just causes, divorced him. His was much the largest and by far the best furnished of the apartments, and with his excessive income and easy daily routine, it might appear that Malice had to entertain little of concern. His immaculate attire, expensive furniture, lavish hangings, and generally ornate decor, might well have soothed a lesser man. In fact, Malice enjoyed them all and looked forward with some satisfaction to their continuing augmentation.

However, he also had his worries. First, though of minor import, he was monitoring the plot being hatched by his brother Moribund and his cousins Ribald and Dorset to resume leather trunk manufacturing on a small scale, using cheap materials assembled by attractive female high school students. Malice actually heartily approved of this venture, although he planned to reshape the related executive bonus program, and, he hoped, to meet frequently and privately with the young women to discuss their experiences in leather trunk manufacturing.

Of greater, but also of not the highest concern to Malice on that hot and rainy, summer night were the rumors he'd heard about his cousins, the Pastors Primus and Secondus Prior and their sudden unexplained increase in income. As senior trustee of the Second Church of the Revealed Truth, to this also he didn't object, but as he smiled his thin toothy smirk and fingered the collar of his striped shirt, he was hoping for an opportunity to participate.

His greatest concern, one that he kept almost hidden from himself, was that he knew, deep inside, that he was far from the best chief executive ever to serve at Prior Leather, and the antics of his brother and cousins were ample proof of their similar status. With the competent Humboldt working only part time, what if something went wrong? Still worse, from just a word or two that Malice had managed to overhear, what if Humboldt had found some other interest and might retire entirely?

&&&

Chapter 7

Humboldt awoke to the banging. He had been struggling with a very bad dream in which he had forgotten where he'd parked his treasured Buick station wagon. Just as he awakened, his cousin Moribund, aided by unnamed strangers, had been giving him purposefully misleading directions, and Penny Rote, of all people, was promising to report the whole embarrassing affair on the evening news.

As he recovered himself, lost for a moment in the dark living room with only the faint glow of the streetlights for illumination, Humboldt finally made out the noise. It was actually alternate doorbell ringing and annoyed pounding on his front door. The rattle and roar of rain on his windows told him that the weather, if anything, was worse. It was just after eleven o'clock and Penny Rote was waiting.

Humboldt rushed to open the door. Penny entered, anchorwoman's head held high, at home in any situation, and seemingly impervious to the rain. To his right, just a glance showed her car parked at the curb. It stood out among the very few others, for it was a very expensive foreign sport utility vehicle. Only Cousin Malice had anything comparable. She tossed her raincoat and umbrella on a nearby chair, and said, cheerfully, "Good evening, friend Humboldt." Then, after a closer look at his attire, she added with a grin, "I see you're ready. Let's wait a few minutes, though, before we go. My weather guy says it's going to quit." With that, she sailed on into his living room, recklessly flipping on light switches as she went. Humboldt followed.

Sitting down in one his mother's antique Victorian armchairs, she surveyed her surroundings, crossed her elegant legs, and launched into an obviously rehearsed statement of her thanks for Humboldt's vital assistance in what she termed, ". . . . this literary venture of mine. I'm so glad to have your help. Maybe I'll even acknowledge it in the book and give you a free copy."

Humboldt shuddered. The situation seemed more dangerous with each passing moment.

Now, she was saying something about, ". . . . in the public interest."

He was startled by her confidence. How could one of those sleazy detective novels, exploiting the setting of a bedraggled old church, be of any concern to the public? At the same time, he had to admit to himself, in his words, that she really was most presentable.

Humboldt had had few female co-workers. Malice was constantly recruiting attractive secretaries. However, those slender young ladies stayed for an average of about three weeks and then were never seen again, except, of course, as plaintiffs in the harassment cases. Humboldt was very inexperienced in dealing with women.

Penny Rote was older, but certainly attractively proportioned. Her thick sandy hair was worn quite short, and, in person, her face showed more than a few freckles. Her clothing was another matter. Apparently ignoring all standards of proper apparel for night break-ins of decaying churches, she was still in what he presumed was anchorwoman attire, light gray pants outfit, light blue blouse, black stockings, and black heels. He wondered whether or not to stress the need for dark colors, pointing to his own as an example. Then he thought better of it, and anyway she was still talking.

"You see, Humboldt, the theory of my book is that there's this big old wreck of a church, and someone is using it as a place from which to commit crimes." She smiled. "Of course, the problem is that I haven't been in a church like yours for ever so many years, and all the other ones I've seen lately are bright new colonial styles. I need to see something really dilapidated, and that's where you come in. That old pile of bricks across the street is just what I need. It's so great that you're getting me inside when no one's around."

Quaking inwardly, Humboldt responded with only a gloomy nod. He was past the point of no return. While trembling at the thought of the disastrous trouble and embarrassment that would follow their discovery, for the moment he was hooked. It may have been her threats about Prior Leather and the Trust, or the anchorwoman aura, or perhaps the freckles had done it.

He was also thinking, just in passing, of a strange circumstance. Penny was determined to use the Second Church of the Revealed Truth as the site of a fictional crime. Why, what a coincidence. He'd recently begun to suspect that his cousins Primus and Secondus were up to something, but hoped they weren't actually using the church itself for one of their nefarious schemes. He already had enough to worry about.

After a few minutes, Penny turned to look out the front window. She said brightly, "Look, Humboldt, I'm sure it's letting up now. Let's get going." She stood up, smoothed her jacket, and led the way out the front door, saying with a gesture in the direction of her rain gear, "Why not grab that in case it starts again." He followed again, now carrying her red umbrella.

Humboldt looked nervously up and down the street. Thank goodness for the dark and stormy night. None of his snoopy relatives would be about after eleven o'clock on such an evening. Humboldt couldn't even put words to the unspeakable shame of encountering a party of those people, dressed as he was and in the company of a notorious television personality.

Penny leaped agilely across the overflowing gutters. Humboldt followed more cautiously. Within a minute, it seemed, they'd crossed Woodhouse in a right diagonal direction, reached the wall in front of the church, and were sheltering under the arch of the nearest doorway, a side door opening, as he remembered, on the corner of the sanctuary.

Humboldt fumbled for the key, enduring, for a few seconds of horror, the fear that he'd left it behind. Then, there it was in his other pocket. At first, he thought it was only sticking in the lock, but then firm metal contact told him that they were at the wrong door. What next? However, Penny Rote merely gave him an encouraging grin, shook her head, said, "This always happens," grabbed his hand, and they sloshed about forty feet north along the wet sidewalk to the farther and main front door. There, the key turned.

The door was heavy, built of massive vertical planks of dark wood, iron bound, and arched at the top. It rasped open on aged hinges. They found themselves in a dingy, rectangular hallway, with, as shown in the glimmer of Humboldt's flashlight, two doors each on the left and right, and a larger pair at the far end. The air was thick with an unpleasant damp mustiness. The plastered walls, originally painted the inevitable institutional beige, were gray with finger marks and grime. The floor still sported a few of last autumn's dried leaves.

To his horror, Penny was fumbling for the light switch. Mercifully, only one bulb was working. Worse, now she was trying the doors on their left and right. They seemed to be locked, and she looked inquiringly at Humboldt, as if thinking he might have more keys.

He explained hurriedly, "From memory, those are just stairs going up and down, the church offices, and a parlor."

Still interested, she frowned and thought a moment, wrote something on a small notepad, then strode on to the far end of the entrance hallway, and pushed open the swinging doors leading into the broad dark sanctuary. Humboldt trudged after her.

Although familiar with it as a boy, he was startled at first by immense black emptiness before them. Above, a dim glow filtered in from the streetlights, and, ridiculously, on his left, an ordinary domestic nightlight was burning in an electrical outlet low on the wall. With this meager illumination, combined with that of his flashlight, the main features slowly emerged. On each side of the center aisle, two ranks of dark oak church pews advanced before them toward the gloom of the chancel area. Even in the dim light, they could see the thick dust everywhere, and that several pews were broken. One of these, in the back row, was leaning forward, tipped against its neighbor. For these hazardous areas, pieces of cord and hand-written signs blocked access to the seats and warned worshipers away. The floors under the ranks of pews were in shadow, but Humboldt remembered them as a dingy sort of brown linoleum, probably the same as that used at his office. The aisles themselves were of glazed green and brown clay tile, now also very dirty, and cracked and worn with use. In one aisle, near where they were standing, a pair of open hymnals lay with their backs upward on the dusty floor. Regrettably, in several other places, spatters of white showed, their nature confirmed by the carcass of a dead pigeon.

At the sound of their first steps, there was a nervous rustling somewhere. Humboldt froze, ready for deeply embarrassing hostilities from some angry night watchman, or worse, the start of the dreaded bat encounter. Then all was quiet. Penny Rote said, softly, "Wow."

On the high plastered walls rising above them, there was now almost nothing except the cracks and grime of years. Especially near the front of the church, Humboldt recalled that there had once been decorations of gold encrusted icon-like figures, and also ornate patterns of gold covering the wooden carvings, rising up from the floor. Now the beam of his light showed only bare surfaces, cobwebbed and cracked plaster, and, in one place, two pieces of cheap plywood, apparently nailed to the wall to cover some sort of damage. Still higher, almost out of sight in the dusty darkness, hung about a dozen grotesque iron light fixtures, supposedly in the shape of miniature churches, but believed by generations of bored Sunday school children to resemble flying dragons.

Saying, "Let's look around," Penny led him down the center aisle, her eyes searching from left to right. She turned, "Say, Humboldt, this is quite a place. What a great setting for a murder or two. Maybe I should start with you." With a grin, she made a pistol barrel of her right index finger, pointed it at him, and whispered, "Bang, bang."

Humboldt cringed. Levity! That was all he needed, when at any moment a lurking night watchman might discover them. He shuddered at the thought of their arrest and the trouble that would cause. His mind nervously formed a newspaper headline, " TV ANCHORWOMAN DESECRATES OLD CHURCH. COMPTROLLER IMPLICATED." That would be the worst.

Penny moved forward toward the alter, glanced at the pair of iron candle sticks, one taller than the other, turned to the pulpit, climbed the steps and assumed a pastoral pose. "Hear me, sinners," she called out, laughing loudly.

Humboldt cringed again. Hoping the distraction would keep her quiet, he shined his light fully upward, illuminating part of the high arched ceiling in a soft glow. Most of it was covered with old-fashioned wood-fiber acoustic tile, very dirty and much stained by water leaks. Here and there, the tiles were missing entirely.

In the center of the ceiling, the searching flashlight revealed a much larger iron light fixture, hanging from a long, black chain, and containing, by Humboldt's recollection, for he'd counted them many times as a boy, forty-seven light bulbs. Above it, from the center of the ceiling, curving off downward toward each corner of the sanctuary, were massive wooden trusses, black in the dim light, and resting at the corners of the sanctuary, on high wooden piers thick with black carving. The church had been built in the days of low-cost lumber and Osgood Prior had seen no need for interior masonry.

Penny, descending from the pulpit, remarked, "This is really great. What else is there for me to see?"

Appropriately for the setting, Humboldt had been devoutly hoping the sanctuary would satisfy her. He said, hurriedly, "I'm not too sure. There's a basement and the tower." He could hardly speak the last words. A dangerous climb up the steep treacherous winding stairs of the tower, assuming the access door could be unlocked, would be the last straw. There was another rustling noise, this time from high up behind the altar, and then the soft call of a sleepy pigeon.

Glancing back over her shoulder, Penny walked back rather quickly, to where he was standing. "Okay, lead on, Detective Prior." She was trying to be funny, but the words still grated.

There was another rumble of thunder, and then Humboldt could hear the rain, again hammering down on the roof above them. Anxiously adopting a 'Not up in the tower' strategy, he said hurriedly, pointing to the right, "As I remember it, there's a basement stairway over there behind the chancel and another one off the entrance hall." He paused, hoping she'd change her mind.

No such luck. Penny asked, "Good deal. What's down there anyway?"

The longer they were there, the more certain he was of damning discovery. He muttered, "Just more old classrooms, a kitchen, storage, and the furnace, I think. I haven't been down there for many years. Probably nothing of interest, I'm sure."

Penny shrugged, "Might as well take a look while I'm here," and took a step toward the door he'd indicated, just visible at the corner of the chancel area. There was a scurrying noise of tiny feet, and again she quickly stepped back to him, took his hand, and then pulled him toward the door.

Humboldt followed across the dusty tiles into the rear vestibule, praying that the stairway door would be locked. Alas, it was not. Penny Rote paused at the top of the stairs, doubtless repelled by the over whelming odors of age and decay wafting up from the church basement. These were unmitigated by even the vestige of a hot dish, for the church suppers had ended more than a decade ago. Then she plunged down the stairs. Again, Humboldt followed her. If possible, he was even more worried, thinking they'd certainly be trapped down below. He was also gripped by an even greater feeling of frustration. She now had his flashlight.

&&&

Now, just for a moment, let us shift the scene back to the residence of another of the characters chronicled in this report. It was approaching midnight, minutes before the last events just described. At the crack of an especially loud clap of thunder, Pastor Secondus Prior stirred in his sleep. His wife, another bland, mostly incompetent Prior cousin, who does not really figure in this account, turned over, muttered a soft, "Wuh," and went back to sleep.

Secondus, for personal reasons, had to get up. He levered his scrawny old body out of bed, pushed his long white hair away from his eyes, and found his slippers. His bedroom was on the side of the Prior apartments away from the church. However, the architect of the building had omitted private master bathrooms, so it was necessary to leave the comfort of the bedroom and proceed along the upstairs hallway. There, passing a window fronting on Woodhouse Avenue, he chanced to look outside. It was still raining, but aided by the streetlights, the great heap of his church was visible in the distance, slightly to his right, an even blacker mass against the dark western sky. However, something looked odd. Just below the church tower, on the huge half-circle of the front stained-glass window, glistening in the rain, another faint ghostly light seemed to be moving.

Secondus differed from his brother Primus and his cousin Malice in not being abnormally suspicious. Although corrupt, his was an optimistic positive forward-looking form of corruption. In his drowsy state, he assumed the flickering glow was some sort of unusual reflected lightning, and anyway he needed to move on to the bathroom. Later, however, he'd remember it.

&&&

Curiously enough, Secondus Prior was not the only person up and about in the aging apartments thoughtfully provided by Osgood Prior for the benefit of his feckless descendents. The Pastor's cousin, the vile Malice Prior, president of Prior and Cousins Leather, was still awake and, in fact, had not been to bed. He was fully and nattily dressed in his invariably expensive casual clothes, and was equipped with a dark raincoat against the storm. He had just opened the doorway of his apartment, and lizard-like, was darting his head back and forth, left and right, searching the ornate over-decorated hallway for signs of any of his inquisitive neighbors. He repeated the process in the lobby, peering out into the rain. Although he would have termed it an appointment, we may say that he was on his way to an assignation.

By way of background, weeks before, Malice had been reintroduced to one of his third-cousins, an eager forty-year-old black-haired divorcee named Temperance Prior. They had met over cocktails at a noisy party at the home of still another relative, and one thing having led to another, had arranged to meet again, privately.

Malice had begun that part of the conversation with the words, "I always prefer to get acquainted more privately, so that we can . . . ," his words trailed off in an attractive hissing lisp.

Understanding perfectly, and impressed by his status as a corporation president, Temperance had said she thought that they should definitely get to know one another much better, where they wouldn't be so disturbed.

Malice quickly responded that he knew just the time and place.

&&&

Chapter 8

  We now return to Miss Penelope Rote and Mr. Humboldt Prior, just where we left them down in the bowels of the Second Revealed Church. Before he could stop her, Penny turned on the light at the bottom of the stairs. They were in a dank and depressing hallway leading off toward the front of the church, its far end shrouded in the gloom. Things seemed even worse down here. The hallway walls and vaulted ceiling were again of institutional beige plaster, even dirtier, damp, and spun with cobwebs.

  Penny wrinkled her pretty nose, and muttered, "Yuck, what's that?"

  There was definitely a very unpleasant odor, something like drains, he thought. There were also streaks of black mold. The floor was dark brick, coated with the scum of periodic flooding. It was not a nice place.

  Thankfully, in the first few feet of the hallway there was only one doorway. This proved to open on the furnaces and steam boilers and thus was of no interest to the intrepid anchorwoman. Next, they encountered the door to the kitchen, also apparently not to be involved in her mystery story. However, about halfway forward along the main hallway, the walls on either side were interrupted by a wide cross hallway, equally dirty, and running the entire width of the church building. Along this depressing passageway, there were more doors. Penny Rote darted from one to the next, opening each, turning on lights, and briefly inspecting the rooms, saying, "Boy oh boy, look at all this old stuff."

  Most were classrooms, empty except for scraps of discarded paper and heaps of broken furniture, coated with dirt and dust, and obviously untouched for many years. In one, on an outside wall, water dripped down. Humboldt followed her, wishing he was elsewhere, but ever recalling the mayhem she'd promised his company if he failed to cooperate.

To his surprise, she seemed most interested in a dingy storeroom, with a wooden floor, slightly raised, presumably against the damp. She exclaimed, "What an old mess. Secondhand boxes full of papers, old books, rotten floor mops, and ancient Christmas decorations all jumbled together."

Humboldt remembered the place, having once been sent there as a boy to bring more blackboard chalk to his Sunday school class. "Yes, he found himself saying, "It's always been a storeroom. The older boys used to smoke down here and once one of them said he'd hit me if I told on them."

Penny frowned. She wasn't afraid to get her hands dirty. After finding the room's light switch, her busy fingers explored several of the boxes, emerging once with a sheet of faded stationery with a letterhead in old-fashioned type. It read, "The Second Church of the Revealed Truth, Primus Prior, Pastor." Using the flashlight for a closer look, she laughingly drew Humboldt's eye to a legend across the bottom of the page, "Timeo danaos et dona ferentes."

Shaking her head, she chuckled softly, finally saying, "Humboldt, what in the world is this?"

Humboldt dimly recalled the story and reluctantly explained. "My Mother told me that when he first came here, Pastor Primus heard the words somewhere and liked the sound of them. He didn't know that 'Timeo' doesn't mean 'Thank you.' She said use of the slogan, 'Beware of Greeks when bearing gifts,' made a fiasco of the church's annual fund drive." He wondered why he was saying all this, still hoping against hope to be charged only as an accessory to the burglary. Awkwardly shuffling his feet, he said more slowly, "Really, it was before my time."

She asked casually, "Is that pastor still around?"

He nodded. "Yes. He helps his younger brother, the current pastor." He said nothing more as the two old reprobates were a family embarrassment.

Penny shrugged, pocketed the misguided letterhead, examined quite a number of other old letters and other dusty papers, pocketed three or four of them, turned off the storeroom light, and led the way back to the main hallway, skillfully dodging the dried-up remains of a long-dead rat. Humboldt groaned inwardly. Now he was involved in actual theft.

Their footfalls clattered on the dirty brick floor, as they explored the other half of the cross hallway, and then moved on toward the front basement stairway, with Penny quickly looking into each room, more than once recoiling with a soft "Icky," at something she saw or smelled.

Once, the beam of Humboldt's flashlight, still misappropriated, showed a room apparently devoted to the accumulation of scrap paper for recycling. To his annoyance, Penny wasted more time there, rummaging through the bags, and for whatever reason, actually reading and keeping a few of the discarded papers. She explained with a grin. "The stuff will be good background for my book."

At the base of the well-worn front stairs, they paused next to a grimy wooden door, obviously another storage closet. To his great relief, it was locked. For the moment, all was quiet. Humboldt was entertaining a new and not trivial worry. What if the batteries in his flashlight failed? Was he supposed to provide spares? For real spies and detectives, that was probably routine.

Then, just at that moment when thank goodness for once she wasn't talking, he distinctly heard above them the instantly recognizable sound of the church front door swinging open and the rattle of footsteps on the floor of the front hallway, directly overhead.

Humboldt froze. Just as he had foreseen, the worst had happened, but who could it be? Was it an ordinary night watchman, an armed security guard, or, most shameful of all, even the police? To her credit, Penny merely whispered, "Don't worry, I know what to do." Without making a sound, she found the switch for the lower hallway lights and plunged them into darkness. Then, they waited, Humboldt rehearsing his first words to the arresting officers.

&&&

There is no need for excessive secrecy in this chronicle, and moreover, simple fairness requires that the reader not be left in doubt. The answer to the question of the nature of the night's second intrusion of the peaceful slumber of the Second Church of the Revealed Truth is an easy one. It is merely that Mr. Malice Prior, as senior church trustee, was naturally equipped with a complete set of all keys. Faced with the imperative need obviously felt by his cousin Temperance for his company in some place of darkness and quiet, free from observation by his relatives or others, one of the well-padded church pews had naturally come to mind.

Intruders three and four, Malice Prior and his third cousin Temperance, had entered the church, hand in illicit hand, oblivious of the fact that they were not really alone. Passing the oak door that opened onto the front basement stairs, they proceeded through the swinging doors into the sanctuary, and employing a pen light that Malice frequently used for such improper purposes, were appraising the cleanliness and privacy of several of the pews well forward along the center aisle. Warming to his task, Malice kissed her on the ear.

Temperance squeezed his arm and giggled, "Oh, you little devil."

&&&

Listening carefully to the footsteps above, moving off behind them into the church, Penny Rote led the still-petrified Humboldt as silently as possible up the front stairway. She quietly opened the door into the entrance hall, closed it behind them, and paused, listening. They could just hear a shuffling noise, a whispered giggle, and more footsteps. Then, the two of them moved quickly toward the front door, their feet rasping softly across the floor.

&&&

Malice administered another kiss and was suitably rewarded. Just at this point, somewhere behind them, the lovers heard other footsteps. Malice reacted with a typically serpent-like escape mechanism. Pushing his companion ahead of him for protection, he darted away to the left and crouched down behind the front pew, thus providing just the amount of time needed for the exit of the first pair of intruders.

&&&

Penny whispered, "It's going to be okay, Humboldt." Then, opening and closing the front church door at fast as she could, she had them outside and across the street in what seemed to him to be only a matter of seconds. The rain still pelted down, and, to Humboldt's great joy, there was no one on the street and no lights in the windows of the rowhouses. Still carrying her red umbrella, he finally dared to breathe. Sheltering in the deep arch of his own front doorway, she reassured him. "Piece of cake, Humboldt my friend. This was nothing to the scrapes we used to have on our old 'TV Investigates Series.'"

A faint hope rose in Humboldt Prior. Might this be all she required? "That's a relief," he said honestly.

Penny patted his arm reassuringly. "You did just fine. Next time it will be much easier."

Humboldt shuddered in horror. 'Next time?' Then she wasn't finished. This was certain doom. Now that the authorities were alerted, a second visit would surely be fatal. Humboldt tried to form convincing words that would explain all this. However, with another friendly smile, and another soft pat on his arm, Penny exclaimed, "Got to get going. I'll be in touch." Then, seizing her umbrella, she ran down his steps, and was gone in a flurry of legs, disappearing into her SUV.

Still struggling to regain his composure and very conscious of the fact that she had kept his flashlight, Humboldt opened his own front door, scuttled into his hallway, and double locked the door behind him. He was safe, but probably only for the moment. Crouching in the front window of his darkened living room, he searched the street. The official police vehicles were evidently parked elsewhere. There were only two or three cars scattered up and down Woodhouse Avenue, but within them no lights showed. The surveillance team, if any, was certainly well hidden. A roar of thunder announced another deluge of rain. Through it, Humboldt thought he saw two figures running away from the main entrance of the church. Curiously enough, they were headed in opposite directions.

And that seemed to be all. There were no wailing police sirens, no glare of accusing floodlights, and no authoritative knocks on his door. Humboldt staggered upstairs. After a hot shower, that he hoped would bring at least some relaxation, he tumbled into bed. Expecting hours of tossing and turning, he instead fell asleep almost at once. For about thirty minutes, all was quiet.

Then, at about two o'clock in the morning, Humboldt awoke with a start and an awful thought. He turned on his light, jumped out of bed, and in his faded pajamas, rushed downstairs. In an agony of worry, he desperately searched his front hall and living room. Yes, his worst fears had been realized. His Minnesota Twins baseball cap, an integral part of his disguise, was missing, doubtless lost somewhere in the church. What a disaster. He'd read of the new science of DNA testing. Apparently, with far less evidence than would remain on the inside of his cap, trained police experts could make a positive identification. It was only a matter of time.

Now virtually convicted, Humboldt began to remount the stairs, resolved at least to enjoy one of the few nights remaining to him in his own home. For some reason, he turned back. There, on the hall chair, a relic of his great-aunt, was even more damning evidence. Through inexcusable carelessness, he'd retained Penny Rote's blue raincoat. However, he next found himself picking it up, shaking out the remaining raindrops, and hanging it carefully in his coat closet. Then he returned to bed and, convinced that there was nothing he could do to escape the fateful knock on his door, he slept soundly for over six hours.

&&&

Later the next morning, there actually was a loud knock on the door of one of the other Prior abodes. This time it was the slender white-headed figure of Pastor Secondus Prior, trying to rouse his older brother, Pastor Primus. This was never an easy task, for Primus usually slept late, exhausted by his multi-faceted suspicions and illicit activities of the previous day. Finally, a nearly identical scrawny white-haired old man appeared at the door, differing from the man seeking entry only in that this one was clutching a faded and none-too-clean bathrobe about his distended belly, the remnant of his once more ample figure of pre-retirement days.

"What the hell do you want at this hour?"

Secondus, out of breath from his hurried arrival, said hushed tones, "I've got to talk to you, something's happened."

Primus, his routine day-to-day suspicions immediately aroused, nodded, and ushered his brother into his shabby living room. "I knew it," he said, "I told you to be more careful." Actually, Primus had no idea of the particular concern that brought his agitated younger brother to his door. His was just a sort of general-purpose response, arising from his habitually suspicious nature, and applicable to many of their recent activities.

Secondus sank into one of the threadbare chairs. "I've just been over at Second Revealed," he gasped. "Look at what I found." He displayed a damp baseball cap. "Somebody was in there last night."

Primus, although also seated, staggered in dismay. Which of their numerous acts of malfeasance or misfeasance might be targeted, and who might be investigating them? He had hoped that the last of their thefts of gold, carefully removed from the decorations of the old church, had receded back into time and the statute of limitations. Then, remembering their highly questionable radio ministry and the unexplained inquiries of which they had indications, he was sure he knew. He muttered, "Secondus, it's got to be the damn radio show."

His brother was inclined to agree. Still active as the senior pastor of the Second Church of the Revealed Truth, he was more closely tied to the peccadilloes of the radio ministry, and had more to lose. However, ever the optimist, he grasped at straws. "You may be right, Brother, but could there be anything else? What about that damn Malice Prior? Sure, he's a trustee, but he's always sneaking around. Twice before, I found him in there. Why one time he even had some girl with him. He had the gall to try to tell me she was interested in church architecture." He snickered.

Anything relating to his cousin Malice was always high among Primus's suspicions. "Could be, but what's he after? When did this happen?"

Secondus shook his head. "I was over there late yesterday afternoon for a few minutes. Everything was kosher. This morning, I went over to check for mail and found the damn cap on the floor by the front door. It wasn't there yesterday."

Thinking further, Primus finally assumed the worst. "It isn't Malice. He wouldn't be caught dead in an old cap like that. It's probably the FBI or the IRS. I've seen that their guys always dress casual when they're on a night raid." Primus, like many of his idle relatives, occupied his ample free time by watching television.

Secondus started. "By God, Primus, you've got to be right. I remember now. I was looking out late last night. I thought just for a second I saw a funny light moving on the front window of the church. Now, I know what it was."

His brother snarled. "Now we're in for it. It's either the Feds or something even worse." He struggled up out of his chair and paced nervously back and forth.

Secondus was appalled. "What in hell could be worse than the Feds?"

Primus, revealing too much reading of dubious religious newsletters and too few regular baths, leaned close his brother and whispered, "I'll tell you what's worse. It's one of the big outfits, the national radio ministries. They're even more crooked than we are. I've always suspected that they'd try to muscle in on our territory. They probably have spies scouting us out and trying to find out how much money we're able to skim off."

Secondus had another worry. "What if they rat on us to the media? We've always been afraid that somebody might call one of those TV investigators about us."

Primus cursed. "I suppose that could f . . . ing happen and we'd have a hell of a mess trying to answer all their damn questions."

Secondus was out of optimism. "What the f . . . are we going to do? Those big multi-state salvation ministries are tough. They're worse than the mob. They'll roll right over us."

Primus, still pacing, pointed a boney finger at his younger brother. "That's just what will happen if we don't get help. We need a partner, somebody just as tricky as they are. Say, I've got an idea. What about that guy who wanted to make some bucks taking pictures of our members? He said he'd cut us in because he was having trouble getting photo jobs at the reputable churches."

For all his worry, Secondus chuckled. "Oh, him. That guy called Tompkins. We had to tell him we've only got a couple of dozen members, and some of them don't want their photos circulating."

Primus nodded. "Yeah, we should get old Stewie Tompkins. He calls himself 'Snapshot' Tompkins. He's slippery as they come."

&&&

Chapter 9

The day had dawned without rain, although last night's drenching left the air heavy with moisture. Humboldt slept on, sweating, but happily oblivious. When, just before noon, he did awake, it was with a strange gloomy confidence. His was one of those states of mind in which the person believes that nothing worse can possibly happen. He was absolutely certain that the police, armed with science, were already full on his trail.

In the course of dressing for work, again in his ill-fitting lightweight summer suit, it suddenly came to him that it was after twelve PM. He was very late for work. More trouble. Then he thought, with almost a devil-may-care attitude, what did it matter? I'm semi-retired. I'll just work in the afternoon for a change. He lunched comfortably on buttered toast and a slice of cold meatloaf, and still in the mood of daring his pursuers, drove downtown in his more conspicuous white Buick station wagon.

Unfortunately, the drive began with an embarrassing incident at the gas station. The clerk mistakenly charged another person for Humboldt's gasoline and made him wait while the mess was straightened out. In spite of the car's air-conditioning, the heat was oppressive, and he had a cramp in the calf of his left leg. What a bad start. Several snarls of traffic delayed him, and in one place, a huge crane blocked most of the street. Waiting there, his leg aching and abused by the smell of hot asphalt and automobile exhaust, Humboldt's worried mind reverted to its fussy corporate comptroller mode. Attempting to be proactive, although not good at it, he began to devise, and prepare for, alternative fates, each turning out to be worse than the previous one. In the final version, Penny Rote's superiors at the TV station, for all of her importance and position of authority, discharged her, turned state's evidence, and not only blamed the burglary on him, but also forced Penny to tell what she knew about Prior and Cousins Leather. Aided by this, all of his previous worries returned.

When you came down to it, Humboldt thought, it was really all the fault of that disastrous amateur writer and his vile fictional detective. The man's reckless use of a real person's name had started all the trouble, and compounded it by supplying all that unwelcome information on police and legal procedure. He wished he'd never heard of any of it.

Thus, it was a no longer fatalistic, but rather an actively distressed Humboldt Prior, who parked his car in the company's half flooded parking lot, and limped his water-soaked way across the muddy street to his office. Not even a friendly wave from Millard or Everett Fillmore, returning from a lunchtime errand, lessened his gloom.

Feeling like a hunted animal, Humboldt climbed the stairs to the second floor corporate offices. He passed the luxurious private office of the president, barely noticing Malice Prior, glaring from behind his partially open door, his head never still. There was really nothing unusual there.

However, next door, where the half-glass walls provided less privacy, he could see that his other cousins, Moribund Prior, general sales manager, Dorset Prior, engineering and production, and Ribald Prior, personnel manager, were having an afternoon meeting. Usually, by noon, one or more of them would have disappeared in the direction of one of the expensive private golf courses for which Prior Leather paid their memberships. Was the meeting a bad sign? All three looked up as he passed, and he hoped they wouldn't ask him to join them.

In the comparative safety of his own office, Humboldt shut the door and relaxed a little. The reassuring familiarity of his drab wood and metal furniture and shabby décor was a welcome change from last night's horrors. What next, he worried? How could he escape the clutches of the police, not to mention those of the relentless anchorwoman?

Seeking refuge in routine, he turned to a pile of payment vouchers, and set out to review and approve. As a business enterprise, Prior Leather was virtually inactive, so there usually weren't many of these payments. The first few were typical of those needed to fund the minimal comings and goings of the various idle executives, only occupying time as opposed to actual business related activities. Another payment, very limited as to description, had been initiated by Prior Leather's attorneys and was in favor of another law firm representing a woman who evidently had proved some sexual harassment claim against the president. This, too, was not unusual.

Two payments caught his attention. In the first, Dorset Prior had requested the purchase of sixteen thousand square feet of something called 'Faux Leathre,' a material unknown to Humboldt, but obviously available from a French supplier at a very low cost. "LES ASBESTO - EXPRESSLY NOT WARRANTED" was stamped on the invoice. In the other payment, Ribald Prior, of personnel, was requesting reimbursement for what he called "interviewing expenses," amounting to almost $150.00. Attached were copies of receipts from ice cream and hamburger shops bearing names such as "Jennifer," "Heather," "Bambi," and "Susie." Humboldt frowned, but had no grounds for withholding his signature. The amounts were modest, even for Prior and Cousins, and the purchase of shoddy goods and the interviewing of young women were not uncommon activities of his cousins. He shrugged, signed, and sighed sadly.

&&&

Although already deeply troubled, had Humboldt been present at the meeting in Moribund's office he might well have done much more than shrug and sigh. When we join the meeting, Moribund Prior, general sales manger, is speaking.

"As I told you this morning, Dorset," he boasted, "I've personally got it all fixed up with Manheimers department stores." He leaned back in his desk chair, crossing his skinny legs in a relaxed manner and gestured toward the ceiling. "I had to use a little persuasion, but they're so damn fixated on their plans for that winter promotion of theirs, that they swallowed it whole. Didn't even blink at the price of $929.95 per trunk and actually raised the order quantity to ten dozen."

Ribald grinned. "That's great news, Morrie. The increase in the order will help offset the changes the president made in our bonus plan."

Dorset and Moribund shook their heads regretfully. They'd been expecting it.

Ribald went on. "How did you kill their first order?"

Moribund snickered. "Oh, f . . k, that was easy. First, I got their advertising guy a little drunk. Then, I just said the first thing I thought of. Something about those first trunks being a model that we used to make for the government, and that we couldn't sell them to him. I hinted at national security regulations."

"So it's all good to go?"

"Yeah. They're going to have ten or fifteen of the big trunks in each store, at least one for each department. Some will be decked out with manikins wearing pretty clothes, and beachwear, and others with some fake green holly stuff and more manikins in red outfits. One will be right next to where they have those dumb Santa Claus guys set up for the kiddies."

Ribald rubbed his hand in his thick oily hair. "Good thing it's for Christmas. Those teenage girls I want to hire are all on summer vacation now, but right after Labor Day, they'll all be looking for jobs to earn money for college. I already talked to several and they'll spread the word. Luckily, two or three were around the high school for cheerleading practice, and I even saw them in their outfits. Hot stuff." His expression reverted to his normal evil leer.

Suspecting that Prior Leather's president, Malice Prior, might be listening next door, and would join them at any moment, Dorset wanted to show that he had his end well in hand. "I've got my end well in hand," he began. "I found the goods we'll need to cover the trunks, once we make those cheap wooden box frames. I got the stuff overseas from a remnants outfit I found on the Internet. It's called Faux Leathre, made in France from some sort of residue. I talked to the French guy on the phone. I couldn't understand him very well, but I think he said something about recycled cardboard, stiffened with some sort of fiber. Reconstituted asbestos, I think he said it was."

Ribald, still thinking evilly of the lithe young bodies he planned to hire as assembly workers, was mildly concerned. "Isn't that stuff dangerous?"

Dorset, always eager to demonstrate the sort of engineering and production knowledge he wished he actually had, shook his head. "Nah. It's safe as anything. When it says 'reconstituted,' it means completely changed. Nothing to worry about."

The others, though in total ignorance, nodded.

Then, Moribund summed up. "Okay, guys. Get everything ready. Dorset, get some more of that cheap wood for the boxes. We'll slap the trunk frames together, tack on that fake leather, add some cheap plastic hardware, and we'll be all set. I'll tell the boss. As usual, Brother Malice is all hot about the damn advance photo shoot for the advertising. He's offered to host it for Manheimers, once we get the first trunk put together. I'll bet he's already been interviewing those voluptuous models."

Ribald actually giggled. "I'd like to be there for that."

Moribund put his finger to his lips. "Keep it quiet. Malice says it's all 'Top Secret,' like in the army, strictly 'need to know.' Especially, for old Humboldt."

Looking uneasily over their shoulders, Dorset and Ribald nodded. Both somehow felt their chances were better, the less 'old Humboldt' knew.

Behind the door that separated Moribund's office from that of his older brother, the president, Malice Prior, there was another sinister nod.

&&&

Later that same afternoon, uptown in the shabby and little-used offices of the Second Church of the Revealed Truth, there were more negotiations that would have added to Humboldt's alarm had he known of them. Secondus Prior, senior pastor, and Primus Prior, pastor emeritus, their thin elderly fames racked on uncomfortable old-fashioned straight-backed church-parlor chairs, were seated on one side of a greasy old mahogany table, waiting in the church for an expected visitor. Both were tired from an exhausting session at the tape recorder. Recognizing an opportunity in the past week's heavy rains, they were planning an extra broadcast on a Biblical flood theme, comparing their radio ministry with an ark, to which each elderly listener should send extra money for provisions.

Primus grumbled. "Hell, brother, when's Stewie coming, anyway?"

Secondus twisted his skinny body, trying to find a less uncomfortable position. "Pretty soon. We're lucky he was in town. Apparently, a few months ago he had a job in one of the suburbs. He said he had to stop by that church today and replace some of the frames he sold to the church members. Something about the gold decoration coming off."

Primus turned away from the table and spat his chewing gum into a far corner of the office. "Well, we know about that, don't we," he muttered with a conspiratorial glance.

Secondus nodded. "Yeah, as if we still had any gold in the church. All the gold leaf is long gone and it was f . . . ing hard to scrape off. I wish we had some more of it, though. If only the old founder, Osgood Prior, had left us some in reserve. Just for a rainy day."

Primus shrugged. The brothers were constantly looking for an angle that would yield some more money. "Damn good time for that, these days with all this rain." At that point, there was a stealthy knock on the heavy oak door of the office.

(Before actually introducing the specimen under consideration, a general word about church photographers is advisable. Almost all are honest citizens, simply trying to earn a living. To do this, they need merely to persuade other reputable people to purchase attractive framed photographs of themselves. These are in addition to those taken to appear in those illustrated church directories that are so helpful when trying to identify the person who greeted us at the grocery store. Endless varieties of high-pressure salesmanship are only incidental to these worthy ends.)

Stewie Tompkins, of Amory, Mississippi, was at the lower extreme of that sales continuum. His merchandise was shoddy, and his supply of pressure tactics was inexhaustible. His out-of-date lens sometimes produced a misty effect, making the members of the congregation unrecognizable even to their closest pew-mates. He always dismissed as a coincidence, the incident of his having allegedly charged for photographing a deceased parishioner who had passed on before his photo appointment. Tompkins merely happened to be in the church at the time of the visitation.

The oak door opened to reveal a lanky rat-faced middle-aged man, with thick short-cut gray hair. His yellowish-green leisure suit, of serviceable double-knit material, appeared to have been designed, decades before, for a shorter but heavier individual. He was wearing orange socks.

His greeting was friendly and familiar, for churches such as Second Revealed seldom called him without some special need. "Heh, Secondus, you old bastard. How yah doing?"

Introductions were accomplished and Stewie 'Snapshot' Tompkins, wrinkling his nose at the musty air, sat down opposite the two pastoral brothers. Knowing a little about their radio ministry, he rather thought they might want special photographs of themselves to send to their listeners. Misguided as such an idea seemed he was already adding twenty percent to his usual prices.

Primus came directly to the point, or at least as directly as possible for one of his suspicious nature. "Mr. Tompkins, I assume you know of our important new radio ministry."

Stewie grinned. "Sure as heck do. Great stuff."

"Yes, ours has been a worthy endeavor. Now, however, I'm sorry to tell you that the forces of evil are arrayed against us. We may be under unfair media scrutiny and also believe that competitors are snooping around, jealous of our pure purposes, and intent on mere financial gain."

Secondus nodded and continued, "Yea, while we seek only to serve our flock and cover our extremely modest costs, we suspect that distant national ministries are preparing to ravage the peaceful groves of our totally charitable garden of spiritual rest for seniors. They would exploit our listeners, clear-cutting our virgin plantings rather than sustaining." The unconscious choice of a lumbering metaphor was doubtless inherited from the buccaneering founder of their church.

Stewie Tompkins smirked. He'd been wrong, but there still might be money to be made. He nodded in agreement and then, lying glibly, replied with inspired phrases. "One of the big national radio ministries, huh. I hear they're all trying to expand to other cities, and aren't fussy about how they do it. They all have strategic plans and hard-nosed management consultants."

Primus shuddered. His worst suspicions were correct, and given the nature of his lesser suspicions, that was indescribably serious. He tried to compose himself. "Mr. Tompkins, we too need a consultant, a younger more active man, who can find out what's happening. Questions are being asked and last night our church, the sacred bastion of our radio ministry, was actually penetrated."

Tompkins, irreverent as some church photographers are, raised his hands in mock amazement. "Wow. So they actually broke in on you. It must be one of the major salvation conglomerates from the southeast. They always mean business and resort to all kinds of shady tactics." He instinctively felt that the more worried the elderly brothers were, the more money would be forthcoming.

Secondus confirmed this. "Through frugal savings, we have emergency funds for such purposes. Shall we say a $50,000 retainer with some of it paid in advance?"

Stewie Tompkins smiled. "Lead me to it, boys. Where do I start?"

Calling on his arsenal of suspicions, Pastor Primus Prior had most of the suggestions. "We need the church watched, especially at night. We need you to hang around at the post office we use and at our radio station. Find out who is sneaking in there and asking about us. Use all your contacts."

Secondus wanted to help. Rising to his narrow height, he said mournfully, "Alas, we also fear it may be possible that the evil forces marshaled against us, with their huge broadcasting budgets, may have bribed one of the local television stations. A secret media investigation, intended to taint and weaken us, may also be underway."

Lying in his teeth, Tompkins agreed with everything they said. As long as they kept the money coming, he was perfectly willing to work day and night, occasionally checking the church, asking a few questions in the neighborhood, and watching the TV news. He was picturing the luxurious motel suite with the well-stocked liquor cabinet, to which he planned to move that very day.

&&&

Chapter 10

At one o'clock in the morning, two or three days after the horrific events described in the previous chapters, Humboldt Prior stirred in his troubled sleep. He had not been resting well lately. First, over-arching all his other concerns was his dread of another call from Penny Rote. He was still cornered and trapped by her fatal knowledge of the Prior Trust, and would have to respond. Her words, "Next time," as though posted in stark black letters on some evil billboard, loomed up before whatever more positive thoughts happened to occupy his mind. At night, they kept him awake.

Things at the office, usually his sole source of satisfaction, had not been going quite as they usually did. He couldn't put his finger on the problem, but something made him uneasy. For one thing, his cousins Moribund and Dorset were frequently together. Not that there was anything theoretically wrong with this, but Humboldt knew from long experience that sales and manufacturing were often at swords points and normally simply tried to ignore each other.

As usual, he attempted to take comfort from the fact that nothing was actually happening down in the first-floor workshops of Prior Leather's derelict factory. However, he had noticed Dorset emerging from the factory area one afternoon, covered with dirt and grease, as though he'd been attempting to use one of the old machines. He passed off Humboldt's polite inquiry with a casual remark that he'd just been looking for something he remembered seeing down there. Then too, one day as he was leaving the office, Humboldt had observed a delivery of several large stacks of wood, each piece about two inches in cross section and about six feet long. Some were full of knots, others were wet and badly warped, and all were coated with mildew and dirt. Dorset was outside with one of the very few actual workers still employed by Prior and

Cousins Leather. He was obviously arranging to have the stacks of wood moved into the factory. What possible use could there be for such rotten material?

Finally, the president, his deplorable cousin Malice, had been pestering him again with peculiar questions. Usually, Malice kept his distance, taking refuge in military jargon about separation of command responsibilities, to avoid contact with Humboldt except on matters strictly related to accounting. These, Humboldt knew his boss saw as a necessary evil, vital to the continued flow of large salaries, but best left alone. Beyond this, unknown to Humboldt was the president's fear of the all-powerful accountants of the Trust, lying in wait at their private offices on one of the top floors of the National Bank. Malice knew they were inclined to listen to his comptroller.

The president's questions seemed to relate to the taxability of incentive bonus payments and even stock option grants and suggested that Malice was imagining a level of profitable business activity unseen at Prior Leather for decades. What was he thinking of? All in all, Humboldt was uneasy.

On this particular night, Humboldt had attempted a quiet evening. Turning to the usually reliable public television, he had enjoyed a program on European rail travel, but had then been betrayed by the programming director, who with obvious ill intent had followed it with a horrid detective story in which the detective himself had been wrongfully charged with a Kafkaesque criminal trespass. That was all he needed.

At about nine o'clock on a warm sultry rainy night, hoping to relax, he had gone to bed early after a hot shower, over-looking the fact that the temperature was still well above eighty degrees. Thus, he found himself sprawled on his bed, too overheated to sleep well, and listening to alarming storm warnings on his poorly tuned radio. He had been asleep for an hour at most, when, as stated, something stirred him.

He knew dimly that he'd been beset by a frightening dream, one in which his cousin Ribald, assisted by a dozen or so screaming teenage girls, had been chasing him through the dark streets of his neighborhood, urging him to appear on a popular television program devoted to unsolved crimes. In his dream, he was unable to run, and his pursuers were steadily gaining on him, chanting, "Detective, detective," over and over. Then the scene changed.

Now, in his next dream, it seemed that a vaguely familiar voice was hectoring him on another topic. Stridently, the voice was saying something about, "Attractive gifts," "Urgent needs," and "Mailing right away." What could that mean? Then he more or less awoke, hot and very uncomfortable, to a rumble of distant thunder.

It was pitch dark and he could hear more rain on the roof. The quavering voice continued, now in the form of unwanted medical advice, with words sounding like, "Mend your neck." Sleepily, he struggled to find the source of the exhortation. Finally, he discovered that his bedside radio was still playing, and on turning his better ear to the sound, resolved the repeated words as "Send your check."

But who was speaking? At first, while the voice was definitely familiar, he couldn't place the speaker. Although it was just across the street from his home, Humboldt had not for years, been present for services at the Second Church of the Revealed Truth. With age, voices alter, but after some minutes of listening to highly unwelcome information about the growing costs of religious broadcasting, he at last determined that the speaker was none other than his own elderly cousin, Pastor Primus Prior.

Specifically, in an old man's scratchy voice, he heard, "So, heed the entreaties of your devoted guide in your journey to the hereafter, your dear friend Pastor Primus, of Second Revealed, coming to you this evening solely through the blessed support of listeners such as yourself." There was a hesitation and a coughing sound. Then the words continued. "Why not use one of the preaddressed envelopes right now. Turn on your bed light, find your check book and a stamp, and keep us working for you with the beyond."

Humboldt sat up. Ranging in tone from a dull rasp to an excited screech, Primus was repeating his theme for the fourth time, clearly tying good things in the listener's after-life to generous gift purchases and contributions supporting the valiant efforts of the Revealed Truth Radio Ministries. Only with such determined electronic advocacy, beamed heavenward at many hundreds of watts of power, could the listener have certainty of the long-term future. With that sure confidence, Pastor Primus intoned, came another, vital to the continuance of the radio ministry. "Beloved friends," he began, "the skyward entreaties supported by your gifts bring also the blessed certainty you'll enjoy in ignoring any misguided questions raised by your children or grandchildren as to the generous amounts you are sending to the Radio Ministries. They mean well, but know not that which has been revealed to you."

Yet, there was more. Humboldt, now even more awake, shook his head in disbelief. Reaching back to ideas from the nineteenth century, Primus was even clumsily hinting that his, alone among radio ministries, enjoyed a form of two-way communication. When all circumstances and conditions were favorable, and radio audience contributions were ample, he claimed it was even possible to hear from recently decreased listeners, or the relatives of living listeners, "Those Lying at Rest in Revealed Truth," as he called them. "Those beloved departed beings, now living on the blissful other side, are unanimous in their sacred endorsement of the Revealed Truth Radio Ministry and recommend further financial support. With such support, communication with the dear departed is definitely possible." After being interrupted by a fit of sneezing, the broadcast ended with a prayer for intercession in the reduction of radio broadcast access fees.

This was in a way, Humboldt thought glumly, just another type of embarrassing nightmare. He'd heard this new venture described casually by his next-door neighbor, after one of cousin Dorset's wakeful nights of indigestion. Primus and Secondus were up to their old tricks, only using more up-to-date technology. His only consolation was that apparently they couldn't afford television. Dorset, gullible as always, had read something about the importance of outreach, and actually saw the radio ministry as evidence of renewed vigor in the Second Revealed Church. At the time, Humboldt, focused as usual on his figures, had tried to pass it off as more or less harmless. Even now, he thought as he turned over, trying to go back to sleep, it really wasn't any worse than what some of his other cousins, Malice Prior and Ribald Prior, were up to almost every day.

Sadly, for Humboldt, the night's disturbances weren't over. Two hours later, still awake he got up to look outside, wondering if it was still raining. The dark pavement of Woodhouse Avenue, usually deserted at this time of night, glistened with rain. However the street wasn't empty. A garish yellow Cadillac sedan was parked directly in front of his residence. Of greater concern, was the man inside who was obviously watching the church. From time to time, a powerful flashlight played across the front of the old building from one entrance to the other. Who in the world drove a car like that? Then he knew. As frequently portrayed on television, it was obvious that police plain-clothes detectives had the area under surveillance. Humboldt shuddered.

&&&

In the mid-afternoon of the day that began with Humboldt's deeply troubled night and early morning, the scene shifts to one of the more dingy units of the Prior apartment building at the north end of Woodhouse Avenue, about thirteen doors north of Humboldt's rowhouse. Pastor Secondus Prior was seated, wearing a stained undershirt and disreputable overalls, preparing a sermon. He was barefoot because of the heat.

If interrupted by the telephone he would have said he was in his study, however strictly speaking, he was in one corner of his crowded living room, hunched over his littered old wooden desk, composing his message for the following Sunday.

Indeed, even more strictly speaking, Secondus might be better said to be compiling or assembling his sermon. He was the fortunate possessor of a well-thumbed book of favorite sermons of a popular mid-nineteenth century southern evangelist, now free of copyright protection. Years before, it had been his practice to simply copy one of the sermons, changing only a few words. Now with the dwindling attendance and increasing deafness of the remaining members of the Second Church of the Revealed Truth, he had adopted a more eclectic method. In this, he used approximately the first quarter of one message and the last quarter of another, thus producing sermons characterized by both variety and brevity. This afternoon, he was almost finished.

Over the noise of his wife's kitchen radio, blaring a popular song, he thought he could hear a disturbance outside. Seconds later, recalling it more exactly, he thought although he was also growing deaf, it had sounded like the scrabbling noise of an elderly man attempting to run up a flight of stairs. Then there was the noise of someone falling against the wall, followed by curses and an exhausted knocking. He went to the door.

His brother, Pastor Emeritus Primus Prior, tumbled into the room, choking, panting, and calling for a drink. Hurrying to his ample liquor cabinet, Secondus supplied an inexpensive local beer, gestured his brother to a chair, and stood by awaiting developments. Primus had his white hair combed and was dressed in a business-like black suit, shirt, and necktie. Only, his mismatched socks, and unshaven thin face suggested unusual haste and excitement.

After another large swallow of beer, he began. "Did you hear what the f . . . happened last night."

Guessing this was a reference to the taped broadcast of the Revealed Truth Radio Ministries, during which he'd slept soundly, Secondus prevaricated. "My wife said it sounded a little different and that you were the only one talking."

"Damn right. The radio station guy called me just before midnight, saying they couldn't find the tape. He admitted they had it, but now it was gone." Primus paused, lost in thought. Then he muttered an especially vile expletive, and added as a typically suspicious aside, "You don't suppose that big national ministry that's after us could have stolen the damn thing?"

Secondus doubted this, but said only, "What did you tell them at the radio station?"

It was warm in the room and Primus was perspiring freely. He wiped his face and growled. "Quite a few damn things, but that's neither here nor there. The question was what to do?" He paused again for emphasis. "Well, I said I'd come downtown, and made it there about ten minutes before air time. The damn young punk was just standing there with his face hanging out. I had to make a decision, and I decided to go on the air myself. Live radio."

Secondus tried to suppress a horrified look and failed, but Primus, his excitement building, missed it entirely. Recovering, the younger of the two white-haired elderly brothers asked cautiously, "How did it go?"

"Pretty damn good, everything considered. I gave them some of the usual comforting stuff, and plenty of requests for dough. Then, I sort of wandered off onto something new that I'd heard of somewhere. Maybe I was too tired, but I found myself saying a few things about that old deal about talking to the deceased. You know, sitting around tables and waiting for knocking noises, when all the time it's the host doing the knocking, and then telling the suckers what it means."

Secondus had been standing through all this, but now he slumped back into his desk chair. "My God, you're talking about mediums and spiritualism and all that."

Primus was recovering his composure and realized that to Secondus, here a proxy for the uninformed public, the topic may have sounded risky and even irreligious. However, with superior knowledge of actual listener sentiment, Primus was also quite cocky.

"Damn right I was, though only for a few sentences. Then the time we pay for ran out. That was when the phones lit up. The station got about a dozen calls. The old bats in the nursing homes just loved the idea of messages from the departed. Some said they were sending an extra check and others wanted to know when we were going to do it again. One old dame even talked about changing her will. Brother, we're onto something big."

Secondus was interested, but cautious. "Maybe so, but we're not mediums and we don't know s . . t about spiritualism."

Primus was undaunted. "It ain't that hard to learn. I went right downtown to the bookstore and got an old book that tells all about it." He brandished a cheap looking paperback with a lurid red and yellow cover. "Meantime, we've got help. When I woke up this morning, I called old Stewie Tompkins right away. He's from Mississippi, so I figured he might know." (As often in this narrative, Pastor Primus was mistaken. People as sensible and practical as the residents of the State of Mississippi, are not especially taken with spiritualism.)

Secondus, however, was impressed. "Did he?"

"Damn right he did. He says his old auntie was a medium. He's coming over to tell us all about it." Primus thought a minute and then went on, obviously forgetting his own age. "This could be it. We'll be giving those crazy old folks just what they're looking for. Their own dear departed sweeties will be telling them how important it is to send us the bucks. It's what the business guys call real value added."

Secondus nodded. He was equally corrupt, but as has been mentioned, his was a more positive form. "It sounds good," he said. "Maybe that will give us the edge on the big national take-over ministry that's snooping around." In his enthusiasm, he stood up and brought each of them another beer.

Then the two brothers sat down to wait for their newly hired consultant, now found to have, in addition to youth and ingenuity, specialized knowledge of the new and promising field that they planned to exploit. Primus was telling Secondus of the certain increase in donations, and Secondus was explaining that there was a good 'tie-in' with one of the figurines they had for sale. As we leave them, a yellow Cadillac is pulling up in front of their apartment building.

&&&

Chapter 11

(Note: At this point in the narrative, the historian owes the reader a technical explanation. In this account of Humboldt Prior, his various cousins, the television anchor Penelope Rote, and the Second Church of the Revealed Truth, certain literary conventions are observed. One of these is that of chapters of roughly equal length. To do otherwise is to court disaster.

Careful readers, noting very large differences in length between successive chapters, immediately suspect that they have been sold or given an expurgated version. That, they will not tolerate. Therefore, in this new chapter, we immediately return to more of the same scene set in the squalid apartment of Pastor Secondus Prior, where he and his brother, Pastor Primus, are awaiting the arrival of Stewie "Snapshot" Tompkins, church photographer and their newly hired consultant in the affairs of the Revealed Truth Radio Ministry.)

&&&

Stewie Tompkins parked his yellow Cadillac at the curb in front of the Prior apartments. For once, it was not raining. However, he did not immediately get out and hurry up stairs to the apartment of Pastor Secondus, where he'd been told to meet the two brothers. A moment's thought seemed indicated.

"Snapshot" Tompkins was usually a cautious man. Although his nickname might seem to suggest facility at haste or ability to make quick decisions, this was not the case. His practice was to think things over first, and today he knew he'd have to be careful, as he was far from on familiar ground. In his normal occupation, that of selling unwanted portrait photographs to church members, he definitely knew 'what was what.' Years of practice told him how to compliment the men on their ladies, and the ladies on their jewelry. He knew how to feel out the situation, learning all about the member's family. Then, almost without thinking, he gushed anecdotes and compliments, each calculated to sell another picture for another relative. Long experience had prepared him with full knowledge of his craft. However, contrary to his emphatic statements to Pastor Primus Prior, Tompkins knew almost nothing about spiritualism.

Beyond a movie that he'd happened upon in 1987, and a dimly remembered newspaper exposure of a spiritualist practicing in Memphis, Tennessee that he'd read in 1995, Stewie was almost at a complete loss. He retained only two ideas. One was an image of people sitting around a table, doing something or other. The other was that there was money to be made. Trying to recall more, he sat for two or three minutes, pondering. Finally, he shrugged. As usual, he'd have to fall back on trickery and deceit.

He ascended the stairs, taking note of the substantial, though somewhat worn carpeting and wall coverings. There was money here, or at least there had been at one time. He found the entrance to Secondus' apartment, listened and then knocked politely. There was a shuffling patter of old feet and the door opened. As was his custom, Tompkins used all his faculties to quickly size up the moods of his clients. Two pairs of elderly eyes returned the favor, looking questioningly from vacant faces, below two shocks of shaggy white hair. Stewie took in the shabby apartment, the scrawny bodies, and the mismatched socks and/or bare feet of his respective hosts and grew more confident. It was going to be easy.

"Hi guys, how are yah?" he sang out. He found a place to sit on a faded sofa, being careful to preserve the crease in the slacks of his greenish leisure suit. Today, he'd added a pink shirt to the ensemble. As he sat down, he found further inspiration on the dusty coffee table in front of him. There lay the gaudily covered spiritualism text that Primus had acquired an hour or so before. His whole plan of attack formed with unusual speed. While Primus and Secondus launched into an over-long rehash of the history of the radio ministry and the events of the night before, Stewie thumbed quickly through the thin volume.

After several minutes, still ignoring the specific purpose of their meeting, Secondus changed the subject, and asked, anxiously, "So, have you found out anything about who is snooping around?"

Still reading, Stewie tried to think. In fact, he'd only driven past the post office they'd told him they used, and had not yet visited the radio station as they'd requested him to do. However, without much hesitation, he fell into his usual mode of exaggeration and lying. "Not too much yet, but my contacts down south tell me two or three of the biggest national radio ministries are sure as heck interested in this region. They want to break in here, where's there's lots of good old dough to be gathered up. That Atlanta bunch, especially, can be mean. We've got to be real careful. Too bad you guys don't have enough bucks to buy up your radio station. That's what they often do."

Primus was horrified. He immediately pictured the fatal interview in which their station manager told them he could no longer carry their recorded programs.

Leaning forward on the couch, and nodding his head for emphasis, Tompkins quickly moved on to safer territory. "I've been watching the old church down the street like you asked me. It's been dead quiet, but I'll keep at it. Those big outfits are tough and there's no telling what they might try." He wanted to be sure the two brothers knew he was earning his retainer.

His words worked. Primus and Secondus looked at each other, dismayed by the frightening prospect, their foreheads furrowed in worry. Primus groaned, "What chance do we have?"

Secondus, more optimistic, was also more combative. He muttered, "We've got to grow our ministry. If we're big enough, they can't touch us."

Primus, encouraged by these words, began to expound on his ideas for sucking more money from their lonely elderly listeners by offering messages from departed relatives and other loved ones. "It'll be a snap," he said. "We'll just add some blank lines to the donation and figurine order form. The old coots will use them to ask a question of their dear departed, and in the next recorded program we'll dream up some kind of answer." He continued for several minutes in the same vein, repeating himself as old men often do.

After enduring this, and having learned a good deal about spiritualism in a short time, Tompkins finally interrupted. "I see you have Jacobson's "Beyond the Passing," he said, gesturing with the brightly covered spiritualism book. " It's one of the best. I've got my copy at home and my old granny had hers for years and years. She relied on it always, and almost wore it out."

Primus stirred, looking pleased, and then more typically, suspicious. "I thought you said it was your aunt who was the medium."

Tompkins had slipped on that, but glibly recovered. "Both of the old gals, actually. They was constantly at it, sometimes working together, sometimes fighting each other over who could bring back the most voices. Granny was better at rocking the table, but for imagination, old auntie was the best in the whole county."

Primus wanted to get down to business. "So you think you can give us some tips to get going on the radio?"

Stewie grinned. "Big piece of cake. Since the seniors are back in their nursing homes, they can't see you. You don't have to sweat dark rooms, ghostly lights, special tables, and wires, and all that kind of s . . t."

Secondus actually rubbed his hands in glee. "Sounds great."

"Sure as shootin' is," Tompkins continued, having quickly scanned several more paragraphs. "The thing is, boys, that you have to use your imaginations and then keep it all real vague. Just give them a lot of old time stuff about peace, happiness, and tranquility. Don't get into any damn specifics. Tell them stuff that could apply to most anybody."

Primus, excitedly sweating in his old suit, was the first to grasp what Tompkins said was the key point. Pounding his fist into his other gnarled hand, he exclaimed, "Hell, the best thing is that they aren't right there in the room with us. If we mix things up, and they do remember it the next morning, we've got a week or two for them to write in again, and for us to think of a better answer."

Secondus nodded. "Better yet, if they're puzzled and do want to ask the departed another question, they've got buy more stuff or send in another gift to the ministry. It's the clear thing."

It was too warm in the room, and Stewie Tompkins wiped his forehead with a handkerchief that had seen better days. "I think you're on the right track. How about I sit in on your next taping, and help get you started?"

At this point, Primus's suspicious nature took over. It might be just as well, he thought, if their new consultant didn't become too familiar with what they were doing. What if, for instance, he got his hands on their vital mailing list of senior citizens in nursing homes? "No," he said slowly, "I think we've got the general idea. My brother and I will try a show or two. Meantime, you check out that radio station and the post office and keep watching the church. Those crooked ministry bastards may try to break in again."

As 'Snapshot' Tompkins was leaving the Prior apartments, his face wore a slight frown. While he was relieved that he'd successfully fooled the old men into thinking he was an expert on spiritualism, he was also a little disappointed. He had, in fact, been interested in their all-important mailing list.

&&&

At about the same time in the afternoon as the just described deeply troubling meeting was taking place, Humboldt Prior was still at his office in the Prior Building. He was not having a good day. Finally drifting off to sleep only after the alarming sight of the police Cadillac parked outside his rowhouse, he had then over-slept until eight-thirty. Skipping breakfast, always a mistake, he'd tried, unsuccessfully, to make good time through heavy traffic on his way down to the office. While engaged in this futile effort, he was free to brood and fell prey to an alarming aberration of thought that will be described later.

Trying to forget his troubles as he reached the corporate offices of Prior and Cousins, and glumly congratulating himself on not having made even worse time because of the traffic, he was greeted by his cousin Ribald Prior, the personnel manager, with a snide remark about accountants keeping bankers' hours. Humboldt attempted to ignore him, along with the vulgar limerick that inevitably followed.

Once seated in the comparative safety of his own office, he dealt with routine papers until almost lunchtime. Given his semi-retired status, he was about to stop work for the day. At that point, he guiltily recalled his very late arrival, and Ribald's sarcasm, and grumpily decided to have lunch and then continue working until mid-afternoon. Now, very hungry, he made still another mistake by eating at a dreary and none-to-clean sandwich shop only a block from the Prior Building. It was really just a few tables in the front part of a questionable liquor store, with the sandwiches wisely prepared out of sight in the back room. Apparently catering mainly to healthy young people with strong stomachs, the place featured thick spicy sausages on hard dry bread, flavored with a suspiciously tart and brownish mayonnaise. Eating slowly, for fear of damaging a tooth, he contrived to finish most of his lunch before losing his appetite. By the time he had trudged back to his office, his stomach was miserable.

On the stairs leading up to the second floor of the Prior Building, he encountered Everett or Millard Fillmore, of the sales department. This polite Swedish gentleman said something that sounded like, "How good it is to finally get that big order." Humboldt wondered if he'd heard him correctly, but feeling worse and worse, he merely said that he agreed. Upstairs, it appeared that his fellow executives had decamped to cooler pastures, and he hoped they would remain there and not return to bother him. He closed his door.

It was a relief to have a day without rain, but with the remaining humidity enhanced by the blazing mid-summer sun, the afternoon heat was oppressive. His office was stifling. Something in his desk chair was failing intermittently, and this was one of those days in which the chair had lowered itself to a position in which, when he was seated, the top of his steel desk was above the level of his shirt pocket. Thus, appearing as a cross bald-headed child attempting tiredly to do office work, he spent the next hour searching for something that had gone wrong in the monthly account closing.

This tragedy seldom occurred, but when it did it was the practice of his bookkeeper to struggle with the problem for several days without asking for help, and then to dump it on Humboldt the afternoon before the figures were due. He set to work, mumbling to himself about how unfair it all was. After virtually redoing the entire closing, and adding up several long columns of numbers on his poky old adding machine, he finally discovered a numerical transposition and marked it. Then, somehow feeling safer in his own office, he summoned his cousin Orlo Prior, the office manager, to return the trial balance and other closing papers to bookkeeping.

Minutes later, with just the slightest satisfaction of having completed this onerous task, for which he would never receive any credit, he was thinking of leaving for the day when the telephone rang. This brought back all his fears. Upon answering with real trepidation, he was only momentarily relieved to find that it was just Cousin Orlo announcing that he had completed his delivery assignment and was leaving on another errand. However, the ringing had done its work and he returned to his morning's new worry. This unfortunate mental quirk was that, while for several days he'd been taking some comfort in the thought that he hadn't heard from Penny Rote, the reality was that the longer he didn't, the more likely he would in the next few minutes. Readers may well dismiss this as illogical, but allowances must be made for his exhaustion and sheltered circumstances. He was not in a condition to reason well.

Thus, when there was, even worse, a knock on the door, he jumped several inches. Perhaps she actually had the gall to come to his office. It turned out to be, of all people, Millard Fillmore back with a question. In his invariably polite voice, still tinged with the Swedish accent of his rural upbringing, Millard asked, "Could you please spare me a moment, Mr. Humboldt?"

Humboldt, nervous and dead tired, was still a good soldier. "Surely. Please come in."

"Sorry, but there's no one else here. Mr. Moribund and Mr. Dorset have been gone for hours, or I'd ask one of them."

Humboldt seethed inwardly. This was typical. With the rain absent, it was only a question of which country club cousins Dorset and Moribund had chosen for their afternoon rounds of golf. He asked, "What's up?"

"A fellow just came up from the shop. He couldn't find anyone here in the front office, so he walked back to sales. There's a big delivery, one of those huge overseas airfreight containers. They want to know, should they just have it placed outside or try to get the contents into the warehouse?"

For Humboldt, as the comptroller and responsible only for accounting, this was a no-win situation. Any answer he gave on a matter concerning inventories or manufacturing risked complaints from Dorset on his return. Then, too, given Prior Leather's inertia, large deliveries of materials were almost unknown. What to do? Humboldt, already care worn, shrugged. What was one more trouble? "Have them bring it inside the warehouse."

Millard thanked him and left.

What did this mean? He remembered the meetings between Moribund, Dorset, and Ribald, the orders for materials, and the delivery of the shoddy looking bundles of strips of wood. Was Prior and Cousins actually going back into the trunk business, and for what hapless customer? Another worry. Then the telephone rang again.

&&&

Chapter 12

At first, absolutely certain that it was the dreaded anchorwoman, he considered the possibility of not answering the call. What if he had just left for the day? Surely, even television newsanchors sometimes found their prey out of the office. However, remembering that his last visitor was the person most likely to answer in his absence, and imagining her reaction to talking to someone called Millard Fillmore, he finally picked up the phone. "Hello. Prior and Cousins, this is Mr. Humboldt Prior speaking."

For all his fussing and worrying, he was somehow surprised at the informality of her words. "Hi, Humboldt, it's your friend, Penny."

The suspense of waiting was over. As distraught as he was, he was also slightly irritated as he'd been expecting something more momentous sounding. However, he had to say something in reply. He sighed. "Good afternoon."

"Say, I've got to take another look at that old church. How about tonight?"

Tonight? Already? The prospect was appalling. He was very tired and far from over his last experiences. Then there was the police surveillance. Although the temperature in his office, if anything, had become even hotter, he actually shivered. Growing more flustered, he asked finally, "Are you sure that's wise?"

Penny was firm with him. "Yes, Humboldt, we have to. Tonight's the night. Something new has come up in my writing project. I have to get back in there. Also, I think I should also check out that funny old apartment house down the street. Isn't that where the minister lives? I'm thinking of using it in my story, too."

If possible, Humboldt was even more horrified. Now she wanted to get into the Prior Apartments. He spluttered, "But, that's way too risky, we mustn't do that. Why, they almost caught us last time."

She seemed without mercy. "No, last time was easy, and this time will be a walk in the park. That goes for both the church and that dingy old dump of an apartment house. I'll see you about eleven."

A burst of late afternoon thunder almost drowned out her last words. The die was cast.

&&&

Humboldt was well placed as the comptroller, in charge of what passed for Prior Leather's bookkeeping department. By nature, he worried and fussed about even the most routine matters. Thus, faced with another late evening of highly dangerous church break-ins, by the time he had made his way through early rush-hour traffic, stopped near his home for one or two errands, and garaged his car, he was somewhere between a dark funk and an absolute tizzy. By suppertime, a veritable swarm of troubles and worries buzzed through his agitated mind.

He'd stopped for fresh flashlight batteries so that, at least, had been taken care of. However, he now realized with growing dismay that he had to again assume his ridiculous burglary costume, but was without the protection of his baseball cap. This, (unknown to him) was still being held by Pastor Secondus Prior as evidence of the suspected nefarious activities of the FBI or some southern evangelical radio ministry. In desperation, he selected a heavy blue wool stocking cap, normally worn only in below zero weather. To this heat source, he again added the dark sweater, the heavy black wool slacks, and the hideous rubber-soled fishing shoes.

Thus outfitted, he sat down to think. Try as he might, he couldn't imagine what he could do to stop Penelope Rote and her most ill conceived interest in his neighborhood as a setting for her mystery fiction. He added to himself that there was already too much of the latter, thank you very much. The whole terrible situation might have kept his mind from his developing concern about the possible plot by his cousins Moribund, Ribald, and Dorset Prior, and his dismay over the Revealed Truth Radio Ministry program he had just heard. However, being who he was, it did not, and he grumbled to himself over them as well.

Later, still stewing, he resorted again to the cold meatloaf for his dinner, adding some heavily seasoned corn chips (bought by mistake), and a salad of aging lettuce that should have been sent to the garbage instead. Even under normal circumstances, this meal would have been at best unwise. Now, combined with his unfortunate luncheon, and gripped by the appalling prospect of another night of breaking and entering, his stomach was a solid knot of turmoil.

Lying on his davenport in his darkened sunroom, trying to recover with the aid of several antacids, and unsuccessfully, to stay cool, he found himself instead grappling with the problem of the yellow Cadillac. This gaudy older car, he was certain, was just what would be chosen as a ruse by plain-clothes detectives assigned to watch for a repeat of the church burglary, especially with a nearby suspect already identified based on DNA evidence from the baseball cap.

At first, he thought explaining all this might dissuade Penny Rote from further research. Then, a horrid dilemma became clear. There was every possibility, as all too clearly explained in the complex stories by his evil nemesis, the amateur detective-story writer, that the detectives were actually investigating something completely different. What if, for instance, they were after one of his cousins, Malice or Ribald, for one of their continuing infractions against the opposite sex? As an alternate crime, that was perfectly likely, but no more so than any one of several of the activities of his other morally challenged cousins, the Pastors Primus and Secondus. Worst of all, what if someone had leaked something about Prior Leather and the Prior Trust?

Thus, in his fevered condition, he concluded he would have to find a way around the surveillance and that he could say nothing to Penny Rote about it. To do so, might reveal more misconduct previously unknown to her, and only hand her another card to use against him. He would have to cooperate with her insane literary efforts. He formed a final ghastly postscript to this reasoning in the form of an imagined explanation he pictured himself giving when questioned after his conviction, by his boss, President Malice Prior, and the all-powerful accountants from the Trust. At that point, he fell uncomfortably asleep for two hours and was only awakened in darkness by a relentless clap of thunder and the roar of a downpour of rain.

He stumbled down the hall to his living room. Cautiously, and without turning on any lights, he peeked out his front window. The heavy rain rattled down, but there were no cars in the street. That was a relief, but the yellow Cadillac might reappear at any time. What to do? Finally, he thought of an idea. Across the street, next to the decrepit old church, was the Prior family's communal garage. Its rear doors opened on a dirty narrow alley that circled north, then east, and then south around the structures located on Osgood Prior's original 1890s Emma Woodhouse Avenue complex of carriage house/garage, church, apartment house, and rowhouses. Perhaps they could walk innocently across to the garage as though intending to take his car. Instead, they could exit the garage into the alley and attempt to enter the church from the rear, assuming as he dimly remembered, there was a door back there and that it could be opened. Unfortunately, Humboldt did not have time to think of things that might be wrong with this desperate plan (there were several), for at eleven o'clock sharp, his doorbell rang. She also knocked.

&&&

He actually hurried to the door. There she was, pretty as ever, as he had to admit to himself, and at least she had brought back his flashlight. Penny was sheltering on his little porch, short gray raincoat belted tightly about her figure, and as before, still dressed for television in a sleek black pants outfit. At least, he thought, she was finally taking his lead in dressing in dark colors.

She shook drops of rain from her sandy hair. "Well, well, friend Humboldt, I see you're ready and waiting," she said brightly with an amused glance at his black clothing. "Let's get going," she added, taking his hand and starting to pull him out into the rain.

"Wait a second," he stammered, "I've got an idea."

There was a flicker of respect in her eyes, and her freckled face relaxed. "Let's hear it, Humboldt. With all your experience, you should know best about this stuff."

That remark was the last thing Humboldt would have wanted to hear, had he been in a state of mind to focus on it. However, grasping frantically at his idea for slightly improving the odds of escaping highly embarrassing discovery by the plain-clothes detectives, her inference about his supposed previous career with the CIA went right past him.

"Remember," he whispered, as they stood side by side watching the rain, "when we used the front entrance last time, they almost trapped us. I suggest it may be safer if we try the rear door of the church." As he spoke, he quickly glanced up and down Woodhouse Avenue, just as he'd seen done on the crime shows. "It looks clear now." They always said something like that.

Penny nodded doubtfully. "Okay, lead on."

Hurrying with her across the wet street to the garage entrance, Humboldt was actually smiling. His own key worked easily in the street door into the garage.

Once inside, Penny stood stock-still. Gazing left and right in the wide semi-darkness, she exclaimed softly, "What the heck is this place?"

Humboldt explained, as they threaded their way through the ranks of parked black Chevrolets. "Now, it's our communal parking garage, but it was originally the barn and carriage house for the rowhouses and any of the apartments whose tenants had horses." In the dim light, they could see along one long wall, patterns of discolored bricks where the long row of horse stalls had been removed. The broad expanse of the garage was almost quiet. Here and there, however, water dripped down from what had been the hay floor, and there was an unpleasant scurrying in a far corner.

Penny jumped and then grinned, sheepishly. "Carriage house, eh? Those old Priors must have been pretty rich."

Preferring not to respond, Humboldt busied himself opening the creaking wooden service door, next to the big overhead garage door that opened on the alley. Almost never used, at first the handle wouldn't turn. Then, finally it opened with a bang, ushering them out into a blast of rain and wind. Penny grabbed for her umbrella. There was more scurrying of rodents very near the door.

Humboldt said, unnecessarily, "I suggest keeping close to the wall." This was obviously the thing to do, as six inches of very dirty rainwater was coursing down the center of the alley, disappearing off to their left, along a slight slope in the direction of HillTop Parkway, the streetlights of which were just visible in distance. It was pitch dark in the alley in front of them. With a less confident Penny Rote clinging to his arm, perhaps because of the rats, he used the flashlight to guide her along the wall toward his boyhood memory of the back door of the church. He was guessing his key to the church would work there, too, but half hoping that it wouldn't. The rain pelted down, and courteously allowing her the most shelter of the wall, he found himself wading through three or four inches of muddy water. The waterproof fishing shoes were definitely not as advertised.

They reached the back entrance to the Second Church, accessible up a short flight of rickety old wooden steps, covered with moss and made more slippery by the rain. At the top, Humboldt tried the key. The door opened on groaning hinges. Touching his hand, and then brushing past him with just a breath of her perfume, Penny Rote moved ahead of him into the gloom of the rear vestibule. Humboldt followed in another mild funk. Once again, she'd taken his flashlight.

Inside, they found themselves in the same dingy back hallway that led to the church sanctuary and the rear basement stairs. Penny Rote, her confidence recovering from the rat episode, wiped her feet on a dirty mat, closed her umbrella, tucked it under one arm, paused, and then with an experienced eye, turned the flashlight on Humboldt's lower extremities.

To his extreme embarrassment, she chuckled, and said firmly, "Those shoes and socks had better come off. They're covered with water and mud. You'll leave all kinds of tracks."

His first impulse was to absolutely refuse. Invading his local church, the domain of his very troublesome cousins, accompanied by a notorious female TV newsanchor, and also barefoot was simply too much. The words 'Certainly not' began to form. Then he saw the wisdom of her words and sulkily complied. For some reason, she seemed uninterested in another visit to the church basement, and didn't even spend much time looking, as they made their way through the huge dark and musty church sanctuary, deadly still except for the roar of rain on the roof far above them, and the sound of their footsteps. (It was the click of her heels actually, as Humboldt was carrying his shoes and socks and his embarrassingly bare feet made almost no sound.) More so on this visit, Humboldt was startled by the appearance of neglect and insufficient funds. The entire church was shabby, and everywhere you looked, something was broken and needed repair.

When they reached the front entry hall, he received another shock. On their previous visit, he'd been greatly relieved to find the church offices and even more so, the stairway to the tower, securely locked. Now, Penny opened her purse and took out a ring of old rusty keys.

She said quietly, "I have to get the flavor of the administrative offices, but last time they were locked. I found these in an antique shop. I'll bet one will fit those old locks. Here, give them a try."

This was even worse. Now he was being forced from his role as an unwilling assistant to that of prime suspect. As he remembered it from TV mysteries, the mere possession of skeleton keys constituted a crime. Still, the even more awful prospect of a television exposé of Prior Leather and the Prior Trust again stifled his protests. He put down his shoes and socks, took the keys and tried first one and then another. The third turned a little, and then, with a loud scratching sound, seemingly audible all the way to the nearest police station, released the aged lock.

Penny pushed the door open and, with the flashlight, began to examine the dusty offices. There were really only three rooms, an outer one, once busy with secretaries hard at work and church members seeking assistance, the minister's shabby office, and the parlor. The latter as has already been reported in this account, featured a battered mahogany table, and stiff high-backed church parlor chairs. Penny muttered, "Boy oh boy, they don't do much in here anymore, do they?"

Frozen in embarrassment, Humboldt said nothing, standing crossly in a corner by a narrow window that looked out on Woodhouse Avenue, still holding his wet shoes, and perspiring in his foolishly chosen heavy dark clothes. Helped by the glow of a streetlight outside the window, he tried to occupy his time glancing at one of a stack of dusty books, found on a nearby shelf. He also watched while Penny did what was apparently necessary to gain the 'flavor' of out-of-date church administration.

She was very thorough. Several times, she picked up a paper from one of the tables or desks and read it, saying, "Boy oh boy, Humboldt, this is just the sort of thing I was looking for." Twice, she had opened a file drawer, rummaged inside, and then put a few papers in her shoulder bag. He shuddered at that, but it was nothing compared to his horror at what happened next.

There was a second glimmer of light outside on the street, flickering through the sheets of rain. He looked out. With awful clarity, he saw the yellow Cadillac slowly looming up from the direction of HillTop Parkway. It pulled up to the curb across the street and stopped. The lights went out. Inside the car, Stewie "Snapshot" Tompkins settled down for a nap.

Humboldt Prior, deprived of the specifics known only to the reader, instead saw the worst. The dreadful situation was developing just as he feared. The relentless plain-clothes detectives were watching.

What in the world to do? The woman had been absurdly overconfident. He spluttered, "My goodness, Miss Rote, there's an unmarked police car with detectives outside on the street. We've really got to get out of here."

To her credit, she did turn off the telltale flashlight. "Let me see," she said, moving softly by him to the window. "How do you know it's the cops?"

He had to come clean. "I've seen that car before, watching the church. That's why I had us come in the back way."

Penny frowned, and then nodded to herself. "Well, I guess you were one step ahead of me. Okay, let's move on to check out the apartments."

They hurried out of the office, Humboldt remembering to lock the door and hand Penny the keys, and through that distraction momentarily forgetting among other things, her appalling insistence on still executing the next trespass on her itinerary. From unbelievable good fortune or the pouring rain, it seemed the policemen weren't leaving the shelter of their car. Without interference, Penny, with the flashlight, and Humboldt, with, as he thought at the time, wet shoes in one hand and water-soaked black socks in the other, walked quickly through the silent church. After an agonizing delay while he reassumed his hideous fishing shoes, they exited the rear door, and cautiously negotiated the slippery back steps. She had stuffed several papers into her large shoulder bag, and Humboldt had also carried away something, though without realizing it.

Once in the garage, although they were safe for the moment, Penny announced, "Okay, Humboldt, so far, so good. You've been great. Now, what about the apartment house?"

Humboldt was shattered. They'd only escaped the police by the narrowest of margins, and she still wasn't satisfied. However, driven by the gnawing fear of discovery, he actually had another idea.

Risking more disclosure of Prior affairs, and stuttering with excitement, he whispered, "Look, all these cars belong to the residents and they all look alike. We ought to take mine, drive it out of the garage and then around the alley behind the apartments. No one will think anything of one of these cars. We'll at least have a chance that way."

Penelope Rote nodded, with an expression that a less frightened person than Humboldt might have recognized as one of growing respect. "Good deal. Let's do it."

&&&

Chapter 13

During the final events of the previous chapter, still slumped in his yellow Cadillac, parked in the heavy rain on Woodhouse Avenue outside the Second Church of the Revealed Truth, Stewie "Snapshot" Tompkins awoke from his refreshing nap. Moments later, he looked left and right, forward and back. Except for the persistent rain, everything seemed quiet. He thought a moment. As one of the very few dishonest church photographers, it was almost never his nature to feel guilt over anything, but now he hesitated. Maybe he'd better actually do something to earn his ample retainer. Specifically, he thought he might as well take a look inside the gloomy old church.

Stewie wriggled into his ancient plastic raincoat, fumbled for something under the Cadillac's front seat, and then darted out of the car and across the street to the entrance to the church, sheltering there from the worst of the rain. Upon his engagement as consultant to the embattled Revealed Truth Radio Ministries, he had been provided with a complete set of keys. He was without a flashlight, but a flicker of lightning helped him with the locked front door. Inside, he turned on the one functioning light in the entrance hall, wiped some of the rain from his gray hair, and then moved straight on into the church, turning on more lights as he did so.

Tompkins had seen hundreds of churches and wasn't very impressed with this one. It was certainly large, but considerably dirtier than most. He didn't spend much time looking around the cavernous sanctuary. He also lacked the hard-edged competence in breaking and entering common in female newsanchors, and therefore had already missed some key evidence. As he continued on to the chancel area, and past it to the rear door, he missed more, including the unmistakable print of a damp bare foot, drying in the musty heat. Proceeding on down the rear stairs to the basement, and through the even dirtier lower hallways, everything seemed in order. He glanced into one or two of the cluttered rooms, ignoring rodents, living and deceased. It was only after climbing the front basement stairway and, a little breathless, arriving in the church offices, that Stewie paused to take stock. At first the light of the overhead fixture revealed nothing unusual. Then he started in surprise at something peculiar lying on the floor next to the door, his hand instinctively clutching an item in the pocket of his trousers.

The item in his pocket was a cheap small-caliber revolver that Tompkins, as customary with church photographers traveling lonely roads with large amounts of cash, kept hidden under the driver's seat of his automobile. Its presence with him now, if known, would have compounded the already enormous woes of Humboldt Prior, now driving at a very slow fidgety pace, along the alley behind the church toward the Prior Apartments. However, Humboldt's agitated state of mind need not much concern the reader who is instead interested in learning what Mr. Tompkins has observed.

The important evidence in question, that Snapshot had by-passed earlier and was now examining, was a pair of very wet and muddy black socks, obviously dropped there by someone. Having seen some of the same television programs as the aforementioned Humboldt Prior, he was next engaged in finding a large envelope in the disordered church office and enclosing the socks for later use. Not really concerned with what they might actually signify, he had merely recognized that they were a usable illustration of the fact that that he was following his clients' orders. As he left the church, he planned on stowing them in his car and showing them to his elderly pastoral clients at the first opportunity.

&&&

Meanwhile, the cautious progress of Mr. Prior and Miss Rote, still through heavy rain, had reached the rear door of the apartment house. Humboldt, preoccupied and extremely nervous, was driving very slowly. He parked the car and looked carefully in both directions, searching for the feared yellow police vehicle. Everything looked safe, but still something felt wrong.

Ignoring the bad weather, Penny Rote bounded out of the car and ran, high-heeled, through the rain to the back door. There was nothing for Humboldt to do but follow her. Inside, she turned to him. "Wow, what a funny old place. Who lives here anyway?"

Humboldt, puffing from the exertion of running and still feeling that something wasn't quite right, said quickly, "Well, actually, the two old pastors, for one thing. Some of my other older relatives are also among those who live here." This was said without thinking, and was something of a fib, as all of the residents were relatives of his.

The back hallway was not unlike the old church, having cracked beige plaster walls, faded tile floor, and a good deal of dust. Without any further questions, Penny poked around for a minute or two, sniffing an odor of burned grease, and reading a crudely printed notice headed "Revealed Truth Radio Broadcast Schedule." Then, ignoring a rusting metal sign reading, "Residents and Guests Only," she pushed on into the front lobby.

Penny exclaimed a startled, "Holy cow," and then said, "Gosh, look at all this." At one time, the lobby had been somewhat more grand. In the middle of the high ceiling, a cracked terracotta floral decoration surrounded the base of an ornate wrought iron light fixture that cast a dim light on a ceiling mural of a surprisingly indelicate nature. More terracotta and murals of faded painted figures crowded the walls right down to the marble floor, also cracked, broken in places, and somewhat dirty. Two Victorian period armchairs stood in one corner and, in view of their obvious age and faded upholstery, were probably authentic. Between them teetered a wrought iron ashtray and a travel magazine protruded from under one of the old chairs.

Penny exclaimed at all this, repeating the phrase, "Great atmosphere," and then, to Humboldt's annoyance, suddenly disappeared up the wide staircase, saying, "Let's check out the next floor," her feet mercifully silent on the thick oriental runner. Moments later, a shocked Humboldt, making distressed noises about privacy, started hurriedly up the stairs after her, only to experience a soft collision with her on the first landing. Even more unnerved by this experience, he heard her say, "Wow, what a funny old dump," and then she hurried back down the stairs.

Minutes later, they were again in the rear hallway, and Humboldt sighed in relief, thinking the evening's dangerous risk-taking might be nearly over. Then Penny asked casually, "I wonder where they put the trash?"

Humboldt blanched at this monstrous inquiry. He'd seen plenty of FBI-based television programs in which the intrepid agents found damming evidence by searching the trash barrels. He started to protest, "I don't know, and anyway, you can't possibly . . ."

However, she was already opening doors, saying over her shoulder, "Now, now, Humboldt, remember what we decided about that funny old leather business of yours. I just need a minute to see what their trash room looks like."

In fact, she apparently needed several minutes. Humboldt waited outside the smelly little room, wondering what in the world he could say if anyone saw them. Finally, she reappeared coughing, wiping her hands, and stuffing what looked like several used envelopes into her cavernous shoulder bag. Again, she said cheerily, "Great atmosphere for my book, Humboldt. It's just what I was looking for. That should do it for now."

His relief in having survived another night of criminal activity surpassed other emotions, so it was with only a vague feeling of unease, that, in view of the pouring rain, he offered to drive her on through the alley and around to where her expensive SUV was parked in front of his rowhouse. He drove cautiously, noting when they arrived on Woodhouse Avenue that no one was inside the yellow Cadillac.

There, she thanked him warmly, patting him on the arm, and saying, "You did just great, Humboldt, even if you claim not to be a retired spy. Not that I believe you, because every so often you surprise me with something really sophisticated. I'm supposed to be the hotshot investigative reporter, but once or twice tonight your long experience showed through. Thanks. I'll call on you again when I need you."

The ascending enormity of these successive sentences left Humboldt speechless. She still thought he was a spy and she wasn't through with him yet. He was glumly shaking his head, as she smiled at him, patted his arm again, took her umbrella, said sweetly, "Actually, it was quite a nice evening," and stepped out into the rain. He watched as she ran along the sidewalk and climbed into her car.

His nightly adventures hopefully over, Humboldt executed a clumsy U-turn, and returned, via HillTop Parkway and the still flooded alley to the Prior communal garage. Parking the car, he dimly recalled putting something in the back seat. Oh yes, it was his wet black socks, as he was barefoot in his horrid fishing shoes, the source, he now realized, of his vague unease. Instead, his hand closed on a hard rectangular object. What was this? Then he knew and the interior light of the Chevrolet confirmed his worst fears. Instead of his socks, he found himself holding the 1898 edition of a thin volume entitled "Building for Truth, Osgood Prior and the Construction of the Second Church of the Revealed Truth."

The whole sad series of mistakes leaped to his mind. He must have dropped his incriminating clothing when he was idly examining this wretched book. That meant that damning evidence was still in the church office, locked there behind a door that could only be opened by a key that had departed the premises in the possession of the extremely troublesome, though somehow quite attractive, Miss Penelope Rote of the evening news. This fatal omission had been overlooked when he reassumed his shoes because, at home, he often went without socks in the summertime.

Now even more certain of apprehension, Humboldt trudged fatalistically out of the garage, ignoring the rain. He also planned to bravely ignore the yellow Cadillac that he believed was driven by the plainclothes detectives who were about to arrest him. However, there was an anti-climax, as that too had departed. So, except for being drenched by an especially hard burst of rain, the balance of his evening was uneventful. For unknown reasons, as he tumbled into bed he was smiling to himself. Perhaps it was that he'd remembered he still had her raincoat.

&&&

For Humboldt, the next morning began with a series of minor disasters. Contrary to his momentary pleasure on retiring for the night, he awakened upset, preoccupied with the turmoil of the previous evening and with a feeling of having half-heard something very disturbing on the radio. At first, he tried to comfort himself with the thought that, after all, he was a long-time member of the Second Revealed Church and what they'd done was really nothing more than some sort of unofficial visit. They had merely entered certain more or less public areas, using a key when necessary. Then he remembered Penny Rote's illegal skeleton keys, her rifling the private offices of the church, and her invasion of the private refuse of the apartments. Why, she even taken some of it away with her. It was at this point that he stubbed his little toe on the leg of the bed. Ouch! It was really all the fault of that blasted amateur writer.

Next, while shaving, he managed to cut the edge of his nose. This absurd injury, with a bandage and residual bleeding, was sure to bring ridicule from his cousins Moribund and Ribald.

On arriving in his kitchen, he was greeted by the sight of the fatal book he'd mistakenly taken from the church offices, now another link in the chain of evidence building against him. Its overlong title, "Building for Truth, Osgood Prior and the Construction of the Second Church of the Revealed Truth," taunted him in gilt lettering.

Preparing his breakfast, he miscalculated the correct reheating of his oatmeal, with the result that a chill lump of it was soon afflicting his digestive system. Lastly, through some misadventure in the assembly process, his morning newspaper had arrived without its news sections. Thus, without reading material to accompany his slightly burned toast, he turned as a last recourse, to the unfortunate "Building for Truth" book, still lying on his kitchen table. He was, after all, interested in local history.

It was soon clear that it was primarily a self-congratulatory and promotional work. According to the custom of the time, after lauding the founder, the author, whoever he was, had supplied the reader with endless favorable accounts of the construction subcontractors and their various work processes. It appeared that every conceivable supplier and subcontractor had his place in "Building for Truth." Laborious descriptions were given of architecture, of excavation, of masonry, of flooring, of furnaces, and of painting and decorating. Materials were described as to quantities and structural properties. As an enthusiast of local history, he recognized many of the names of the businesses that had participated, although most were now long defunct. However, in the thirty or so pages he managed to actually read, one unknown firm, a mysterious "Acme Company" was mentioned quite a number of times, always very favorably. What in the world was that?

With insufficient sleep, an upset stomach, a bleeding nose, and in danger of arrest at any moment, he had absolutely no desire to leave for the office. However, it had to be done. Dressed in his blue wool suit in spite of the weather, he emerged hotly from his front door, only to dart back for his umbrella. It was still drizzling.

Outside, the gloomy street was more or less deserted, free in any event, of the yellow Cadillacs favored by the detectives. The dark red brick and blackish-green wood trim of the rowhouses and apartment building glowered damply down on him as he trudged wearily over to the garage. The enormous window-eye of the huge church building glared accusingly. It was not going to be a good day, and moreover, the "Acme Company" reference was bothering him. He'd seen it somewhere else.

&&&

On arriving at the offices of Prior and Cousins Leather, Humboldt immediately found himself enmeshed in one the president's rare staff meetings. His cousin Orlo Prior, the office manager, who reveled in his occasional inclusion in these tedious affairs, was lying in wait to summon him. Inside the president's luxurious private office, facing a row of expensive guest seating, the president himself, Malice Prior, sat coiled on his slightly elevated, throne-like executive chair. Humboldt's other cousins, Moribund Prior (sales), Dorset Prior (production and design), and Ribald Prior (personnel), were already seated. Moribund leaned his scrawny body forward, and whispered something to his brother. Overhearing, Ribald's fat face contorted in a snicker.

Malice made an uncalled-for remark about semi-retired accountants who were lucky to be able to come in when they pleased. Ribald laughed at this, adding a vulgar reference to Humboldt's injured nose. Then Malice, his broad gray-haired head darting from side to side, said in his usual mock-military manner, "Men, we're going on the offensive."

Orlo, toadying, said loudly, "We're right behind you, boss, just lead the charge." It was one of his usual vapid remarks.

The president went on to describe the Manheimers' trunk order in extravagant but general terms. He placed undue emphasis on the photo shoot, involving the beautiful female models, saying, "Dorset, as soon as you can possibly get one of the trunks slapped together, we're bringing in the girls for some pictures. Those will really help Manheimers get going with their advertising." He licked his lips.

Malice also explained in detail what he termed the amended Prior Leather bonus plan and the percentages allocated to each executive, his own being much the largest. He smirked, "Now that I've provided the leadership and arranged the sale, it's important that you managers be motivated to complete the detail work on a rush order like this." Dorset and Ribald looked cross but resigned to the inevitable.

Moribund reminded the group that the order was now larger. "I've got them up to ten dozen of the large, display-type steamer trunks and, at the price of $929.95 each, we should clear about $96,000 for the bonus plan."

Humboldt could see that Malice, his tongue darting in and out in concentration, was attempting unsuccessfully to calculate his personal fifty percent share of this amount, but said nothing to help him.

Dorset Prior, who at least looked like an executive, then launched into his report on the manufacturing plans, describing the arrival of the necessary materials. "We've got the wood and the hardware," he explained. "For the outside of the trunks, I've obtained a new artificial leather product, imported from France."

It's reconstituted, so it's perfectly safe, yet durable, fire resistant, and very inexpensive."

Having begun to suspect the questionable quality of the materials Dorset was planning to palm off on their long-standing customer, Humboldt nearly asked a mild question. However, Dorset quickly continued, expressing his disappointment that the start of production would have to wait until what he termed the more economical "student workers" were available.

At this point, Ribald, grinning wickedly, broke in saying, "Not at all, Dorset. I've managed to arrange things so that a half-dozen of the best young women, all high school cheerleaders, will actually begin work next week."

The president perked up at this, telling everyone to, "Go on red alert." With that, the meeting ended.

Humboldt, holding a handkerchief to his injured nose, plodded back to his office, hoping for a restful day, and still trying to recall where else he'd heard of the "Acme Company."

&&&

Chapter 14

At much the same time as the last of the events chronicled in the previous chapter, Stewie "Snapshot" Tompkins, having alerted Pastor Secondus Prior to his pending visit by telephone, was knocking on the apartment door of his senior client, Pastor Primus. It was a little after ten o'clock in the morning. The door opened to reveal the unappetizing sight of an unshaven elderly man, rubbing his scraggly white hair, and attempting, at the same time to tie his dirty blue bathrobe around his skinny body. Averting his eyes from this unpleasant scene and trying to avoid taking deep breaths, Stewie Tompkins walked past his host into the dingy living room. Pastor Secondus, who had just arrived, hurriedly dressed and gasping for breath from his haste in negotiating the stairs, followed him immediately. It was not an attractive scene.

Giving time for his clients to compose themselves, and hopefully finish dressing, Tompkins inquired with disinterested politeness about last night's recorded radio show. Pastor Primus responded to this with enthusiasm. He began, "It went off damned great. We'd recorded the usual praying bit and gave the old folks a touching message about that Bluebird figurine you bought too many of, Secondus, the one where the wings come off. We told them that if they buy one, the bird is a symbol of their thoughts going straight to their deceased loved ones. It should really bring in the bucks, and was a great lead-in."

Secondus agreed, "I was listening, and remembered that part from our recording session. I knew it would sell. Then I fell asleep. How about the rest of it?"

"Smooth as silk." Primus smirked and explained the rest of the program to their consultant. "We had recorded some crap about a spiritualism call-in and my brother changed his voice higher to fake being the caller. Then, we cooked up an answer from the old gal's sister about giving us money. That was about all we had on the tape."

Secondus laughed. "Yeah, they taught us that in minister school. Changing your voice sometimes helps in your sermons. What else happened?"

"Luckily for us," Primus continued proudly, "I was down there at the radio station last night during the show, because I had to bring them the new tape with the spiritualism s . . t on it. As I say, we're lucky I was, because we got a real live call to the station from some old goof in a nursing home. He said he was desperate to figure out what to do with ten grand he'd saved, and only wished he could talk to his dear departed wife about it. I thought fast, went on the radio, live, and asked a few questions just for atmosphere. Then I said I'd been trained as a spiritualistic medium, and called for silence while I tried to contact the old guy's wife." Absorbed in his performance, he paused.

Still avoiding any deep breaths, Stewie waited for something to happen. It was almost unbearably stuffy in the crowded apartment, and whatever Secondus had had for breakfast obviously wasn't agreeing with him.

Finally, as if coming out of a trance, Primus continued. "Well, first I knocked on the table a few times, and the radio microphone picked that up beautiful. Then, I said the old buzzard's wife had come through to me and told me to tell her dear hubby that 'there was no need for gold where they'd be together, and he should give the bucks to the Second Church of the Revealed Truth'." He grinned sinisterly. "I figured that made it kind of neutral, see, like the Radio Ministry ain't asking for the money for itself. The caller started to whimper and said that's just what he'd do. I'll bet the check's already in the mail." Gleefully, Primus rubbed his boney hands together.

Secondus concurred. "We've got a real winner here, Stewie, and we're gonna try it again right away. That's why it's so important to block whatever that big national salvation broadcast outfit is trying to pull on us."

From his position at the lowest end of the spectrum of church photographers, Tompkins felt nothing but high approval of these sordid events. Sleepy and momentarily distracted from the real purpose of the meeting, he was trying to remember the details of the spiritualism stunt with the thought of advising certain other struggling churches along the same lines. Then he roused himself. "That's the very thing I've got to tell you about. Something else has happened. I was on watch last night, just like you told me, and look what I found by the church office." He displayed the dirty black socks.

Primus and Secondus recoiled in disgust. Secondus spoke first, "What the hell were they doing there? What can it mean?"

Primus, always suspicious, added in a voice of alarm, "It almost looks like some kind of mob warning, like that time where they put a cow's head in the guy's bed. It scared him near to death, and rightly so." (Primus misremembered the exciting scene from "The Godfather," but his version was equally shocking to his brother.)

Secondus gasped in fright. "My God, if the mob is involved too, we're sunk for sure."

Stewie needed to calm them down a little. After all, if they became too alarmed they might simply call in the police, ending his lucrative consulting engagement. "No, boys, I don't think that's it. I'm sure it must have been a spy for one of the national radio ministries, nosing around. Maybe his feet were wet and it was a dodge not to leave footprints or something." Stewie was actually partially correct about this.

Secondus seemed to agree, but Primus was doubtful. He thought a moment. "Another idea is that is was that damned cousin of ours again. That bastard, Malice Prior, has always been trying to sneak some woman in there. Maybe he got lucky and forgot to put his socks on again." The two brothers chuckled evilly at the thought.

This also wasn't what Stewie wanted. "Nah, I'd have seen that." This was a lie, for he'd been asleep in his Cadillac for the most important part of the evening. "I'm sure it's a guy from one of those southern take-over radio ministries. We'll have to be even more careful. From now on, I'll have this with me at all times." He pulled his old pistol from his leisure suit jacket pocket, and brandished it in front of the startled old clergymen.

It has been well said by someone or other, that there's nothing like a firearm to get your listener's attention and agreement. Both old pastors nodded. Primus muttered, "I guess you're right, Stewie. Just keep watching. If you need more for expenses, let us know." He was thinking of the ten thousand dollars coming from their elderly listener.

Stewie Tompkins departed almost immediately, depositing Humboldt's neglected hosiery in the nearest trashcan.

&&&

At his office in the Prior Building and later at home, the balance of Humboldt's day had been up and down. He was somewhat more relaxed after a quiet hour of approving vouchers, something he was good at, and that did not involve any direct contact with his relatives. Slumped back in his office chair now repaired and back at its usual height, he took refuge from the prospect of his imminent apprehension by the police detectives, by planning additional routine administrative projects. These included the possibility of recycling or trashing a year or two of the firm's oldest accounting records, stored on the otherwise unused third floor, to make more room for newer records that were piling up in the outer office. It was time to get busy with this.

Although it was not at the top of his mental list of troubles, he was also worried about the Manheimers trunk order. The unfortunate emphasis on attractive young female workers was routine for the president and the personnel manager. However, there was something else he half-remembered. What was it?

Then, his cousin Dorset Prior had interrupted him. Dorset seemed a bit nervous, and paced back and forth before he sat down. First, he asked Humboldt, "What did you think of the meeting on the big Manheimers order?"

Humboldt was carefully noncommittal, but, hoping to learn something, he cautiously inquired, "What exactly is the 'artificial leather' you plan to use? Is that the foreign shipment that arrived in the big container, whose invoice was marked 'Not warranted,' with an oblique reference to asbestos?"

Dorset answered glibly saying that, "In France, for all reconstituted products containing substances that formerly were theoretically harmful, a warranty is not customary."

Humboldt nodded as if in agreement, although now he was even more worried.

The next of Dorset's inquiries pertained to insurance. "Have we ever thought of taking out product liability insurance?"

Humboldt answered carefully, "Having virtually no products, that's a type of coverage that Prior Leather hasn't believed it needs to carry."

Dorset's final observation was, "I suppose a foreign manufacturer would be required to assume liability for defective or dangerous raw materials used in products sold in the United States. For instance, what if there was a very remote possibility of long-term respiratory damage to employees and customers?" This was probably added only to create some sort of vague verbal record of Dorset's assumption, in case there was any trouble later on.

However, Humboldt, finally on familiar ground, wisely recognized this as an attempt to shift blame for a potential future problem. It was Dorset's practice to do this by claiming to have discussed the matter with someone else and not to have received any objections. Humboldt realized that he was doing this again, and would, if later confronted with a dangerous liability resulting from the artificial leather, claim that Humboldt himself had given him his approval.

There were several things Humboldt would like to have said about this. However, what he actually said was simply that he would look into it. Dorset thanked him, and strode out of the office, saying he hoped the rain would stop before his tee time.

&&&

At home in the afternoon, matters didn't improve. Next door, several of Dorset's children were screaming and apparently throwing themselves against the common wall between the two rowhouses. It was hot and uncomfortably humid, and the arrival in the mail of one of the numerous history journals to which he subscribed, added to his distress by featuring a lengthy article of the lurid 1910 trial of a notorious burglar. The sentence had been thirty years in prison.

Humboldt tried to rest in the late afternoon, and actually fell asleep for nearly two hours. He awoke to the sound of more rain, with an empty feeling in his stomach. Finding little or nothing remaining in his larder, he crossly sallied forth again, umbrella in hand, and purchased a number of staple foods at a nearby supermarket. He gloomily carried several heavy bags of these groceries through the pouring rain from the garage to his rowhouse, thoroughly soaking them and himself, in the process. Dried off, and hoping to cheer up, he cooked one of his favorite dishes and then settled down to an early supper. There, at the table, he again encountered the unfortunate history of the construction of the Second Church of the Revealed Truth. Delving deeper into this aggrandizing tome, he found more references to the mysterious "Acme Co." Where was it that he'd seen that name?

He was dining earlier than usual, and so didn't foresee that the television would be playing the Six PM, Channel Seven News. There she was again, Penny Rote herself, with all of her fashionable appearance and panoply of newsanchor splendor. She was speaking mostly about crimes, including a major highway project that she said was riddled with incompetence and graft between certain politicians and the construction company. It was at this point, with her reference to a contractor and grounded on his reflections on record storage procedures earlier in the day, that he finally recalled where he'd seen something about the Acme Company. It was lettered on a box of old files on a dusty shelf at the far back corner of Prior Leather's own third floor record storage room.

Perhaps that Acme Co. had been a construction company that his ancestor had formed to build the old church across the street. Over the decades, such self-dealing was all too common in the Prior family business affairs. Humboldt was so enthusiastic at this discovery, that when the telephone rang for the first time, he forgot and answered it at once. It proved to be the first of five calls from those pesky teenaged girls, deliberately spaced at twenty-minute intervals, each asking "the great detective Prior," for help in locating certain missing articles of wearing apparel or cosmetics, and giggling when he asked them please not to call anymore. It was simply more persecution, sounding to someone much more experienced than Humboldt as if it was part of a sorority initiation ritual. At about nine o'clock, the calls ceased, and he wearily climbed the stairs to bed, mentally abusing the negligent mystery-story writer and his ill-chosen fictional detective with the name of a real person. It was still raining hard.

Hoping for a forecast of better weather, he fiddled with his radio, put on a pair of striped pajamas that were too big for him, and then tumbled, exhausted, onto his bed. To his subsequent surprise, he fell asleep almost at once, and slept soundly until one AM, awakening in a sweaty fluster over something on the radio. Nearly four hours of sleep, added to the noise of the rain and the afternoon's long nap, now kept him awake. He listened more carefully.

&&&

After a series of commercial messages devoted to dubious over-the-counter drugs, a now all-too-familiar voice, interrupted by the coughs of an elderly throat, said haltingly in a rasping monotone, "Beloved listeners, those who wait beyond . . . ," pause, " . . . are more than anxious, nay lovingly anxious, to respond to your sacred inquiries. However, answers may be obtained only under the pure auspices of the Revealed Truth Radio Ministries, assuring the best possible conditions for our effort to pierce the veil of what is to come. We seek only to serve our beloved listeners. Brother Secondus, what further have we this blessed evening?"

Humboldt shuddered. They were at it again.

Another elderly voice croaked, "Why Brother Primus, we have a dear communication from a fine little lady listener who signs herself as 'The Widow Perkins.' She calls upon us for assistance in reaching out to her dear brother, Walter, who passed on thirty years ago."

This first voice asked, "Has she received one of our lovely Bluebird of Hope figurines?"

The answer croaked, "Not as yet, dear brother."

There was the sound of someone rustling papers, another cough, and then several banging noises. Then, the first voice returned, saying, "Many answers such as you seek, dear Mrs. Perkins, have already been given to those who wait with us here on the Ministries radio program. However, for you dear friend, the distance in years is very great, and much that happened long ago now stands between you and your beloved departed brother. He can scarcely hear your call, and begs us to tell you that aid is needed. Thus, if you will only allow us to send you, postage paid, one of our cherished Bluebird of Hope figurines for only $29.95, the fragile wings of this beloved avian messenger will surely support your call. A fresh order blank is in the mail to all of our listening family." There was probably more, but Humboldt turned off his radio in disgust and tried to sleep. Yes, they were at it again.

&&&

In any historical account, so-called primary sources add greatly to what is being recorded. Even in cases such as this, with an excess of reticence, secrecy, suspicion, and distrust on the part of most of the participants, original documents can sometimes be found. Thus, the historian, for whatever light it may shed on what has been taking place, offers the following original memorandum. As it was undated, we cannot be absolutely certain of the precise sequence in which to place it, however analysis suggests it was written at about this point in the story.

```
"Intra-Office Memorandum
    Hi    Boss:    Remember    that    special
investigative  report  that  I  mentioned  a  few
weeks    ago.    Here's    a    quick    update.    My
research  is  going  well.  I  found  an  insider
who  knows  a  lot.  He's  a  little  odd  and  hard
to   figure   out   at   times,   but   I   think   he's
legit.  Anyway,  he  is  working  out  better  than
most   sources,   given   that   I've   haven't   been
able  to  tell  him  the  real  story.  As  to  the
```

subjects, they're even worse crooks than I thought. I'll have it wrapped up soon and I think you'll like the result. I'll see you about it in just a few days."

&&&

Chapter 15

It was a few days before Humboldt could find time to conduct his research of the old Acme Co. files that he thought were stored on the third floor of the Osgood Prior Building. First, he was busy all Friday morning with his accounts and then with a silly request, relayed by the secretary from his cousin and boss, Prior Leather's slithery president, Malice Prior.

The secretary said shortly, "Mr. Humboldt, Mr. Prior wants you to check with our attorney to see whether or not we can predate the incentive bonus checks and issue them in advance of the actual date of the award? In other words, Mr. Prior asks if the bonus eligibility is solidly assured, why wait?"

While this seemed a question for Ribald Prior, as personnel manager, Humboldt knew there was internal tension about the bonus plan. He called the attorney, with whom he'd had friendly contacts for decades. After expressions of sympathy, the attorney, who had nightmares about disbarment after almost every contact, direct or indirect, with his client's president, answered that, "Unfortunately, Humboldt, that wouldn't be legal. You can't do it." Humboldt gladly told the secretary this. It was another of his "small victories."

Next, a weekend intervened. It was full of rain and once disrupted by an extremely annoying long distance telephone call. It was from a confused employee of a national bookstore chain, who had left only her name and telephone number on Humboldt's aging answering machine. Not knowing who she was or what she wanted, he had returned the call, only to discover that she was planning a local book signing for the wretched author of those mystery stories that featured an amateur detective regrettably called Humboldt Prior. This further confusion of names was just another example of the unfairness of the whole situation, clearly calling for judicial correction. It took the real Humboldt several minutes to explain that the actual author's name was something else. Then, after the call, he fretted for twenty minutes more, wondering if this, at last, might be ground for litigation and the collection of punitive damages. After all, he'd spent his own money straightening out the mess. Gloomily, he decided his costs were too small. His final reflection on the subject was that at least it hadn't been Penny Rote, with more night adventures in store for him. He said this to himself two or three times.

Vowing to not answer any more telephone calls, he spent the rest of the day cleaning the front portion of his basement. This was an ugly task, as the power cord on his vacuum cleaner wasn't quite long enough and he had to resort to his broom and dustpan. He even moved some of the old trunks and suitcases belonging to his late parents that covered almost the entire wall of the basement nearest the street. Someday, he'd have to really go through them. The trunks hadn't been touched for decades and were covered with cobwebs, dust, and grit from his basement walls. After cleaning for over an hour and transferring much of the dirt to his own person, he gave up, saying to himself that he'd like to see that high and mighty fictional detective do some real work like that. It was hot in his basement and an odor of musty dampness was coming from somewhere, probably from the deep recess outside his front basement window.

On Sunday, for reasons impossible for a rational observer to understand, and after gazing out of his front window for many minutes, he actually decided to attend services at the Second Church of the Reveal Truth. Perhaps he was trying to steel himself and prepare for what he feared would be another night visit, in company with the determined Miss Rote. Or, perhaps there was a different reason. Dressing in his blue suit in spite of the heat, he found a break in the rain and marched across Woodhouse Avenue well ahead of the usual ten o'clock time. The street was deserted.

The dark red bricks of the outer wall, and those of the garage and decrepit church within it, were still wet with rain. An ominous urban crow circled above, and then perched blackly high on the roof of the tower.

Reaching the main doorway in a less-confident frame of mind, he was confronted by a faded hand-written message, unnoticed on his previous nocturnal visit. This explained that, in consideration of the difficulties elderly members seemed to have in reaching the church on time, services were now at ten-thirty on alternate Sundays. The door was locked and a sudden downpour was turning the street behind him into something on the order of a high-pressure car wash.

Without thinking of the highly embarrassing difficulty he'd have in explaining his presence inside, he reached for his key to the church, fumbling for its distinctive tag. To his horror, it wasn't with the rest of the jumble of other keys and pocket money he'd transferred to the blue suit and in the next instant, he clearly remembered seeing Penny Rote with the key to the church as they'd parted after their last visit.

Ignoring the drenching rain, he literally ran back across the street to his house and stayed there the rest of the day.

&&&

On the same weekend during which Humboldt was struggling with the misdirected telephone call from the national bookstore, another of his relatives, likewise resident in the glum complex of dark red brick rowhouses and apartments on Woodhouse Avenue, was also bedeviled by that same instrument. Specifically, Malice Prior sprawled in his sumptuous apartment and cursing the golf-preventing rain, was engaged in resisting temptation.

Malice has been well introduced earlier in this history. His antecedents were as the son of the deceased leatherworks executive and incredibly corrupt state senator Mendacious Prior. Malice was also the younger brother of Malevolence Prior, US Army, who had been shot for excellent reasons, by a firing squad of his own army. We've known Malice as the wealthy president of Prior and Cousins Leather Works, with his tall, lean figure, distinguished broad forehead, and over-long gray hair. We have described his characteristic and expensive casual dress, and have hinted as to his extravagantly decorated apartment, crammed with luxuries of every kind, including those of art, electronics, and upholstery. His excesses as to money and women are also on the record. Less explicit, but equally important, are what might be termed his pre-mammalian self-protection instincts. These were front and center as to the telephone calls.

His forty-some year old black-haired female third cousin, Temperance Prior, had been calling him repeatedly. Even without consideration of her heavy breathing, it was still easy to conclude that she definitely wanted to see him again. Malice had been avoiding her, except for brief encounters at one or two of the Prior family cocktail parties, where close bodily contact was impossible. While he was strongly attracted to his well-endowed and over-heated cousin, his experiences that night in the church were seared on his memory. His shock at finding himself fleeing on foot in heavy rain had stayed with him. His near discovery by what Malice assumed to be a late-working custodian, had been what educators call a teachable moment that Malice did not want to repeat. His hypothetical reaction to the knowledge that what they had actually nearly encountered was a television anchorwoman exceeds imagination.

For some reason, Temperance was insisting on repeating their tryst in the old church. She'd said, "It's the only place, darling. Our snoopy relatives are all over the city, but they're never in church and certainly not at night." She repeated this to Malice more than once during each phone call, often with added words such as, "Darling, we've got to get together right away," and "I want you right now!"

At first, he pleaded other engagements. Then he even claimed to be ill, alluding, with embarrassing specificity, to treatment by his urologist. She kept on calling. Perhaps it was the repetition, or perhaps it was her hints about what she planned to wear and not wear. Anyway, on Sunday afternoon, Malice finally capitulated, agreeing to meet her at the less conspicuous rear door of the church on Monday evening. He thought he was being clever in appointing ten o'clock for the rendezvous, believing that this earlier time would avoid another encounter with the notional custodian. He was, of course, mistaken in this.

&&&

Monday morning dawned partly sunny. Woodhouse Avenue, still wet from the seemingly endless rain, at least appeared clean. Humboldt, benefiting from his recent grocery shopping, enjoyed a cheering and nourishing breakfast, although the history of the church construction was on his table as a reminder of his predicament. He'd heard nothing from Penny Rote for a few days, but was still cornered by her threat to reveal all concerning Prior Leather and the trust, if he refused to assist with her researches for the mystery novel she planned to write. When you came down to it, he said fussily to himself while brushing his teeth, mystery novels were at the heart of all his troubles. If it were not for that loathsome amateur writer and his foul detective, none of this would have happened. There ought to be a law against naming book characters after living persons. Humboldt was in danger of becoming fixated. Perhaps the only thing preventing this, beyond his no-more-than-average willpower, was his other growing fixation. He was becoming more and more obsessed with Penny Rote.

In honor of the improved weather, he intended to drive his treasured Buick station wagon. Just as he entered the garage, he saw the enormous hindquarters of the Malice Prior Cadillac limousine disappearing out into the alley. It was a reminder that he didn't welcome. The city fathers, in their wisdom, had selected this busy Monday morning as the best time for closing the main east-west downtown thoroughfare for road repairs. The resulting traffic delay caused ample time for consideration of what he mentally termed "the Manheimers display trunk trouble."

Clouds were forming in the sky overhead as he summed up the situation, automatically placing assets (unidentified as yet) on the left and liabilities (many) on the right. By now, it was obvious that his Prior cousins Moribund (sales), Dorset (manufacturing), and Ribald (personnel), were planning to pull a fast one on Manheimers, one of his city's most respected retail enterprises. Worse, they had the full support of the company president. Confronted with situations like this, Humboldt's usual strategy was to lie low and hope that the incompetence of his fellow executives would cause their venture to collapse of its own weight. Would that work here? Things seemed to be moving ahead pretty fast. What about Ribald's plans to recruit a manufacturing work force consisting entirely of innocent teenage girls? Nothing good could come of that. What to do?

Humboldt reached the Prior Building just as the rain began again. Attempting a late-middle-aged sprint across the wet parking lot, he strained his left knee and merely nodded to Millard Fillmore who seemed about to stop him for conversation. He hurried up stairs and dodged any contact with his co-executives. He was hoping for a quiet morning.

There were, thank goodness, no waiting phone calls and only a few papers needing his attention. This wasn't necessarily a good sign, for difficult matters often piled up on the desk of the president. Malice, when agitated had a tendency to subside into a pout, and look at nothing for days. Only later, would the problems tardily arrive in Humboldt's office.

&&&

By ten o'clock, he was finished and was free to finally investigate that box of old files pertaining to the mysterious Acme Co., evidently the self-dealing construction company that had built the Second Church of the Revealed Truth. Taking the only key to the third floor record storage, his prerogative as comptroller, he also removed his suit jacket and collected an older one from its hanger behind his office door. The old files on the third floor, unheated for decades to save money, were notoriously dusty.

He climbed the long flight of stairs, opened the locked door, and quickly found the Acme Co. files, stored in the back on a high shelf, just where he remembered them. They were covered with cobwebs. Using an old rag he made an attempt at removing these, and carried the box to an old table and chair that stood near a very dirty window. Now for some real "detective work" that solved real questions, not the stylized activities of the false Humboldt Prior, the product of the diseased thinking of that amateur writer. Humboldt was, after all, a historian, and in addition to his accounts, digging through old papers was one of his few proficiencies.

It was soon apparent that this was only a portion of the construction files that must have once existed. In addition to, regrettably, two more copies of the "Construction of the Second Church" book, there were only a few bundles of old papers. These pertained to what is nowadays called the "punch list" phase, when the completed structure is subject to final inspection by the owner, with lists made of errors, imperfections, and needed changes. Now that his interest was aroused and he had the time to look, Humboldt had to be satisfied with these.

Yes, it was clear that for whatever reason, probably his personal financial interest, old Osgood Prior had acted as his own general contractor. His bold signature, often under the word "Disapproved," appeared on many of the dried-up, dusty pages. Although some of these were requests from the demanding new pastor for more improvements to the new church, Humboldt had to admit that overall, Osgood had been quite generous with these.

Osgood had been frequently at odds with his subcontractors, criticizing delays and cost overruns. Memos flew back and forth between Osgood, his hapless stenographer, and the subcontractors. Several of these recounted obscure, though colorfully-described difficulties with the finishing of what the masonry subcontractor, an obvious German named Fredrick Guttberg, called in labored English, 'un watering' of the 'stone lined out going,' whatever that was. For over two years, through his stenographer, Osgood had complained of leaks, flooding, and expenditures far higher than promised. At first, Guttberg responded that these difficulties were inevitable, and that he'd done his best to provide good work. Still very dissatisfied, Osgood insisted that Second Revealed's pastor be contacted for a full inspection and report. As far as Humboldt could tell from the file, this was never completed. Finally, a copy of a telegram sent to Florida by Osgood's long-suffering stenographer read, 'Mr. Osgood Prior at St. Augustine: Dear Sir: Today's Press reports that Mr. Guttberg has died. What are your wishes?' Uncharacteristically, Osgood failed to pursue the poor man's estate. About one hundred years later, on his visit to the church basement with Penny Rote, Humboldt thought he might have seen evidence of the same water problems.

Sitting at the dusty old table, his mind dwelt far too long on that visit. After an hour or so, he had finished with the files. He concluded that while there wasn't much information about the Acme Company, what there was might be of some historical interest, but only that.

&&&

Later that evening, after a simple supper and a reassuring review of his personal financial reports, Humboldt finally began to relax. A glance at his personal financial situation was usually comforting. His parents had left him reasonably well off. His decent salary from the trust, via Prior and Cousins, and his frugal lifestyle, had further augmented his situation. Maybe he should just completely retire and thus avoid the inevitable tarnish of the Manheimers trunk affair. However, he thought just before dozing in the big chair in his library, he'd still have the Penny Rote imbroglio.

His telephone rang at about nine o'clock, but at first he slept on. The caller was persistent. Sleepily awake, he tried to focus. Somehow, it seemed too late for those pesky teenage girls, supposedly seeking help from the fictional Humboldt Prior. He finally answered the call with a cautious, "Yes?"

It was her voice. Penny said, half laughing, "I'm glad I caught you at home. When you didn't answer, I thought maybe you were out on the town with one of your lady friends."

This shocking inference, directed at a semi-retired bachelor comptroller, was almost too much, but her tone of voice was friendly enough and he was relieved it wasn't one of the teenagers. He replied cautiously, "How are you this evening, Miss Rote?"

"I'm just super, thanks. Right now, I'm out and about, and calling you from my car. Then I have my news show to do, but I have to see you later on, at about eleven."

Sputtering, he started to protest.

"No, no," she said soothingly. "I only want a few minutes of your time. I'm almost done with my book research, and simply have a few more questions. Will that work for you?"

Humboldt thought at first that she was suggesting that they meet somewhere, perhaps in a bar near the TV station. He had a poor impression of such places, filled with cigarette smoke and noisy reporters. "I don't know . . ." he began.

She reassured him. "It's okay, Humboldt. I'll stop by at your place. Just keep the light on for me." She chuckled again, and was gone.

Humboldt was no longer sleepy, but a little less worried. Whatever further toils were in store, at least he was apparently safe from the nameless perils of a further visit to the old church.

However, in the dark skies over Woodhouse Avenue, another thunderstorm was brewing.

&&&

Chapter 16

(Historian's Note: The events to be chronicled in this chapter and the next, present the historian with a challenging task. He must chronicle a complex series of inter-actions involving several of the principal characters. Most of these characters were unassociated with one another and wished to remain so. It is also necessary to introduce another participant, with his own brief but important role to play. Events taking place more or less simultaneously, must, for clarity, be described sequentially. The serious reader may wish to take notes and, perhaps even diagram the actions and locations of the various parties.)

&&&

The first series of events surround Miss Penelope Rote, driving in her expensive sport utility vehicle, toward the Eastern end of HillTop Parkway. It was already raining hard and she hoped it would let up by the time she reached her destination. She planned to arrive there at about nine-thirty PM, Monday evening. It is regrettable to report that again Penny had not been strictly truthful with Humboldt in her earlier phone call. She was, in fact, not going to be performing her ten o'clock newsanchor duties, but instead was planning another secret visit to the Second Church of the Revealed Truth, this time alone. Her substitute newsanchor would say that she was "on assignment."

Ever since their first visit, she had the vague recollection of having seen a stack of files pertaining to the Revealed Truth Radio Ministries, half-hidden behind some boxes of envelopes on one of the top shelves of the church's basement storeroom. She wanted to examine these for reasons not related to her stated project of writing a mystery novel set in an old church.

Indeed, this was another area in which she had not been fully accurate in her statements to Humboldt. The files were marked "Accounts," and "Taxes," the later presumably being the information returns filed with the revenue authorities by most tax-exempt charitable organizations. Her reason for being eager to examine these files was one that began to trouble her, as she had come to know and like the real Humboldt Prior. Whether or not he was a semi-retired operative of the Central Intelligence Agency, she still was not sure. However, she was sure that he was helping her a great deal, that she was actually enjoying his company, and that she wanted his friendship. She recognized that he had gone to considerable trouble and risk on her behalf and now wished she had been more truthful as to the real objects she had in view.

In plain fact, she was not writing a mystery story at all. Instead, she was personally investigating the Revealed Truth Radio Ministries, preparatory to exposing the foolish iniquities of Pastors Primus and Secondus Prior in a lengthy featured segment on her television news program. The Ministries' accounts and tax reports were among the last evidence she needed. She strongly suspected that they would reveal misappropriated funds and misused charitable income. She believed that Humboldt would be dismayed by this deception and she felt badly about that.

It was raining heavily as Penny parked her SUV on HillTop Parkway, under a streetlight at the point at which the alley behind the church and communal garage entered the Parkway. Her stylish black raincoat, worn over a dark sweater and slacks, was belted tight against the storm, and the black scarf covering her sandy hair was pulled forward to disguise her well-known freckled features. She got out of the car, wrinkled her pretty nose at the downpour, and hurried down the alley toward the back door of the church, skillfully dodging the worst of the rain puddles.

It was much darker in the alley and she immediately had recourse to one of her TV station's official flashlights, a powerful model issued to each investigative reporter. She held Humboldt's key to the church in her other hand. The great dark bulks of the communal garage and nineteenth-century church loomed up menacingly on her right. Cautiously, she climbed the rickety wooden back steps of the church, being careful not to slip, just as Humboldt had warned her. The key now worked quite easily in the lock of the rear door, and she soon found herself once more in the rear hallway of the decrepit old church.

Peering into the towering sanctuary, illuminated only by the feeble light shining in the huge half-round window, high in the wall in front of her, she shivered at the dark emptiness, wishing not for the first time, that she had Humboldt with her. She took a deep breath, steeled herself as a good newsanchor must, returned to the rear hall, and then headed down the steep rear stairs to the basement. There, she walked quickly along the main hallway, trying to ignore the musty darkness and certain disturbing odors and scurrying noises. She turned right at the cross-hall to find the door of the storeroom. There, she risked the dim overhead light bulb, and went to work. Again, as a good investigative reporter, she was equipped with a commodious shoulder bag, for use if it proved necessary to borrow any of the files of accounts and tax reports. However, she preferred to take as few as possible, for legal counsel had advised her that recent court decisions did not look kindly on such actions, however newsworthy.

The structure of the huge old church creaked and groaned in the strong wind and Penny could hear the drip of water from several directions. The Radio Ministries files were covered with spider webs, and once something with legs skittered across her face. She quickly wiped it away. It took her about thirty minutes to look through the old files. She was not a trained accountant (it tardily occurred to her that Humboldt was and would have been of real help in this), but it was easy to see that the amounts being reported to the tax authorities as donations and miscellaneous sales revenues were far less than those shown in the handwritten financial statements. The figures for the pay of ministerial staff were also far less in the tax reports. Once, she jumped nervously as something thumped on the floor overhead. Again, summoning true newsanchor resolve, she selected a dozen of the most incriminating pages from the files and stuffed them into her bag. She turned out the light, closed the door, and walked quickly back to main hallway. Her watch told her it was a little after ten o'clock. She would be very glad to be out of the dank church basement and back to the safety of her car.

&&&

Stewie "Snapshot" Tompkins had been having a difficult day. First, there'd been trouble with one of his other local church clients. For several years, Stewie had been serving the photographic needs of one of those huge suburban mega-ministries, "Rising to the Skies of Love Reformed Church." It was located, surrounded by acres of convenient asphalt parking, in a former supermarket, at one of the older shopping malls. "Rising Church," as it was locally nicknamed, had been enjoying four-figure membership growth annually, and now had over ten thousand members. Most of them made extremely generous weekly contributions and also gladly purchased extra pictures from Tompkins' annual photographic sessions that were preliminary to new editions of the church directory. For Stewie, that was one of the benefits of such rapid growth, for the annual reissue of church directories, with photographs, was rare in his business. Tompkins secretly shared the profits from the directories and extra photos with the senior minister, one Jimmy "Already on the Way" Johnson, through a secret scheme of kickbacks in cash.

Early that morning, Snapshot had received an urgent telephone call from this valued associate, conveying the bad news that Rising's second-most-wealthy member, a land developer named Jackie "Acres of Happiness" Johnson had passed away. This Mr. Johnson had been the minister's brother. Speaking from his elaborate vacation home in another state, Minister Johnson described one of his brother's last requests. This was that a family photograph be taken at Jackie Johnson's funeral with the embalmed body of the deceased standing in the center of the front row of the group picture, supported by a tall candlestick or perhaps a coat rack. "Acres of Happiness" Johnson had allegedly suggested that the photos be sold to raise money for the church. Neither "Already on the Way" Johnson nor Stewie Tompkins saw anything inappropriate in all of this, and Stewie agreed to assist with the arrangements in the absence of the surviving brother.

However, the trouble arose later in the morning, when meeting with the undertaker, a partner of one of the city's most reputable mortuary firms, selected by mistake in the absence of the senior minister. This outraged funeral director, speaking on the basis of decades of integrity, flatly refused and threatened Stewie and the associate minister with the Department of Health should any further attempt be made to make such a deplorable use of the dead man's body. Snapshot Tompkins estimated his lost income at something over $5,000.

Next, he had had to hurry his yellow Cadillac through the rain back to the central part of the city, in order to attend a conference on Woodhouse Avenue with Pastors Primus and Secundus Prior. For greater privacy, they met in the church offices, and Stewie was glad to trade the peculiar odors of Primus's apartment for the musty damp of Second Revealed.

The old brothers were in a confident mood. Primus exclaimed, "We're really going great guns and it's all that spiritualism s . . t. Our latest Revealed Truth Radio Ministries programs brought a record level of Bluebird purchases, calls for spiritualistic advice, and cash donations." Primus had been continuing his researches into spiritualism and added, for those interested in that subject, "I've found out that death is termed 'the Great Change'. I'm planning to work that into our next broadcast."

Secondus had chanced to read something about corporate buyouts in his newspaper, and was wondering if they should simply counter whatever "southern takeover ministry" was after them, with an offer to sell. "After all," he added, "they seem to have quieted down the last couple of days, and maybe this would be the time to strike a deal with them."

Recognizing that this offer, and its bemused rejection, would inevitably mean the end of his highly lucrative consulting assignment, Stewie had to fight the idea.

"That just won't work, boys," he explained to the two elderly pastors. "I know those big southern outfits. They'll see it as a sign of weakness and smell 'blood in the water.' The only thing to do is to redouble our vigilance. They're just getting ready to make another move. I'd better watch the church all night from now on."

Pastor Primus nodded. He was always suspicious of deals. He blew his nose and then spat into a far corner. "You're damn right, Snapshot boy. You can't trust 'em. Watch this old dump all night, if necessary. When it starts getting light, you can always catch a nap on that old couch over there."

Pastor Secondus seemed unconvinced, but shrugged and dropped the subject. Stewie Tompkins felt that, for the moment, he had things under control, and departed for his dinner and a short nap in his spacious motel suite.

Thus, it was just before ten o'clock Monday evening, when the worried and generally frazzled Stewie Tompkins again parked his yellow Cadillac in front of the gloomy Second Church of the Revealed Truth. He'd tried unsuccessfully all evening to reach his other major local church client, "Already on the Way" Johnson, in hopes of persuading him to pick another undertaker, more amenable to group photographs. Finally, he was informed that the minister's private jet had already taken off.

Stewie walked quickly through the driving rain, opened the front door of the old church, entered, and locked it behind him. The massive structure moaned and shuddered in the storm and somewhere in the rear of the building, there was what he hoped was only a tree branch clattering against the roof. It was an ominous and frightening night.

Stewie had absolutely no intention of actively watching the church for the entire night. First, he locked himself in the office. Then, after patting the hard form of his old pistol, secured in one coat pocket, he found a whiskey flask in another, took a long reassuring drink, and settled down on the dusty couch, tucked away in an alcove of the church parlor. Ignoring the odor of the decaying upholstery, he soon fell asleep. It was then a little after ten o'clock.

&&&

It is difficult to feel sorry for Humboldt's cousin, Malice Prior. We have spoken of his high position in the business world, and of his wealth and exaggerated sense of the importance of dress and style. Readers have also been made aware of his vile personality and appalling attitude toward women. He is not a sympathetic character.

However, after learning of his experiences just after ten o'clock on the same Monday evening, fair-minded readers may feel just a little sympathy. All day, Malice had been anticipating his tryst with his third cousin, Temperance Prior. Her eagerness to see him had dwelt so largely in his mind, that in his day's business dealings, such as they were, he'd been unusually short and even more inept than usual.

Huddled in the pouring rain, he had been waiting on the slippery back steps of the Second Church of the Revealed Truth since about nine-fifty. Visions of his moments with the seductive Temperance had clearly formed, and he was ready for action. Even the activities of a prowling urban raccoon failed to distract him.

Then, a minute after ten, she appeared, at first only a dim but recognizable silhouette under the streetlight at the HillTop Parkway end of the alley. She moved nearer, swinging provocatively as she walked. Malice actually drew a deep breath in anticipation and excitement, as he savored the attractive outlines of her full figure. However, on closer inspection something looked wrong.

When Temperance finally climbed the steps into the dim light by the rear door, and pressed herself close to him, the full scope of the sartorial disaster was all too clear. Probably hoping to further excite him, she'd come dressed as a "punk rocker." Malice shuddered. There was no appearance more likely to annoy his exaggerated sense of good taste. She was wearing gold high platform shoes, black mesh tights with pink sequins, and a very short, greenish-brown dress with more pink sequins. Her hair was also dyed pink and heavily perfumed. Several fake tattoos decorated her forearms where they emerged from her orange plastic raincoat.

Choking down his dismay, and driven by his reptilian instincts, Malice still managed to greet her effusively with a warm embrace, and using his official key, opened the door and quickly ushered her inside. His sole concern, even under such unlikely circumstances, was not to be seen in the company of the orange raincoat. The stronger light in the back hallway didn't improve matters, but he reasoned that the affair wouldn't have to be a prolonged one. Still holding her, he skillfully moved them on into the dark church sanctuary and to a more or less comfortable place on one of the first pews. Temperance giggled and kissed him passionately, at the same time doing something with her hands. Malice responded appropriately, raising his assessment of the duration of the affair to a full half-hour. It was then about ten-five.

&&&

Thus, to recapitulate, we find ourselves with Miss Penelope Rote, investigative newsanchor, feeling more and more alone, just reaching the center point of the main basement hallway of the Second Church of the Revealed Truth. She was hastily escaping the scene of her investigations of the Revealed Truth Radio Ministry.

At the same time, a worried and somewhat nervous Mr. Stewie "Snapshot" Tompkins, low-grade church photographer, armed with his old revolver, and locked in the church offices, had just fallen soundly asleep.

Next, also at the same moment, an annoyed Mr. Malice Prior and an excited Miss Temperance Prior have just begun their activities in one of the front pews of the same church.

The final party to the confused and violent events that were about to unfold must now be introduced. This participant, in a study more scientific than this one, would be designated as "Male Brown Rat Number 176." He was about twenty-seven months old. His right hind leg was lame from one of his countless rat battles, and he was already the sire, grandsire, or great-grandsire of nearly three hundred progeny, living and deceased. Number 176 was a polished veteran of church affairs, and while not technically a member, was well accustomed to sharing the edifice with human beings, clerical and secular. A few minutes earlier, he had come upon a discarded throat lozenge lying on the dusty floor near the main doorway. He was now politely devouring it outside the entrance to his residence, a hole in the baseboard of the rear wall of the sanctuary, under a heat radiator.

All this time, Mr. Humboldt Prior was dozing in his library across the street.

&&&

Chapter 17

The penultimate event of those described in this and the preceding chapter was a very strong gust of rain and wind that roared northeast, along the alley behind the Second Revealed Church. As Malice Prior had been preoccupied with his plans for his female third-cousin, he had not remembered to close the rear door properly. Therefore, between ten-ten and ten-fifteen that fateful Monday night, the door blew open with a very loud crashing bang.

The consequences varied. Penny Rote, Malice and Temperance Prior, and Rat Number 176, each being busy with their own affairs, either didn't hear the loud noise, or ignored it. However, the curious fact was the Stewie "Snapshot" Tompkins, locked in the church office, somehow heard the noise, and was roused from his sleep. He had been restless and beset with a very bad nightmare. In it, his favorite local church client, Jimmy "Already on the Way" Johnson, minister of the Rising to the Skies of Love Reformed Church was accusing him of taking his deceased brother's place in the group photograph. Money damages were being demanded. It was not a pleasant dream.

Tompkins rolled upright and opened one eye. Where was he? The door banged again. Groggy and only half-awake, he staggered to his feet, put on his shoes, and set off to investigate. He experienced a brief and painful encounter with the office door, that he had no recollection of locking. Then, stumbling, he arrived at the main entrance to the church sanctuary.

Downstairs in the center hallway, Penny Rote heard his footsteps and froze. Malice and Temperance were still busy with their private matters. Rat Number 176 was too polite to take any notice, except to remark to himself that there certainly had been a noticeable increase in night traffic within the church.

Making a minimum amount of noise, Snapshot Tompkins pulled open one of the center doors and peered cautiously into the great, darkened void. He sniffed the musty air. Was there something different? Perhaps he smelled Temperance's heavy perfume, or heard just the slightest breath or other noise from those on the front pew, for, now actually suspicious of real intruders, he pulled his old pistol from his coat pocket. He had never fired the weapon, but had been assured by the gentleman from whom he'd purchased it at a roadside stand outside of Little Rock, Arkansas, that it was loaded and in fine working order.

It was at that point, that an overly excited Malice Prior, experiencing extreme frustration with some article of his partner's unfortunate clothing, let out a vile and audible epithet. Alarmed, Tompkins flinched and then ducked his lanky form down behind one of the rear church pews, banging his knee noisily in doing so. "Holy smokes," he muttered to himself, "somethin's really goin' on."

These understandable but unnecessarily noisy actions were, in turn, too much for the good manners of Rat 176. Common courtesy required that he quickly absent himself from private matters that did not concern him. This, he proceeded to do, unfortunately because of his injured leg, making a loud scrabbling noise three or four feet directly behind the now highly stressed church photographer. Stewie's erroneous conclusion that he was now being threatened from two sides, though regrettable, was also understandable. However, his subsequent actions cannot be endorsed.

In point of fact, the now thoroughly frightened photographer began an agitated crawl back in the direction of the church office, cursing loudly, and at the same time discharging several random revolver shots, each banging off in a different direction. CRACK! CRACK! CRACK!

Their love-making thus violently interrupted by his noisy retreat from the sanctuary and by the much greater noise of the first pistol shot, Malice and Temperance, ignoring their respective states of undress, leaped upright, and began yelling in fright and running toward the rear exit. Temperance, handicapped by her sequined tights, tripped almost at once, but Malice was still standing when Stewie's third shot grazed his right arm. Screeching another even louder and viler epithet, Malice immediately joined his cousin on the floor. There, staying low to avoid further gunshots, they continued a spectacular high-speed scramble until they reached the back door. In spite of the heavy wind and pelting rain, they were very glad to find it open.

Once in the comparative safety of the alley, Temperance brought some sort of order to her clothing, and then helped Malice with his. The rain still pelted down, but neither paid any attention to it. Malice, clutching his injured arm, now actually oozing a little blood through the sleeve of his expensive jacket, was begging Temperance to rush him to the nearest hospital emergency room. Temperance was agreeing to do so, and at the same time was dragging her hysterical paramour with her down the alley in the direction of HillTop Parkway where her car was parked. Obscured by the pouring rain, they soon disappeared.

Much the same may be said for Male Rat 176. He definitely preferred the church quiet as it now became. Pleased with his situation back behind the baseboard and with his hunger temporarily satisfied by the lozenge, he simply went to sleep.

In the church office things were quite different. Stewie Tompkins had just completed one of the fastest escape-crawls in the history of the Second Church of the Revealed Truth. Recovering his composure, he remained at the ready, barricaded behind the locked door of the office, that he'd reinforced by a large desk that he somehow had managed to drag against it. He, too, much preferred the church quiet.

However, after further and more mature reflection, Snapshot Tompkins was not fully pleased with what had just happened. Looking back on it, he realized that he had panicked and that his recent performance could have been much improved. In his photographic vernacular, considerable retouching would be required before the recent events saw the light of day. He was already plotting his next move.

&&&

The same cannot be said for Miss Penelope Rote, the badly frightened newsanchor, last reported frozen in mid step, half way on her path back along the church basement's center hallway. What should she do? At first the choice seemed clear. There were several sharp, cracking blasts of noise, seeming to come from above and behind her. As almost all newsanchors of her age, Penny had never heard real gunfire, but was willing to trust her guess that this was what it would sound like. She instinctively started running along the grimy hallway toward the rear of the church, slipping in her expensive shoes and gasping for breath. This was not the way investigative journalism was supposed to be.

Within seconds however, even worse noises erupted above and in front of her, in the direction in which she was running. These were merely the natural reactions of Malice and Temperance Prior to being surprised in the act, fired upon, and in one case, slightly wounded. Nonetheless, they were the fearsome sounds of running footsteps and of real human voices, obviously wild with fright, and threatening even more danger ahead. She had heard nothing like it in the newsroom.

Penny skidded to a stop, tripped, fell, and banged her head on the wall as she did so. Recovering in seconds, she bravely got to her feet, shook her head to clear it, and then heard the last of the excited yells and curses of Malice and Temperance, exiting by the rear door. Escape in that direction seemed blocked, but thank goodness she had managed to hold onto her official Channel Seven flashlight. Turning to shine it behind her, along the basement hallway and recalling the existence of a second stairway and front exit in that direction, she set off, again running as fast as she could. Once more she tripped, losing one shoe, but recovered and continued on.

Unfortunately, she reached the foot of the front stairway, only to be greeted by the obviously dangerous sounds of a cursing church photographer dragging a large desk across the office floor in order to barricade the office door. Out of breath and now even more frightened and whimpering a little, Penny finally took refuge by hiding in the lower hall storage closet that she and Humboldt had found secured on their first visit. Why it was unlocked, she had no idea, although Humboldt, had he been present (as she now fervently wished that he was) would have explained that his cousin, Mildred Prior, sometimes cleaned portions of the church on late Monday afternoon and Tuesday morning.

Inside the deep narrow closet, with the door securely locked behind her, Penny slumped down into a sitting position, felt dizzy from her two falls, wondered vaguely where her other shoe had got to, and fainted.

&&&

She was awakened minutes later by more ominous noises from upstairs. These were, of course, the sounds of a reenergized and more confident church photographer pulling a heavy desk away from the office door, but it is just as well she didn't know this. In a moment, the sound of footsteps, first overhead, and then worse, coming down the stone stairs to the basement, gave Penny quite enough to worry about. It is axiomatic in newsanchor circles that, while the evidence of a successful investigative burglary can be glossed over in the afterglow of an award winning journalistic 'scoop,' an unsuccessful one, in which the reporter is apprehended and turned over to the police, is a very different matter. She had to get out of there.

The fearsome footsteps continued, now right outside the locked closet door. She scarcely dared to breathe. The hall light came on, penetrating her hiding place with a faint glow. Next, the footsteps clattered away along the brick and stone floor of the center hallway of the church basement. A surprised southern accented voice exclaimed, "What the hell is this?" It was, of course, the voice of a church photographer discovering a woman's expensive shoe where none ought to be, but she didn't know this either. The footsteps moved away, presumably to the far rear end of the hallway. She had to get away!

Perhaps it was the stimulus of probable discovery or that she used her flashlight. Either way, for the first time she saw there was something very odd about the rear wall of the storage closet. In fact, it looked like another narrow door made of strong vertical planks, dark with age. Further scrutiny revealed that the lock of the first closet door actually worked from both sides, seemingly unnecessary for a closet. Was this originally another exit from the old church leading to the outside and escape?

Penny Rote, although frightened, battered by falls on stone floors, and half shoeless, was still quick witted. It took only seconds of thought for her to put two and two together. Stepping cautiously over a pile of rags, pails, and mops, and past an aged vacuum cleaner, she quickly found the handle of the second door, unlocked it, and pulled it open. Above, the glare of her flashlight revealed the moss and cobweb-covered stone arch of a recessed doorway, an opposite rock wall, and little else. The rough and extremely dirty, wet stones of the wall showed dimly in the light and Penny could smell the odors of damp, decaying vegetation, dirt, and so forth. Looking down, she saw a narrow stone doorstep and beyond that a pool of black muddy rainwater, full of rotten leaves, among which regrettably, another dead pigeon was floating.

Another yell from the security guard forced her next move. Coming closer, she heard the magic words, "I know you guys are there. I've got my gun and I'm gonna shoot again." At this, in desperation, Penny slid her feet out onto the narrow doorstep and started to turn to her right hoping for some sign of steps leading upwards to escape, at the same time pulling the heavy narrow door closed behind her. For a person in her situation, this was done with considerable agility, but didn't allow for the missing shoe and decades of slime on the stone step.

Somehow managing to limit herself to a soft plaintive yelp of alarm, Penny slipped off the step and into about a foot of filthy water, rising in the heavy rain preparatory to seeping into the basement of the church, just as it had ever since the time of Fredrick Guttberg over one hundred years before. Her next stagger found nothing solid, and this time she fell forward and downward into a deeper and even more disgusting pool of very filthy and smelly water. Perhaps it was the water that caused her flashlight to suddenly go dim.

Gasping for breath and more frightened than ever, her searching hand somehow found not a stair step, but rather an iron bar affixed to the opposite stone wall. Then, to her amazement and joy her other hand, although still grasping the fading flashlight, managed to find another bar above it, forming, she frantically guessed, the rungs of a escape ladder. With much effort, Penny managed to pull herself up out of the water. Once she nearly fell, but with strength she didn't know she still had, Penny, encumbered with flashlight and shoulder bag, struggled up the iron ladder, out of the flooded areaway, tumbling finally into a mass of thick scrubby bushes at the base of the front wall of the church. There she lay, soaking wet, covered with dirt and wet leaves, gasping for breath and trembling with fear. At least, she could no longer hear the man with the gun.

At that point, her official Channel Seven flashlight failed completely. Behind and below her was an armed southern church security guard, one of a class of men notorious for their lack of appreciation of investigative journalism. Desperate, and hoping for some miracle, she pulled herself up, pushed through the bushes, staggered through tall wet grass, along a slippery sidewalk, and to her immense relief, found herself on Woodhouse Avenue just across the street from Humboldt's rowhouse.

In seconds, she was pounding on his door, calling out hysterically, "Help me, please, help me!" in a scared very un-newsanchor-like voice. She repeated this several times, and then collapsed, huddled against the door, alternatively calling for help, and sobbing hysterically. It was then, approximately ten thirty-five on Monday evening. For what seemed to her like hours, Penny pushed against the heavy door, her fists pounding on the thick boards. However, it was actually only a few moments before the door opened!

&&&

Snug in his library, on a particularly stormy summer night, Humboldt Prior yawned. It was about ten thirty-five and, he thought fussily, he still had nearly a full half-hour to wait, assuming Penny was on time. She had insisted on seeing him again at eleven o'clock after her news show. What now? Just to talk things over, she'd said, but it was still another intrusion. How he wished that darn detective-story writer had never been born. He tried closing his eyes to relax. No, that didn't work.

Somewhere in the distance, apparently just outside his house, someone was yelling something. This was rare on the normally quiet Woodhouse Avenue. Frowning, Humboldt got up and trundled through his front hall into his dark little-used front parlor. He looked out, but could see nothing. However, he could still hear the yelling, sounding like the word "Help!" repeated several times. What did that mean? It was a bit late for the noisy games of the troublesome children of Dorset Prior, his next-door neighbor. However, he supposed he'd better investigate.

Grumpily, he went to his front door. The noise, now sounding more like someone crying, was coming from outside it. Again, he heard the hysterical words, "Help me! Help me!" He pulled the door open.

Humboldt leaped backwards. From the other side of the door, an apparition rushed to him, crying out, "Oh, Humboldt, thank God it's you." The apparition was extremely wet and covered with mud and grime, and he also quickly realized that it was female, wearing only one shoe, and clutching a leather shoulder bag and a large flashlight. The latter facts were even more apparent because whoever she was, was clinging to him, sobbing, and crying, "Don't let him get me!"

Miraculously, it seemed to be Penny Rote, early for once. Shuddering, she looked up at him, mumbling words like, "I never thought I'd get out," and "He said he had a gun." The latter words caused Humboldt to reach past her and firmly close and firmly bolt the door.

&&&

Afterwards, she was surprised at how competent he was. A life-long bachelor, Humboldt knew all about pre-cleaning and drying wet and muddied clothing. Sequestered in his spare bedroom, Penny was equipped with a bathrobe and towels, and shown the way to the bathroom. She emerged a half-hour later, showered and now much more presentable, to find her sweater, slacks, and raincoat, more or less dried, and thoroughly brushed.

They were reasonably wearable and he had even supplied a brand new slipper in place of her lost shoe. It was, however, much too large.

Downstairs, secure in the big chair in his library with a cup of hot tea, she sighed and exclaimed, "Dear Humboldt, I can never thank you enough. You've saved me, and now I'd better come clean. I fibbed a little earlier this evening. Actually, I wanted to get into that damn old church one more time and got trapped there by some guy with a gun. That old lower doorway behind the closet was my only chance. Thank goodness, I've got what I wanted and won't have to go there again. My book research is almost finished. You've been a real friend and a great help. Now, I don't think I'll need to bother you again." Elaboration followed, but still didn't include her real objectives in searching the old church.

When she seemed to have nothing more to tell him, Humboldt nodded, and politely suggested that, in view of the late hour, that he escort her back to her car. She seemed reluctant to leave, but then finally said, "You've been such a dear, and you've helped me so much. Now I've got great stuff about the old church and it's going to be a terrific setting for my book. Thanks ever so much." Then she sighed once more, smiled at him, and said she guessed she'd better go.

The rain had stopped and they set off together towards HillTop Parkway. Penny was still encumbered with shoulder bag and flashlight, and was limping because of the oversized slipper. It never occurred to Humboldt that their appearance in the dark of Woodhouse Avenue would look highly suspicious to anyone chancing to glance out at that hour. He was actually thinking he was sorry she hadn't stayed longer, that he was also sorry she no longer needed his help, and that, all in all, it was a beautiful night. He was not without his susceptibilities.

&&&

Chapter 18

Humboldt's next day started well. For once, the rainstorms had moved east and the morning was sunny, fresh, and clear. Even the gloomy red brick buildings that crowded over Woodhouse Avenue were improved. What he thought of as his 'rescue' of Penny Rote after her dangerous predicament had given him a sense of mild well-being, something on the order of one of those days on which his monthly accounts balanced at the first closing.

On reflection however, and remembering his researches in the third floor record room, he was quite sure that her secret escape route from the armed security guard must have been always intended as an emergency exit from the church basement and only later fecklessly converted into a storage closet. As he ate his breakfast, he opened the boastful history book, "Osgood Prior and the Construction of the Second Church," and found faint marks on a drawing that seemed to represent the exit passage. Humboldt stuffily thought that its present condition might be a useful deterrent, if Penny ever wanted to visit the church again.

One sore spot, however, was that he was quite certain that last night he'd again heard on his radio, the voice of his disreputable cousin, Pastor Primus Prior, assuring some credulous elderly nursing home resident that the purchase of a ceramic figurine would enhance spiritualist communication with her departed loved ones. How much lower could they get?

Celebrating the fine weather, Humboldt again drove his treasured Buick station wagon to the office, dodging the worst of the traffic by a pleasant detour that took him along the river. But then, on his arrival in the Prior Leather executive offices, things took a turn for the worse. His third cousin, Orlo Prior, the office manager, intercepted him. "Nice morning, Mr. Humboldt, the boss wants you right now. You're to wait in his office for a big meeting. We tried to catch you on the phone, but you were already gone."

Humboldt thanked him politely for this unwelcome news, but detoured to his own office to put down his briefcase and pick up pencil and paper. The latter might be useful just in case, although it very seldom transpired, the president might actually say something important. Or incriminating. On arriving in the president's sumptuous domain he found his cousins Moribund (sales), Dorset (production), and Ribald (personnel) already in attendance. Ribald was obviously in fine form, his fat body shaking as he finished an extremely coarse description of the work uniforms he'd ordered for the female high school cheerleaders he had hired as temporary production workers. Humboldt shuddered inwardly. "Plenty of skin," was only one of the terms Ribald used.

Dorset, typically, took little issue with this, except to insist, "You damn well make sure that the costs aren't charged to my budget."

Moribund, as the president's brother, was anxious to display superior knowledge. He explained, "The boss will be just a bit late, he had a little accident last night."

As if on cue, the door quietly opened. Malice Prior slithered into the room, scowling, and favoring his right arm that was in a sling. Gingerly, he eased himself into his raised executive chair, darted his head back and forth, swallowed something, and hissed, "Okay, men, it's time to go over the top. It's the big show. Dorset and Ribald tell me we're all set to start slapping those damn cheap trunks together." Just then, his private telephone rang. Malice glared at his four listeners and picked up the receiver. Again in a hissing tone, he said, "Yes?"

They heard a high-pitched female voice starting to say something, and then Malice angrily gestured his subordinates out of the room. Humboldt, always courteous, was the last. As the heavy door closed, he heard Malice snarling, "I told you a goddamn 'thank you' last night. What more do you want?"

Relying on someone else to reconvene the meeting, Humboldt headed for the safety of his own office, hoping for solitude. The Manheimers steamer trunk order had become a real worry, and he had been hoping it would somehow go away. However, Millard Fillmore, chief clerk of sales, followed him with the same subject in mind.

After an exchange of greetings, Millard apologized, dithered a few moments, made some general remarks about the fine weather, and then finally asked a formal business question. "Mr. Humboldt, as I said, I'm very sorry to bother you about this, especially when you're waiting for an important meeting. However, I'm uncertain about those special oversized 'Made by Prior and Cousins' labels we're having printed to stick on all those trunks for Manheimers. We want them to show well on the television commercials."

Humboldt, wearily anticipating some minor query about an account number for the voucher, answered shortly, "What about them?"

"Well," Millard continued, "When I told Mr. Moribund that printing the warning part in red ink would cost extra, he said to leave it out." (Moribund was the company's general sales manager and promotional items such as labels were his responsibility.)

It was sunny outside, and indoors it was getting warmer by the minute. Humboldt heartily wished both he and Millard Fillmore were somewhere else, speaking to other people. It even occurred to him that another session with Penny Rote might be preferable. This thought surprised him. Then, somewhere in his mind, something clicked, and he recalled Dorset's vague references to liability. He asked carefully, "What warning is that, Mr. Fillmore?"

"Why, the one about the asbestos, that Mr. Dorset requested just to be sure we would be covered in case that foreign process he calls 'reconstituting' didn't work."

Humboldt thought quickly. Obviously, the cheap artificial leather product that Dorset had purchased in Europe contained asbestos fibers. No wonder it was so inexpensive and that there'd been all that secrecy. But, after all, this was quite typical given the level of incompetence in the Prior Leather executive suite, and Humboldt had faced that sort of thing before. Disgusted, but not wanting to alarm Millard needlessly, he merely said, "You did well to ask. I'll handle it." Millard thanked him and disappeared.

Humboldt waited a moment. What was best to do, and how quickly? As has been explained, his range of competences was quite narrow. However, he did possess a finely honed skill at protecting the assets of Prior Leather and the all-important Prior Trust. Even a class-action lawsuit based on asbestos poisoning wasn't the worst of the possible claims to which the perverse activities of his inept cousins had exposed the firm. He walked hurriedly to his desk and picked up the special phone. Fortunately, he knew the chief accountant of the trust would be in his office.

It took only a few brief sentences to explain the situation. The elderly chief accountant was a shrewd man of considerable influence, who regarded Humboldt as Prior Leather's only significant asset. He chuckled mildly. "It's all that bad weather," he said evenly. "I suppose your cousins needed something to do because the rain is keeping them off the golf courses.

"I'll have the Chairman of the Trustees call Malice right away," he continued. "Maybe that will impress him. He'll tell your fine cousin the project must be stopped at once and also tell him that since there's nothing in this year's budget plan for the display trunk venture, unless Mr. Humboldt, you personally okay them, all the costs to date will have to be offset against the president's own salary budget. That should make him think." Humboldt thought he heard another mild chuckle. He didn't really welcome this added gratuitous exposure to Malice's crocodilian financial views, but he knew from long experience that the chief accountant's plan would work perfectly.

The four executives waited patiently. Humboldt was actually working in his plain office, and Moribund, Dorset, and Ribald were clustered outside Moribund's door loudly telling jokes of the type likely to give rise to sexual harassment litigation. Dorset could see the light on the secretary's telephone console indicating use of the private line. Once it went dark, but then came on again almost immediately. Finally, Orlo Prior called them all back to the president's office.

Malice was obviously upset. He swore under his breath, and his head darted back and forth. Licking his lips, he snarled at his brother, "Morrie, you've got to figure out some damn way to cancel that f . . . ing Manheimers order again. We can't do it. That's final."

Moribund, Dorset, and Ribald gasped, and the latter, rising, even asked, "What the hell happened, boss?"

Malice Prior answered that reckless question with a stream of vulgar abuse that would have been immediately familiar to, for instance, Male Rat Number 176. His final words were, "Fire all those damn girls." Ribald shrunk back into his chair and apologized.

Next, Malice turned on Dorset, hissing, "Haven't you ever heard of asbestos poisoning, you numbskull. Send that damn fake leather stuff back where you got it. Tell then we'll sue if they don't refund every cent of our money."

Finally, angrily dismissing the others, Malice turned to Humboldt. "Damn it, I hurt my arm last night and now this mess. Can you find a place for the costs those idiots have spent so far."

Humboldt nodded politely and said, "Yes." He had won another of his "small victories."

&&&

The rest of Humboldt's day was less satisfactory. It appeared that the wasted expenses of the aborted Manheimers deal would put the company slightly in the "red" for the month, and this was never easy to explain to his unscrupulous colleagues. Leaving the office at about one o'clock and sweltering in the heat, he had to stop at three different grocery stores to find edible looking bananas. Then, in the early evening, he was extremely depressed to receive still another of those pestering calls from someone allegedly believing him to be the prominent amateur detective, Humboldt Prior. This ill-informed person, calling from Arizona and apparently induced to do so by some prankster at his office, was insisting on sending him some papers supposedly supporting a claim to a treasure buried somewhere in Mexico. The caller said he wanted him to leave for the border immediately. Humboldt finally untangled himself from the foolish caller, but it wasn't easy.

Again, it was all the fault of that inept writer. Why in the world did he have to choose Humboldt's name for a fictitious character? Surely, common courtesy required at least that local directories be checked before made-up names were used. Federal privacy protection legislation was obviously needed. Humboldt fumed about this all evening.

The night wasn't any better. More rain was moving in and, again, he fell asleep listening to a so-called weather forecast. This was one of those full of vague warnings, but when you thought it over, didn't really say how much rain was going to fall or when it was expected to begin. Following an unfortunate habit that he'd developed in recent weeks, he failed to turn off his radio.

He awoke with a start in the early morning hours. Something bad was going on. He listened more carefully. Yes, it was just as he feared.

The elderly voice of his cousin, Secondus Prior, rasped from the radio. "Yes, dear listeners, your caring servants at the Revealed Truth Radio Ministries have again reached out beyond this mortal realm, reached out over the ether, on your behalf, to those who wait on the other side. What messages of comfort do you have for our beloved friends, dear Brother?"

There were several bumping noises, as if someone had stumbled against a table, and then Pastor Primus Prior came on the radio. "Thank you, dear Brother Secondus, and thank you, dear friends. Yes, with your treasured support I have once more been able to extend your voices past the chill of the grave, to bring your words seeking reassurance to those who have passed over. All is well, and they send each of you spiritual hope of the bliss to come."

Secondus replied, "What blessed relief to hear your words, Pastor Primus. Were there any special messages?" Yawning sleepily, Humboldt feared that there would be.

Next, there was a choking sound, and someone muttered something about, " . . . . a glass of water." After a minute of 'dead air,' Primus's elderly voice went on. "Yes, indeed, dear Brother Secondus. For our cherished friend, Martha Larson, who listens to us in her semi-private room at Rising Arms of Rest, a care facility of the Rising to the Skies of Love Reformed Church, a dear message has come from the great beyond. Knowing that she has been worried about her savings account, her dear departed sister speaks to her with words of comfort and welcome. The 'Great Change' is coming and the money will not be needed in the bliss soon to be received. However, for you, dear Martha, and the rest of those who wait, even greater assurance can come by conveying such funds to our Revealed Truth Radio Ministries, thus availing those like yourself of support in continuing our ministry of outreach to those who have passed."

Secondus added an "Amen, Brother Primus," and then repeated the "Bluebird of Hope" figurine commercial. Humboldt gasped. Even considering the assorted villainies of which these particular cousins had been capable, this was much worse than he had imagined. It was the worst yet, in fact. He snapped off the radio, turned over, and tried to sleep.

&&&

The next day was difficult for both of our principal protagonists. For Humboldt, it began with a temporary stoppage of his second floor toilet, a dreaded event that he finally managed to correct without an embarrassing call to the Trust's official plumber, still another distant fourth-cousin, unkindly nicknamed "Plunger" Prior. Then, at the office, he found his oily cousin, Ribald, with another of his off-color suggestions.

Barging into Humboldt's office, Ribald began with an unsubtle snicker. "Say Humboldt, you old so and so, I was speaking to the boss about something yesterday afternoon. He asked me to follow up with you."

Humboldt, already on guard, and knowing that it was quite possible that Ribald was lying, cautiously answered, "What were you speaking to him about?"

Ribald smirked. "Well, we were just wondering if we could still hire two or three of those gal cheerleaders. We could use them around the office as interns, brighten up the place and so on."

Humboldt thought quickly. How could he stop this? It was difficult to imagine a less suitable working environment for young women. Then he remembered Dorset's vague concerns about liability. That might do it. He answered, "It could be possible, as long as we have plenty of insurance to cover anything that might happen to them. I'm sure you can cover the premium cost in your personal budget."

Ribald recoiled in dismay. Prior Leather's departmental overhead budgets were notoriously restricted and were used by his cousins mainly to cover club memberships, and so-called business lunches. He had no margin left for the risks of cheerleaders. His face fell. "Well, okay, I guess we can't. Thanks for the info."

The rest of Humboldt's morning was similar, and, looking out of his window, he could see the rain had begun again.

&&&

For Penelope Rote, prominent television newsanchor, at first the day looked more promising. She and Andrea Anderson, her producer, had scheduled an important ten o'clock meeting in the executive suite. Their appointment was with the news director, Kenny Sidebotham, a vapid relative of Channel Seven's East Coast owners. She liked him well enough, but viewed his approval of her planned radio ministries exposé as a mere formality.

Kenny Sidebotham was tall and narrow-headed, with a well-trimmed light beard, a vacant stare, and an expensive gray suit. He welcomed the two women into his plush corner office, seated them in armchairs of a distinctly modern style, and offered coffee. "What awful weather," he exclaimed. "It's as bad as the Nor-Easters we get at our summer home in Maine." Then he listened as Penny began her presentation.

"Kenny, we've got an absolute knockout here," she said. Then, she outlined her planned news special, showed him several of the damming papers of the Revealed Truth Radio Ministry, that had somehow happened to come into her possession, and played a tape recording of one of their recent radio broadcasts.

Andrea, guessing correctly that their boss didn't know, briefly explained what spiritualism was. "Mr. Sidebotham, it used to be more common. Some con-artist pretends to be able to speak to the dead and collects money for doing it."

Penny summed up. "It will be a real public service to get those old crooks off the air. What do you say?"

Kenny Sidebotham gazed at his glamorous visitor, wondering about his first impression, which was that she was too old for him. He stroked his beard, and, finally shook his head. "Not quite ready, I think, Penny old girl. My boss in New York, when I was a trainee, used to say, 'Kenny boy, remember it's television. Always show them live footage.' You need film of those old crooks doing their thing. In fact, you need a sting. Get one, and you'll be all set. Hop to it." Then, as the two women stood up to leave, and after a moment's weighing of the possibilities, he added, "Say, Penny, I've got a couple of tickets, and was wondering . . . ."

Penny and her colleague fled his office, their heels clicking rapidly in the marble hallway. Alone, minutes later, Penny Rote seethed in two or three different directions. She couldn't quite say which was the worst, the silly dismissal of her excellent news special, or the ghastly social invitation. However, she had to get the exposé of the Radio Ministry on the air. The criminal taking of money from the elderly had to be stopped and she knew it would be great television. All she had to do was set up a sting.

She pondered for a moment, smoothing her skirt, and sipping her fourth coffee of the day. Nothing came to her. Then, from the back of her mind, a memory arose. She recalled the TV coverage of a famous FBI sting operation in Washington, DC. It involved a congressman and an extremely silly, if not out and out comic, middle-eastern gentleman. He was an older man in a funny outfit, impersonating a wealthy, but inept businessman seeking to buy influence. Naturally, she thought next of Humboldt Prior.

She chuckled to herself, smiled, and thought of how much she wanted to score over her boss, Kenny Sidebotham. Humboldt would have to help her again. About twenty minutes later she picked up the phone. He answered on the first ring.

&&&

Chapter 19

Humboldt was flustered by Penny's unexpected request for another meeting. The fatal call had come at eleven-thirty AM, just as he was getting ready to leave for the day. She seemed a little hesitant, and simply said, "Hi Humboldt, this is Penny Rote. How are you doing today?"

He answered nervously, "Okay, I guess, Miss Rote. And you?"

"I'm fine, Humboldt, thanks to you. I don't know what I'd have done without you the other night. Thanks a million. You're such a dear." She paused and then gave him the bad news. "Anyway, I need to see you just one more time, Humboldt, please."

"Golly, Miss Rote, I don't know," he replied, jumping to a natural conclusion. "It's a big risk going back into the church just for more atmosphere for your book."

She tried to reassure him. "No, no, Humboldt, I'm through breaking and entering, I promise. I just need your help in meeting with someone. Please meet me at the Pike House at noon. This will be the last time, honest."

This sounded a little better. Perhaps she merely needed his help as a business executive or as a historian. "I'll meet you at twelve noon, then," he said, "and we'll see what I can do to help."

It was starting to rain again, when, thirty minutes later, he parked his Buick. He'd had time to think of several less favorable possibilities. However, he was still stymied by the risk of her exposing Prior Leather and the Trust and their unusual financial arrangements. Worse, these arrangements were horribly distorted in her fantastic theory that, along with the mystery-adventure stories featuring a fictional Humboldt Prior, they were part of a Central Intelligence Agency cover plan.

Nonetheless, things did seem different now. Perhaps it was still her pretty face or perhaps it was his memory of the moment when the terrified Penny had clung to him after her escape from the church. Anyway, he hadn't argued quite so much, and she had said, "Please."

He entered the restaurant, tried to decide which of the moth-eaten mounted hunting and fishing trophies he most wanted to avoid, and then selected a booth toward the rear.

It was crowded in the Pike House. Groups of hungry people hurried in, shaking off the rain, and soon occupied almost all of the booths and tables. He saw no one he recognized and hoped that the crowd would provide some sort of cover. He realized, not for the first time in this aggravating series of adventures, that he was thinking like a spy, or at least like the one portrayed, also as 'Humboldt Prior,' in those deplorable books by the amateur writer. He still couldn't imagine how that man could face himself in the mirror.

He saw Penny Rote appear, hesitate, then wave to him and hurry, with her lithesome walk, through the packed tables. She was smiling. "What a day," she exclaimed, tapping the rain off her umbrella, hanging up her raincoat, and sliding into the booth next to him. "I'm really glad you could make time for me on such short notice." She was wearing a sheer summer dress and he could smell her perfume.

Humboldt said something polite, and then they dealt with the hovering waiter who had followed her to the booth.

It wasn't until they were well into their ham sandwiches that the actual reason for their meeting finally emerged. Penny turned to him, and said softly and tentatively, "Humboldt, you've been a real friend to me. Now I've got to take a chance. Remember that mystery book I told you about?"

Humboldt nodded. "Yes, I do. How is the writing coming along?" With all his trouble with the other amateur mystery writer, the fact that she was writing such a book only added to the unfairness of the whole thing.

Penny sighed, and spoke very hurriedly, as if trying to get her words out all at once. "Well, that's just it. I'm not actually writing, at least not a book. Humboldt, please, hear me out. All this time, I've been fibbing to you. I'm not writing a book at all. I'm investigating those crooked preacher cousins of yours and that awful radio program of theirs. I'm working on a special report about them for my evening TV news show."

Shocked at first, Humboldt frowned at her disclosure. Then he thought a moment, and discovered that he was actually glad to hear it. He wasn't sure the Trust would welcome an exposé of the old preachers, but they had finally gone way past all boundaries with their spiritualism tricks. This would serve them right. And anyway, at least it wasn't another mystery story after all.

He actually smiled. "That's very interesting, Miss Rote."

Beside him in the booth a dark cloud of apprehension rose toward the ceiling of the Pike House and drifted off in the direction of the kitchen. Greatly relieved, Penny smiled warmly and said quickly, "Thank goodness, Humboldt, I was so afraid that you'd be angry with me and my little fib. Now I need you to help me again, just this one more time." She leaned closer and lightly kissed his cheek.

The cloud of apprehension had stopped in mid-air, turned around, and was returning to Humboldt when the kiss intervened. He started to say, "You assured me . . . ," but then changed his mind. He hadn't seen the freckles that close before. He asked tentatively, "What do you need me to do?"

Then Penny told him about the sting and about Mr. Chandra Nomorpour, the wealthy Indian businessman. After some thought, she and her producer had finally conceived of this absurd person just before she called to meet Humboldt for lunch. The unfamiliar nationality would put the corrupt radio ministers off their guard. The dark skin would work for the station's make-up department, and they thought the high and excitable voice would be fairly easy for Humboldt to learn. His normally nervous and fidgety state would go well with Mr. Nomorpour's distress at finding himself alone in a strange land, having to invest tens of millions in an iron mine without the treasured guidance of his just deceased father, the revered billionaire, Mr. Chandatra Nomorpour. The family name had come to Penny as she thought of the endless rain. She concluded, "All you have to do for me, Humboldt dear, is pretend to be Mr. Nomorpour for a little while. We'll give you a great disguise and tell you what to say. It will be easy."

Humboldt listened nervously, having every intention of an absolute refusal. However, he found himself unable to do so. He weighed his cousin Primus's suspicious nature against Secondus's more trusting approach. Along with the vile Malice Prior and the obscene Ribald, the ministerial brothers had been bedeviling the more ordinary members of the family for decades. Now, they were getting older and were probably over confident of the success of their despicable spiritualism scheme. He found that he agreed with Penny that the Revealed Truth Radio Ministries absolutely had to be stopped.

To his amazement, he found himself asking, "I've never acted a part before, do you actually think I could do it?"

Penny Rote grinned. "Piece of cake, Humboldt, my friend. Just leave everything to me."

&&&

At about the same time, there were further developments concerning the Second Church of the Revealed Truth and its Revealed Truth Radio Ministry. While without gunfire, fleeing suspects, or female newsanchors escaping by hidden doorways, they were nonetheless important. Stewie "Snapshot" Tompkins had spent much of the previous days trying his best to "frame" the wild events of Monday night. In other words, he was planning to lie about them.

There were several risks. When surprised by what he now realized were a couple of mere trespassers, he had foolishly restored to gunfire. What if some neighbor had heard this and reported it? Worse, what if his bullets had damaged the church in some way or, worse yet, had wounded one of those relatively innocent intruders he'd heard escaping through the rear door? He had hardly slept.

Then there was the woman's shoe he had found in the grimy lower hallway and the other vague indications that someone had been down there. These and all the other recent events were obviously totally unconnected with any sort of radio ministry takeover, but maybe he could still make something of them. His $50,000 security retainer was being paid in installments and he couldn't afford to have the old brothers lose confidence in him. His troubles over the funeral of the brother of Jimmy" "Already on the Way" Johnson, senior minister of Rising to the Skies of Love Reformed Church, might be bad for his photography business. He needed the money.

With his story finally ready, he had called Pastor Secondus Prior, chatted for a few minutes, and then suggested a one o'clock meeting at the church. He hoped he had planted a seed or two with the more credulous of the two brothers. It was still raining lightly as he parked the yellow Cadillac. The main door of the church was unlocked, so he guessed they were there before him.

Stewie was still wearing his greenish leisure suit, now somewhat the worse for having been slept in several times. The two brothers, one shaved, and one not, were in their usual daytime attire of over-worn shirts, rumpled old slacks, and down-at-the-heel shoes. Meeting in the church office, the picture they made was, again, not an attractive one.

After greetings, Primus began the meeting. "Did you happen to hear our last show, Tompkins? It was a record. Through the spirits we managed to land an entire savings account. Some old gal gave us nearly thirty thousand bucks. That will come in real good to us." He licked his lips in anticipation.

Secondus agreed. "We're getting into the grove and there's no telling how far we can go. Brother Primus has turned out to be a swell medium."

Tompkins made a respectful comment. This was right up his alley.

Primus muttered something intended to sound modest, and then asked, cautiously, "Well, Tompkins, what's this about? What's on your mind?" He was always suspicious of anyone to whom he was paying large sums of money.

Stewie took his cue. He pulled Penny's high-heeled shoe out of his jacket pocket and placed it on the table between them. "We had another incident in the church a couple of nights ago. I handled it okay, and I found this downstairs. Since then I've been completing my investigations."

Both brothers shuddered at the additional evidence, but Secondus, at least, forgetting he was dealing with a crooked church photographer, was impressed by the professionalism of finishing the investigation and only then furnishing a complete report. Primus was still frowning.

"Yeah, several of them tried to sneak into the church Monday night. I was on watch and surprised them in the act." He paused for emphasis.

The startled brothers waited.

Stewie continued excitedly. "I called them on it, and one of them actually took a shot at old Stewie. Of course, that didn't stop me, and I chased them back out again. Later on, I actually saw two of them limping away down the street. I think they was hiding by the front porch of one of them places over there." He gestured in the general direction of the rowhouses.

The brothers were relieved. Secondus asked, "Did they get anything?"

"I don't think they had time, but this dame's shoe means we're in more trouble. I've got to watch even more carefully."

Primus, his mind on the savings account and trying to think of an even better trick for his next broadcast, finally attended to the question of the shoe. "Well," he rasped, "what the hell do you think it means?"

Stewie Tompkins had his answer ready. "Real bad trouble. I'm hearing there's a secret action-group within one of those big Texas radio ministries. They use real glamorous gals as confidential field prospectors, paving the way for takeovers of local church radio. They entice some of the local clergy guys that way, and they'll do anything to get what they want."

Secondus was horrified, but at the same time, intrigued. "Glamorous women as church radio takeover specialists? What next?"

Primus nodded slowly. He was not as trusting as his brother and had been beginning to wonder about their security consultant. However, he merely said, "Okay, Stewie, keep up the good work. Go get some sleep now. You'll probably have to be up all night from now on."

Stewie agreed and left the office. He was confident he had kept the brothers sufficiently worried. Penny Rote's lost shoe was deposited in the trashcan outside a coffee bar where Tompkins stopped on his way to his next appointment.

When they were alone together, Primus turned and snarled at his brother. "Secondus, somethin' don't smell right. That Tompkins might be okay and he might not. We've got a lot at risk if it is one of those southern takeover ministry outfits, but maybe it's just some damn kids, or burglars, or even that fool Malice Prior and one his girl friends. Baseball caps and old socks and ladies shoes don't sound very high level to me. We've got to cover all the angles."

He paused, thinking. Could he trust his brother to handle it? Then the thought of the savings account and others like it grew larger. He had his priorities. "Okay, Brother Secondus, listen up. We'd better check with the cops. You call downtown and tell them we think we're had a couple of break-ins at Second Revealed. Don't say nothin' about the f . . . ing radio show."

Primus hesitated. They'd better be a little more cautious in another direction, too. "And keep that damn Malice Prior out of it. Since he's a damn trustee we can't risk getting him upset. But be sure to tell them we want their best detective. Got that?"

Secondus, more and more worried, wiped his forehead. "Yes, I've got it. I'll get on it right away."

Primus eyed him suspiciously. "Be damn sure you do. Now, I've got to get home and think. We need a new angle for the spiritualism deal. Somethin' that will pull in even more dough." Primus stood up slowly, rubbed his back, cleared his throat, and shuffled out of the office.

Secondus Prior walked over to the desk and found the telephone directory. The phone itself had been disconnected as an economy measure, but he had his grimy old cell phone. Having, for decades, tried to avoid the police, he now wondered how to approach the call. They needed the best detective or investigator possible, one that could sort through anything from one of the dreaded takeover ministries to some kids just looking for a thrill. Then he recalled one of his favorite television shows of a decade or so before. Yes, they were surely the best investigators. Knowing nothing of jurisdictional matters, he found the listing and carefully keyed the number of the local office of the Federal Bureau of Investigation.

&&&

Coincidences do occur, even in historical chronicles such as this. Several months before, two or three influential conservative congressmen had, in a public hearing, grilled the Deputy Director of the FBI, complaining of discriminatory media and other harassment of various of the newer non-denominational churches. As is normal in such cases, in due course a lengthy internal FBI directive was issued. This memo, demanding increased attention to so-called anti-religious initiatives directed at autonomous theological bodies, went to all FBI field offices.

Scholars will never know whether or not this obscure language was understood as intended, or if it made any difference to Special Agent William Boat, when he received the telephone call from the allegedly aggrieved Pastor Secondus Prior, of the Second Church of the Revealed Truth. Perhaps, as things had been a bit slow in his section, the investigation would have proceeded in any case.

Special Agent Boat identified himself and said, "Thanks for calling us, Pastor Prior, how may we help you?" Then he listened carefully.

Secondus still had a reasonably good memory and covered much of what had been happening. "Well, we've had a series of petty break-ins at the Second Church of the Revealed Truth. We employed a trained security guard, but now it's become more serious. Monday night, they broke in again and actually fired shots at him before he chased them away. Later, he saw two of them making away dnow the street. Mr. Boat, we need your investigation to assure the sanctity of our sacred premises."

On request, Secondus also supplied Agent Boat with the address of the church, the names and addresses of all parties even remotely concerned, including neighbors who might have seen something, and even the local address of Snapshot Tompkins, the referenced security guard. As instructed, he said nothing at all about the radio show or the dreaded takeover ministries.

Having nothing much to do that afternoon, Agent William Boat began at once. He telephoned the obvious key witness, security guard Tompkins, but found him absent. (Stewie was, in fact, in a distant suburb, again attempting to patch things up with Pastor Jimmy "Already on the Way" Johnson.)

The next morning, wanting to use his time efficiently by attending to his staff personnel development duties as well as the investigation, Agent Boat gathered up two trainees, Probationary Agents Michael Dinsbury and Clarence Omsworth, and set forth in one of those nondescript FBI vans to drive over to Woodhouse Avenue.

&&&

Chapter 20

Once away from the influence of his lunch with the attractive Penelope Rote, Humboldt began to feel he had made a serious mistake and was now in an even worse predicament. How could have he ever agreed to such a thing? He faced the daunting prospect of having to appear, dressed up as an Indian businessman, in the dangerous deception she was planning to practice upon his cousins Pastors Primus and Secondus and their Revealed Truth Radio Ministry. However, after stewing about it all afternoon, that night he slept quite soundly. He had concluded that he would just have to handle it somehow.

The next morning dawned on a positive note, as the skies were blue, with only a few white, puffy clouds. On another positive note, his breakfast was interrupted by a welcome call from the Trust's maintenance supervisor. They were finally coming to replace the carpet runner on his stairway. Could he kindly remain at home for a few minutes longer and let them in? Although mildly annoyed with anything that altered his daily routine, he readily agreed. In exchange, the supervisor promised to remain with the carpet layers, watching them until they were finished.

Because of the delay in his regular departure, Humboldt actually glimpsed the FBI agents' van turning onto Woodhouse Avenue, as he, for his part, was exiting the alley onto HillTop Parkway. He continued on his pleasant drive to the office, again taking the longer route along the river, totally unaware of the agents' subsequent activities.

These began with a visit to the Second Church of the Revealed Truth. Finding the keys hidden under the doormat where Secondus had promised to leave them, the FBI agents entered the front hallway. Administratively, they were well prepared for their task, having plenty of forms and clipboards for their field notes, and a laptop computer for instant wireless transmission of their findings back to headquarters.

Agent Boat was disappointed. "What a dirty old dump," he exclaimed. "Well men, we have to take the good with the bad. Let's give it a good going over just as you've been trained. Agent Dinsbury, you and I will take the big room ahead. Agent Omsworth, you search the offices."

After their first pass through the dusty dilapidated sanctuary and into the rear hallway, Agent Dinsbury reported to his superior. "There's dried mud on the floor back there." This was, of course, also true of many other places on the floor, and the agents lacked any technology to distinguish between recent dried mud, tracked in by Malice and Temperance days before, and other tracks many months old.

After searching the office and finding nothing, Agent Omsworth joined the other two in the sanctuary and the two trainees were then dispatched to check the basement, while Agent Boat entered the work done thus far into their computer. The trainees returned from the basement twenty minutes later, covered with grime, and without having discovered anything out of the ordinary, much less the hidden emergency exit. Omsworth reported, "There's nothing but old junk down there." Next, however, he redeemed himself by the sharp-eyed observance of something amiss in the front of the church. "Look boss, isn't that a bullet hole in the front of the litany desk?"

"Great work, Agent Omsworth," Boat responded, proceeding to direct an exhaustive search for the bullet. The three agents crawled all over the front of the church, acquiring more grime in the process, but finding nothing. In fact, Male Rat 176 had already secured the bullet, thinking it would add interest to the decor of his otherwise sparsely furnished quarters.

While the agents produced a lengthy and thorough record, a careful reading of it would reveal that they actually found little of real interest. This was partly because the church was generally so messy as to obscure traces of specific recent activity, and partly because Secondus, and an extremely angry Primus Prior, berating his brother for having called the FBI instead of the local police, had spent the previous late afternoon and evening removing all evidence of their manipulation of the church finances and any stray papers pertaining to the radio ministry.

The three agents ended their visit to the church after about an hour. Agent Boat ponderously summed up their findings, saying, "Well men, we can say that we've confirmed that one or more persons have improperly entered the building and have, by way of discharging a firearm, done willful damage."

Their next assignment was to interview one of the nearest residents across Woodhouse Avenue. It was from the vicinity of the front steps of this rowhouse, that Pastor Secondus Prior had told Agent Boat that his security guard had observed two of the suspect individuals limping away toward HillTop Parkway. The assumption was that one of them was injured, for the possibility that the limp was caused by a man's oversized slipper on a woman's foot was too remote to even occur to the FBI agents.

The residence across the street, the address of one Humboldt Prior according to their growing file of notes, was found unoccupied except for a crew of carpet layers and some sort of maintenance supervisor. This person was very familiar with the extended Prior family. After the agents identified themselves and sought information, he answered, "Yeah, that's him, Mr. Humboldt Prior. He lives here. He's down at his office. It's at Prior and Cousins Leather Works, on the far side of downtown."

Agent Dinsbury, with commendable initiative, had removed an extra church directory from the office. He interjected, "Look here, Special Agent Boat, in this roster the senior church trustee, a Mr. Malice Prior, is listed as the president of that firm." Upon inquiry, the supervisor confirmed this also and said that the individual in question would probably also be at his office at Prior and Cousins.

The three agents glanced into the front rooms of Humboldt's house and observed that they seemed dusty and little used. Agent Dinsbury shrewdly remarked, "What are the chances he would have even been in here late at night? How could he have seen those escaping burglars lurking in the shelter of his front steps?"

The maintenance supervisor obligingly confirmed this as well, saying, "He don't hardly ever go in there."

Agent William Boat and his associates caucused in their van, while completing their notes and computer entries. Probationary Agent Omsworth had read the memo on anti-religious initiatives. "Agent Boat," he said, "it says we're supposed to contact what it calls the lay-leadership as well as the clergy. Who would that be?"

Agent Boat explained that, "In this case, they're talking about that senior trustee fellow, so the next logical step is to proceed downtown and interview both the senior trustee and the possible witness at their common workplace, thereby saving the FBI both gasoline and time."

&&&

Thus it was that Mr. Malice Prior, president of Prior Leather, and a potential defendant in a whole series of sexual harassment and other criminal actions, received from his cousin and chief clerk, Orlo Prior, the appalling news that three FBI agents were in the outer office and wished to speak with him.

Panic ensued and Malice's lizard-like escape reactions took over. He instantly cleared his expensive desk, picked up his empty briefcase, placed it conspicuously on the center of the desk, and otherwise positioned himself as a busy executive about to leave for an urgent conference elsewhere. Orlo ushered the three men into Malice's domain. There, they saw a tall distinguished looking businessman, with a broad forehead and long wavy gray hair. He was favoring his right arm and was obviously on a tight schedule. Credentials were exhibited and introductions were made.

"I'm Mr. Prior, president of the company. I'm glad to see you men," he said. "I'm delighted to be of assistance to the FBI, although, unfortunately, I'm just leaving for an important out-of-town meeting. Please be seated for a few minutes." Then, his head darting back and forth, he politely asked, in a soft, hissing voice, the purpose of their visit.

Agent Boat explained that, "It has to do with trouble at the Second Church of the Revealed Truth," and gave further details. He concluded, "So, it looks like they've had a series of break-ins. The Director wants you to know we're on it and will do our best to find those responsible, whether it's snooping news reporters, atheist vandals, or otherwise. Two of them were actually seen escaping down Woodhouse Avenue. Unfortunately, we don't have good descriptions."

Malice was enormously relieved to hear that the case merely involved desecration of his church, and that the focus was on the street in front of the church and not on his own hurried transit of the alley behind it. He thanked them profusely. "Men, I don't doubt that you'll get to the bottom of this outrage," he said, again pleading an urgent conference. He also had a twelve-thirty tee time.

As the agents were leaving his office, Malice had one of his rare inspirations. "Say," he added, "My comptroller, Humboldt Prior, lives right across the street." He went on with a chuckle, "He's a real early-to-bed guy, but maybe he saw something."

The agents, again conducted by Orlo Prior, moved on in the direction of Humboldt's office. They did not observe someone in an ugly gray-green suit running in the opposite direction, down the stairs as fast as he could go. Malice Prior was leaving the building.

&&&

Given the circumstances, Humboldt was relatively well prepared. Orlo hadn't been able to resist retailing the startling news of the FBI visit, and had done so at the first opportunity. As often, when not dealing with his accounts, Humboldt jumped to the wrong conclusion. In a nutshell, he saw the FBI visit as the end result of the DNA testing of his lost Minnesota Twins baseball cap and his missing socks, assuming that such high-tech matters were the province of experts from Washington, DC. He had no idea that they merely wished to ask if he had seen any strangers escaping down Woodhouse Avenue.

What to do? Whether from closer acquaintance with Penny Rote, or from their momentary embrace after she escaped from the old church, he had but one growing and noble conviction. He would have to take the blame! In his sixties, his life was largely over, while she was younger and had a great reputation to lose. If anyone was to be arrested for breaking and entering, or for who knew what other crimes they'd committed, it should be him. He had his story ready.

For their part, although rapidly building an impressive case file, the FBI agents saw their visit to Humboldt's office as entirely routine. Probationary Agent Dinsbury had had some contact with corporate accountants and viewed them as, "Old fuddy-duddies who don't ever look beyond their noses." He had previously expressed this view to his companions without meeting any disagreement. Their visit was just a matter of formality, asking if the subject had seen anything last Monday night.

Orlo Prior ushered the three men into Humboldt's office. He hoped for the chance to listen outside, but Agent Omsworth shut the door. Special Agent Boat made introductions. "Good morning, Mr. Prior. I'm Special Agent Bill Boat, of the FBI. This is Agent Dinsbury and this is Agent Omsworth. This isn't a big deal, we'd just like your assistance with a question about last Monday night." Agent Dinsbury was already adding the term 'nondescript' to his mental notes about Humboldt.

Humboldt smiled and invited them to sit down. Having seen it many times on television, he was ready for this tactic. They always began that way, with an innocent sounding inquiry. He nodded. "I'll be glad to help if I can."

Agent Boat continued, somehow even more reassured by the Spartan surroundings of Humboldt's office and the neat piles of papers on his desk. "We're checking on a series of break-ins at the church across the street from your residence. Last Monday night there was also some vandalism, so it's getting more serious. Two of the suspects were seen, later on, leaving the area on foot along your street, walking toward HillTop Parkway. It was quite late, but we wondered if, by any chance, you saw anything?"

Humboldt quivered inwardly, but from decades of fending off Internal Revenue Service examiners, gave no outward sign. These FBI men were tough and cleverly trained. He wasn't ready for the fact that someone had seen the two of them, as he walked Penny to her car. Whoever it was had mistaken them for the other intruders that Penny thought had escaped from the rear door that opened onto the alley behind the church. On the other hand, there was not one mention of the DNA evidence or that he, personally, was a suspect. Apparently they also had no knowledge of Penny Rote or her investigation, and saw the whole affair as only a series of burglaries. While at some point, he still might have to execute his plan and confess with his prepared story of unauthorized nocturnal visits to the church for quiet and meditation, apparently that could wait a little longer.

He tried to parry the question as, God forbid, he had read of that loathsome fictional amateur detective doing. "Going away down the street, did you say?" The effect of this was only to convince his visitors that he was also hard of hearing.

"Yes," said Agent Bill Boat more loudly, "We think they were getting away from the church that way. Did you see anything from your front window at around eleven-thirty."

Humboldt answered, inwardly pleased that he was telling the literal truth, "No, sorry, I wasn't looking out my window at that time."

Agent Omsworth muttered under his breath. "Waste of time. By then the old guy had probably been asleep for hours."

The agents added a few more lines to their notes, and Agent Dinsbury keyed something into their laptop computer. They thanked Humboldt, gave him their business cards, and departed.

Humboldt gave a sigh of relief. Obviously, he was still a suspect, but perhaps the FBI's scientific evidence was inconclusive. He resolved to await further developments. He also decided not to tell Penny about the FBI visit. It was part of being noble.

&&&

Later the same afternoon, Primus and Secondus Prior were busy in the latter's apartment, taping another program of the Revealed Truth Radio Ministries. Their show was now more popular than ever, interlarded with spiritualist guidance from the dear departed, especially for those listeners having liquid assets. When they were nearly finished, there was an interruption.

Primus growled at Mrs. Secondus for bothering them, but agreed to take the telephone call. He listened for a minute or two, and then excitedly said, "Yes, certainly. So you telephoned our radio station?" There was a pause. "Yes, my dear friend, a personal session at night would be entirely in order. We find those bring great comfort and the spirits are most communicative in those late hours. Who is the beloved from whom you seek guidance from beyond the Great Change? Oh, I see, for him as well?" There was a much longer pause. Then Primus spoke again, nervously fumbling for a pencil. "How do you spell that? How much? Oh indeed, for a pending important conference with his investment bankers? In that case, as he is fully engaged until then, please, invite your dear stricken employer to be at the radio station at one o'clock, early next Monday morning. Thank you very much, and may your own quest for blessed guidance be, in due course, fruitful also."

Primus was so excited that he could hardly put down the telephone. He threw his hands in the air. "Who do you think that was, Brother Secondus?"

Secondus looked blank. "Who?"

Primus continued. "I'll tell you who it was. It's our big chance. That caller was a foreign sounding dame. I'd say she was British, very sophisticated and refined. Anyhow, she's nothing less than the personal secretary to the billionaire Indian steel magnate, Chandra Nomorpour. I've heard of him, of course, as you would if you paid more attention to the business news."

Secondus was confused. Their own market niche was that of senior citizens calling from their nursing homes. He stammered. "What did he want?"

"To see us for advice, of course, you dummy," Primus sputtered excitedly. "Oh, she played it crafty at first, pretending she was the one wanting to communicate with the departed, but I was too sharp for her. It comes out that he's a guy in his sixties and has just lost his aged father who always made all the big decisions. You know how those old billionaire Indian families are. He's over here to buy an iron mine up north somewhere and he's scared to death to act without a word from his deceased father. It's the ideal set up. The gal said he'll gladly pay a big fee to us, maybe into the high six or even in seven figures."

Secondus jumped up. "Wow. What a deal. Our first live one, and for millions of bucks." The elderly pastor was literally dancing with glee.

Primus gestured him back to his chair. "Get busy, damn it. We've got to finish taping, and then get some crap ready for the silly fool."

&&&

Chapter 21

All in all, by Saturday it had been a complicated week. It was with a distinct feeling of pleasure that Humboldt recalled his experiences of last Monday night, culminating in his unexpected rescue of Penny after she escaped from the old church. He was also pleased with his success in thwarting his cousins, Malice, Moribund, Dorset, and Ribald, and their scheme to defraud the respected Manheimers department store with asbestos covered Christmas display trunks, assembled by victimized high school girls. However, from there on, it had been all down hill.

He still couldn't imagine how he had come to agree to help Penny with her crazy plan to perpetrate a 'sting' on his cousins Pastors Primus and Secondus Prior during a 'live' episode of their deceitful Revealed Truth Radio Ministries. He crossly scolded himself for recklessly consenting to portray a ridiculous Indian billionaire called Chandra Nomorpour, who was seeking spiritualist help in contacting his deceased father. What folly! He could readily think of half a dozen horrid consequences of such rashness, each worse than the last.

He lost more and more sleep trying to think of some way out of this mess. Some ideas had emerged, but short of self-immolation or leaving the country, he could think of none that would stop the relentless newsanchor in her pursuit of a blockbuster TV news exposé. He would just have to hope that something would come up.

Lastly, there'd been the visit from the three FBI agents. Although, in retrospect, it seemed that disaster had been narrowly averted, they were well known to be very persistent in their investigations. After stewing about all this most of Saturday, he was even toying with the idea of contacting Special Agent William

Boat and confessing to breaking and entering, with a request for immediate sentencing. This would solve both problems.

Against all this recent turmoil, the improved appearance of his new stairway runner and the fact that Dorset's children were being less noisy next door, were only minor consolations.

Saturday evening was worse. Distracted by something on the television, Humboldt had burned part of his supper, but had eaten it anyway. Thus, his stomach was upset when another deluded detective story reader called him. This person, speaking from Des Moines in a high irritating voice, started right in with an especially distressing inquiry about the fictional Humboldt Prior. Would it ever end? What if that spineless writer kept at it for years and years, convincing more and more readers that there was a real detective or espionage figure of that name? It had happened with Sherlock Holmes. However, politely as always, he simply answered again that there was no such person, thus, in a way, denying his own existence.

In spite of all his troubles, he was fast asleep in his big chair when her call came. It was warm in his library and the patter of more rain may have soothed him. At first, he only managed a tired and confused sounding, "Hello."

"Hi, Humboldt. It's Penny Rote. We're on for tomorrow night, or rather early Monday morning. That's when they're on the radio."

For a more than middle-aged man, who had been sound asleep, this was at first mere gibberish. Then he remembered. "Oh dear," he said. "I don't see how I can do it so soon. I'll have to study up somehow, read some books or something."

Penny was firm. "Now, now, Humboldt, you know I've got everything covered. You'll do fine. Just be at the station at about nine o'clock tomorrow, Sunday morning. We'll talk you through it, get your voice right, and fix up the hidden camera and sound equipment. You'll need a big briefcase for that, but my producer has found one you can use. The wardrobe, hair, and makeup lady will be in at eleven for a dry run of that stuff." Outside, there was an ominous crack of thunder.

Humboldt was still sputtering. "But . . . ," he began.

She knew how to handle him. "It will be okay, Humboldt, and you know how much I need your help." She also knew enough to repeat the address of the TV station and suggest that he write it down. Then, with the parting words, "Remember, run through and equipment at nine and makeup at eleven. Now I've got to go." She quickly ended the call.

Humboldt sat stock still except for the shuddering. This was even more hideous than he ever thought it could be. In his worst moments, he had only pictured himself sitting quietly in a corner while Penny, also in disguise, told Nomorpour's story to his cousins, the would-be spiritualists. Now he faced an ascending scale of horrors. They had to get his voice right, so that meant they actually expected him to do the talking. He'd be carrying hidden cameras and recorders, so that probably meant he'd be alone. And, maybe worst of all, he'd be wearing some sort of makeup.

That hadn't occurred since an awful afternoon long ago, during his fifth-grade Sunday school pageant. Some of his make-up had gotten into his mouth and had tasted awful. When the time came for his Bible verse, he had gagged instead of speaking. Even his teacher had laughed. What could he do now?

Humboldt had only meager knowledge of parts of his own country, let alone of India. Desperately trying to prepare himself, he somehow dredged up hazy recollections of movies, one featuring an actor playing a ridiculous 19th century style Indian gentleman who finally disappeared, hurrying off-stage saying something about snakes. Later, being the type of person he was, there was only some of this that Humboldt would happen to remember.

&&&

The next morning dawned hot and sunny, and comprised for Humboldt, a mounting series of indignities. He was a reasonably tolerant and thick-skinned individual, but nothing in his years as Prior Leather's comptroller had prepared him for the rough and tumble of television broadcasting. It had, he thought in retrospect, some of the worst aspects of his old Sunday school class.

Responsibly dressed in his blue suit, he arrived as ordered, at nine o'clock at the Channel Seven studios, a sumptuous array of expensive new buildings in one of his city's more remote neighborhoods. As it was Sunday morning, the lobby, although open, was deserted. He stood for several minutes admiring its steel, glass, and marble luxury. After all, if no one came to attend to him, he could hardly be blamed for not keeping his appointment. Finally, his conscientious nature got the better of this discreditable subterfuge, and he located a call button on the edge of the vacant reception desk. This almost instantly produced a bright competent young woman, who identified herself as, "Andrea Anderson, Penny's producer." At that moment, Humboldt found the alliterative name somehow appropriate for television.

Andrea continued pleasantly. "It's great that you're here on time, Humboldt, we've got a lot to do." She led him through an absolute labyrinth of hallways, studios, and cubicles, until they reached a room marked 'Reserved for Miss Rote.' She unlocked the door. Inside he found a plastic table on which something sticky had been spilled, and several folding chairs. There were no windows and the air-conditioning wasn't working very well. The walls were bare except for a 'whiteboard.' (These tools of modern business meetings were unknown at Prior and Cousins, but Humboldt had once seen one of them at an accounting seminar). On the board, someone had written 'Operation Revealed' in red marker, together with an outline of the day's activities. An unflattering stick-figure cartoon had been added. Handing him three or four sheets of paper, she left him to, as she chirped, "Learn the outline and think about how you are going to say it."

Humboldt shivered in spite of the heat, but diligently sat down to read. Each sentence was more appalling than the last. He was to state that he was Chandra Nomorpour, a business executive from India. He had just arrived in the country to purchase an iron mine, and now his aged father, upon whom his fabulously wealthy family relied for all important business decisions, had unexpectedly passed away. He, therefore, needed urgently to communicate with his father and had come to these revered spiritualist experts for assistance. He would pay ten million rupees for this help. A footnote advised that was equal to, the writer thought, about $250,000.

How could anyone in his right mind be expected to say any of this? And, even more impossibly, how could anyone else believe it? With rising panic, Humboldt looked at the heap of files and envelopes on the table. From one of the latter, jutted a pink bundle of what was obviously some sort of crude counterfeit foreign currency. This was the last straw. How could they possibly expect him to use that? Even his elderly and extremely greedy cousins wouldn't be fooled. Helplessly, he reread the papers, perspiring freely and regretting his suit and necktie.

Then the two women bustled into the room, Penny, happily saying, "Hi, there, Humboldt," and Andrea carefully carrying a large leather briefcase. Both were barelegged in comfortable shorts and lightweight tops. Another injustice. Repeatedly, they made him stumble through the outline script, telling him he had to convey his story in his own words. After about six attempts, all of which he judged dismal failures, Penny pronounced herself satisfied.

Then, walking to the far side of the room she whispered to Andrea, "How about the voice?"

If he heard correctly, Andrea's response was even more humiliating. "If he can raise it about an octave, it will sound even sillier."

Trying to ignore this insult, Humboldt dutifully tried again, mimicking his hazy recollection of the Indian gentleman in the movie. To his amazement they said it was perfect, and turned to the matter of his equipment. Andrea put the large leather briefcase on the table in front of him. It was of the old-fashioned 'top open' type that ordinarily stands upright. She and Penny Rote demonstrated the tiny lens aperture, the small video camera mounted inside, and the tape recorder, adding that, of course, the case would be locked and the equipment running when they let him out at the studio.

This disagreeable confirmation that he would be alone in this horrid enterprise, washed over Humboldt as he listened to Penny's next question, "If the case is locked, where does he put his money?"

Though impressed by Andrea's competent answer, "There'll be plenty of room in the pockets of that funny looking baggy outfit we've got for him," this preview of the absurd foreign clothing he would have to wear was still another blow. Penny showed him the bundle of fake rupees.

He started to remonstrate. "I don't think . . . ."

"No, no, Humboldt, really, it will be fine. The money will be wrapped. When the session is over, you hand it to them and then leave. We'll be waiting outside in the car and have you away from there right away. I've done this before. It will work, I promise. Trust me." She smiled at him and then had him do his lines once more.

Wardrobe, hair, and makeup, in the person of an abrasive middle-aged woman named Barbie Benson, arrived at a quarter to eleven. The three women stood at the doorway, staring at him. He heard obnoxious phrases such as, "So skinny, he won't fill out his costume," and, "Not much hair is there?" and, "Well, if I fix the makeup even darker . . ."

After that, it was pretty much all a blur, except Penny's final instructions. She exclaimed, kindly, "Humboldt, you've been a real dear about all this. You'll do just fine, and I'll be ever so grateful. Now, be sure to be back here at eleven tonight."

At that moment, Humboldt felt somewhat reassured. However, when driving home, fretting, and more and more alarmed, something else occurred to him. Andrea Anderson and Barbie Benson? What odd sounding names. What if they were aliases? That despised writer, the font of all his troubles, was always giving characters fake names. It was a sure sign of real danger. On the other hand, Penny had said, 'I'll be ever so grateful.'

&&&

That afternoon, in a very different broadcast studio, other preparations were underway. The studios of the Revealed Truth Radio Ministry were actually only a squalid little room in the cramped spaces of Radio Station RCK, a decaying medium-wattage facility located east of downtown. In fact, it was not far from Prior Leather's building. The station's proprietors had welcomed the Ministry's early morning broadcast as it earned them a modest fee, and saved the trouble of airing a taped program of commercials for dubious medicines. For daytime programming the station owners persisted in their belief that an audience still existed for locally produced 1950s rock music, intermingled with weather forecasts.

Having to go through the motions of Sunday services at the Second Church of the Revealed Truth, followed by their usual large noonday meals, Pastors Primus and Secondus had been unable to reach the studio until mid-afternoon. They arrived at about three o'clock, encumbered by a large roll of black cloth, some candles, and a badly scratched glass crystal ball, formerly part of Mrs. Primus's collection of paperweights. They, too, had to prepare for Mr. Nomorpour's visit.

They'd never entertained a person seeking spiritualist advice live in the studio before, as their nursing home listeners, even those who telephoned, were necessarily in their rooms in the small hours of the morning. Primus muttered, "We've got to make the place look authentic. That crazy Mr. Nomorpour probably goes to mediums all the time."

At Secondus's request, Stewie "Snapshot" Tompkins, errant church photographer, met them there. More alert observers than the two elderly pastors would have noticed he was wearing a new shirt and tie and that his leisure suit was freshly cleaned and pressed. They assembled around a dirty wooden table, empty except for two grimy microphones and an out-of-date tape player.

Primus asked, suspiciously, "What's new on your end, Stewie?" He was more and more certain that their troubles at the church were in no way related to takeover attempts by southern radio ministries. Now, he wanted an explanation. However, he overlooked the possibility that the FBI agents had already questioned his consultant.

Stewie Tompkins replied with assurance. "Nothing much as to the church. I told them FBI guys all about the break-ins and explained that it might well just be kids fooling around." Then he grinned in a certain sneering way, a warning familiar to those church officials who questioned his photographic sales tactics. "I just casually mentioned that we didn't really think it was one of them big southern radio outfits. That possibility was news to the FBI boys, but they was real interested."

Tompkins was much more skilled in deceit than either Primus or Secondus, and he had the brothers cornered. The last thing they wanted was Federal attention to their radio show. Stewie's threat was obvious. Any trouble about the money they'd paid him, and their radio ministry would be mentioned again. Primus subsided.

Still under the misimpression that Snapshot might be an experienced spiritualist, Secondus made one more attempt. "Stewie, we've got a big one late tonight. Some rich guy from India is coming here for advice. Maybe, with your experience with the spirits, you could lend a hand?"

Primus glared, but Stewie Tompkins simply shook his head. "Nah. I think this just about does it for this job. I gotta be heading home to my old gal down in Mississippi." He thanked the brothers and immediately left the studio. Knowing something about mail fraud, he also wished to avoid any further contact with the Radio Ministry or the Federal authorities.

He had a second reason for ending his consulting engagement. Given the strain of nights spent waiting in the church and his new and better opportunity, their money was no longer attractive. At his last meeting with Minister Jimmy "Already on the Way" Johnson, of the Rising to the Skies of Love mega church, he'd been introduced to Johnson's nephew, the son of his brother, the deceased real estate developer Jackie "Acres of Happiness" Johnson. This very prosperous young man, Joey "Acres of Success" Johnson, was now starting to manage his late Father's real estate development empire. He would soon need an entire new portfolio of photographs.

It was a relieved Stewie Tompkins, who, having found the disreputable old pastors too much even for him, soon turned his yellow Cadillac onto the southbound interstate.

The old white-haired brothers struggled to prepare the studio, hanging the black cloth on the walls, and arranging the candles and glass ball on the table. Stewie's words of warning bothered them. Secondus said worriedly, "What if the FBI does ask more questions? It makes Mr. Nomorpour's money look even better. It might be our last big chance."

Primus, covering the table with more black cloth and pricking his finger on a thumbtack in the process, only snarled.

&&&

Chapter 22

As ordered, Mr. Humboldt Prior reappeared at Channel Seven at eleven o'clock Sunday evening, this time having replaced the blue suit with more casual attire. It was a dark cloudy summer evening, and threatened still more rain. There were only six or seven cars in the wide parking lot in front of the main building. The huge girders of the television broadcast tower, rising behind the station, were just a blur in the misty night sky. Penny, whose status as a senior weekday newsanchor usually freed her from Sunday night duties, was waiting in the lobby. She was fetchingly dressed all in black, and her bright freckled face welcomed him with a warm smile of greeting.

"Humboldt, its so wonderful to have you here to help me. I can never thank you enough for what you're doing. We're pretty well set for tonight. Let's get started."

For just an instant, he rebelled at the sheer lunacy of the whole affair, but she was already walking quickly toward the far door, and he supposed, as usual, there was nothing to do but follow her.

Literary discretion requires the historian to pass a veil over Humboldt's regrettable experiences of the next hour or so. Little need be said of several more dry runs of his intended appeal for help to his unwitting cousins, the crooked spiritualists Pastors Primus and Secondus, or of his reaction to Andrea's suggestion that he would sound even more peculiar if he tried to make his voice break once or twice. Likewise, his clumsy attempts at learning the correct orientation of the briefcase, so that the hidden camera would to be pointed at the corrupt hosts of the radio ministry, are left to the reader's imagination. He did not show at his best.

Following these preparatory steps, he was passed on to the harsh clutches of makeup specialist Barbie Benson, though he now doubted that was her real name. Again, the details of his embarrassment at disrobing in front of her, his discomfort at pinpricks as his costume was adjusted, his ignored protests at having some sort of smelly brown ointment smeared into what hair he had left, and his shiver of stark horror as he glimpsed his half-made-up face in the mirror, are all matters beyond the scope of this history.

The writer will only say that when, at about mid-night, Mr. Chandra Nomorpour emerged from the secret recesses of the Channel Seven studios, the overall effect was mixed at best. Humboldt first saw the appalling results reflected at him in the glass windows of the lobby. His sole consolation was that he was certain that there was absolutely no possibility of his being recognized.

Beginning from below, they had encased his feet in some peculiar looking slippers of gold and green leather. Men's hosiery had been omitted entirely, but dark brown makeup had been applied to his feet, ankles, and shins. His body was covered, thank goodness, by a loose-woven and baggy white coverall-like affair, apparently manufactured for obese housepainters working in hot weather. Over this, went an equally baggy lightweight high-collared jacket, tan in color, and intended by its tailor for a much larger man. One large inner pocket was stuffed with the counterfeit rupees. His face, except for his eyes and lips, was now colored a very dark grayish brown, as was his hair, thickly coated with a nasty and adhesive brown oily substance, and swept up to anchor a squarish white cap of the type worn by the late Prime Minister Nehru.

Penny Rote and Andrea Anderson, trying not to laugh, followed him closely through the lobby, obviously planning to forestall any further attempts at escape. Andrea had the all-important briefcase. Of course, it was raining again. Penny, always resourceful, immediately sensed the potential for damage to Mr. Nomorpour's makeup and costume.

"Humboldt, we're going to need your umbrella."

He responded in dismay. "I'm afraid it's in my other car." He was driving the nondescript Chevrolet in a final pathetic attempt at anonymity.

Thus, Andrea had to run back into the studio, and, after minutes, emerged carrying an expensive-looking black umbrella that she said she'd taken without permission from the office of Mr. Sidebotham, the news director. Humboldt, now in the nadir of his descent into shame and embarrassment, was secretly glad that now someone else might also be in trouble.

Sheltered by the spacious umbrella, they hurried across the wet parking lot, shoved him into the back seat of his own car, buckled his seatbelt, and set off to make television history. Penny Rote was driving.

&&&

It took them nearly an hour to reach the wretched old building housing Radio Station RCK and the broadcast studio of the Revealed Truth Radio Ministries. Andrea had insisted she knew the way, but only succeeded in embroiling them in a labyrinth of abandoned warehouses and railroad tracks, blocks away from their real destination. Finally, recourse was had to Mr. Nomorpour's local knowledge, and at last, the Chevrolet pulled up in front of the radio station. It was still raining hard.

Humboldt sat frozen in place, but Penny Rote reached back, smiled at him, and patted his arm. Andrea got out of the car, opened the rear door, efficiently started the camera and recorder inside the briefcase, closed and locked it, and handed it to him. She stepped aside, and somehow he found himself climbing out and opening the umbrella, at the same time clutching the incriminating briefcase. He squared Mr. Nomorpour's shoulders, and mechanically putting one foot in front of the other, trudged grumpily across the sidewalk to meet his fate. Now appearing as he did, it seemed as though nothing worse could possibly happen.

&&&

There were no windows facing the deserted street, but the shabby door of the one-story brick building was not locked. He dodged a puddle of rainwater, stepped inside, and found himself in a drab dirty and ill-smelling hallway, the walls of which were plastered with tattered pictures of forgotten rock musicians. Hearing muffled voices behind the door to his right, he knocked on it. The elderly voices stopped, something hard fell to the floor, and there was a mutter of foul language. He therefore assumed his pastor cousins were within.

He pushed the door open and, his nerves on edge, quickly observed several things. Two old men, dressed in faded black clerical garb, were standing at the far side of a rickety wooden table. He had not seen the brothers close up for several years. However, their low foreheads, nearly identical weak faces, prominent chins, shocks of unkempt greasy white hair, and generally dissolute appearance made them instantly recognizable as his elderly cousins, Primus and Secondus. Someone had attempted to drape the walls of the room with a wrinkled black fabric, and two lighted candles supplied most of the feeble illumination. What looked like a crystal ball had been apparently just retrieved from the floor and was still rocking in its place on the black-covered table, next to a pair of microphones.

One of the old men greeted him. "Ah, here is our dear friend and fellow seeker of what is beyond the Great Change. Welcome, Mr. Nomorpour, please enter these sanctified and purified premises."

The other old man impatiently waved him toward a dirty folding chair, placed facing them at the table.

Humboldt never received all the credit he deserved for Mr. Nomorpour's success that night. His first unrecognized contribution was his instant realization that even the best of tiny hidden video cameras require sufficient light to function. Unbelievably, as he thought afterwards, he found himself excitedly waving his umbrella, and yipping in a high singsong chant, "Oh yes, yes, welcome, but not in the dark, please, please. In the dark, men steal from other men. My own honored father said to me, 'Chandra my son, never meet on business in the darkness. Even your guardian serpents cannot help you there'." The gratuitous reference to "serpents" was said without thinking.

Pastor Primus Prior looked chagrinned. The ceiling lights were turned on, and Humboldt had won another of his "small victories."

The three men took their seats at the table and Humboldt placed the briefcase on it next to him, correctly oriented on the first try. Secondus added further words of welcome, and said that they understood that their esteemed fellow seeker, their brother in the spirits, Mr. Nomorpour, wished guidance on an investment decision. Secondus started to say more, but Primus shushed him, saying, "So you wish to hear from your revered parent who has passed on to the other side?"

Mr. Nomorpour then launched into his rehearsed opening remarks, doing them somewhat differently, but nonetheless fully satisfying the elderly radio ministers as to his identity, veracity, and good intentions.

Continuing in a squeaky voice, he entreated them. "Ah yes, most assuredly I, the humble Chandra Nomorpour, am all alone in your favored land, having to encounter clever bankers from whom I seek to obtain necessary funds. Being uninformed in their ways, I know not what to do, and desire guidance." He concluded, again in his high-pitched singsong, "So, so, I seek from your excellent selves just a few words of instruction from my honored father, the great deceased billionaire Chandatra Nomorpour, the mighty founder of Nomorpour Enterprises. I would learn his advice as to the desired purchase of the mines of iron." He hesitated, trying to recall when Penny said to flash the wrapped bundle of counterfeit rupees. Finally, he reached inside his loose jacket, found the money, nervously struggled to pull it out, nearly upsetting the all important briefcase and video camera, and finally placed the package of currency on the table in front of him. Whatever shortcomings the speech may have had were more than offset by the appearance of the cold hard cash.

Primus nodded, muttered something to Secondus, and then closed his eyes preparatory to going into a trance, just as he'd seen done in a 1920s movie he had recently studied. Secondus accompanied this by softly humming a familiar Protestant anthem, spiritual enough in its way, although not absolutely appropriate for the circumstances or the presumed religion of Mr. Nomorpour and his deceased father. Minutes passed. The atmosphere of the small room became oppressive with candle smoke and the odor of pizza coming from somewhere else in the studio building.

At last, the humming stopped, and Primus, in his role as both medium and the "control" so common in 19th century séances, opened his eyes. He coughed and spoke haltingly. "Dear Mr. Nomorpour, we have again succeeded with the spirits. They speak to you from far away, beyond the Great Change, and from far above the serene peaks to the north of your beloved homeland of India." (Primus knew the location of the Himalayas, but as he thought they were called the Andes it is fortunate that he didn't attempt to name them.) He continued in his raspy voice. "From the revered spirits I bring you words of comfort and reassurance." He rose to his feet and pointed his scrawny arm at Mr. Nomorpour, waggled his finger, and went on. "The blessed words of your beloved Father come to you from beyond the grave. You will be firm with the bankers, will obtain more than ample funds, and then will invest as he directed you, withholding only an additional ten percent as an offering to those who aided the spirits in giving this guidance." Feigning exhaustion, he sank back into his chair.

Humboldt was momentarily petrified. Mr. Nomorpour had received no instructions about an additional ten percent commission. However, as a long-service comptroller, he was well accustomed to dealing with such greedy requests from consultants. He said in Mr. Nomorpour's squeaky chant, "Ah, yes, certainly, certainly, yes indeed. I agree to an additional commission, yes, yes, of course." Humboldt was on more familiar ground. He added shrewdly, "Payable only after I purchase the mines of iron."

That seemed to satisfy the medium, for Primus turned to Secundus, and said something about getting the regular taped program on the air. Then he turned back to Mr. Nomorpour, nodded in the direction of the bundle of counterfeit rupees, and then of the door. He said gruffly, "Well, I trust we've been of satisfaction." Then he stopped, looked round, listened, and said sharply, "What's that damn noise?"

Now, Humboldt and Mr. Nomorpour were in real trouble. Suddenly, a scratchy buzzing noise had started coming from the briefcase. It was obviously some failure of the camera or recorder, but only Humboldt was aware of this. Again, although no one else ever knew it, one remembered part of his attempt at preparation to portray an Indian gentleman saved Penny Rote's TV special report.

Incredibly nervous, but somehow inspired, he jumped up quickly. "Ah, yes, yes, my friends," he said hurriedly in his highest lilting voice, "there is your first payment. Now, I perceive without doubt it is the restlessness of my guardian ceremonial cobra, that I always carry at my side." He gestured in the direction of the briefcase.

The two elderly brothers recoiled in alarm.

Mr. Nomorpour went on, excitedly, "He is hungry. I must hasten to attend to his worthy needs." With that he seized the briefcase and the umbrella, said over his shoulder in a particularly high voice, "Men, you have been very good men, now I go," and rushed out of the door. It was still another of his "small victories."

Primus and Secondus each grabbed for the bundle of fake currency. Secondus, being a little younger and spryer got it in his hands first. Primus snarled at him about attending to their regular taped show, seized the money from his distracted brother, and although almost entirely ignorant of counterfeiting or US/Indian currency exchange rates, began to count it.

Outside, the rain had stopped. Mr. Chandra Nomorpour, soon to disappear from this history, emerged hastily from the RCK building, stumbled across the cracked and uneven sidewalk, almost losing one gold and green slipper in the process, opened the back door of the Chevrolet, toppled inside, mumbled, "I think it went mostly okay," and fainted.

&&&

Approximately ninety minutes later, Mr. Humboldt Prior reappeared from the warrens of the Channel Seven studios. He had suffered more nameless indignities at the hands of the merciless makeup specialist, Barbie Benson, but at least was free from almost all vestiges of Mr. Nomorpour. The exception was an unhealthy looking grayness of complexion that persisted for several days. Penny Rote and her producer, Andrea Anderson waited for him in the quiet deserted lobby.

Andrea yawned and exclaimed, "That was great work you did, Humboldt. Our technical guys say the video and audio you got are just perfect for us. Stay tuned to Channel Seven at ten tonight." Then she hurried away, back to her production work.

Penny Rote came closer to him. "Humboldt, my dear friend, you were wonderful. My special report is going to knock their socks off, and do a world of good besides. I still can't figure out whether or not you're an ex-spy, but you sure did the job. Thanks ever so much." With that, she threw her arms around him and planted another kiss on his ex-Indian cheek. She added protectively, "Now drive home carefully and get some rest," squeezed his hand, and also hurried away, back into the maze of offices and technical rooms behind the lobby.

Humboldt drove home, a prey to mixed feelings. His arrival in the Prior communal garage and then at his rowhouse was unobserved as church photographer Snapshot Tompkins was no longer on watch from the church window, and his cousins, Pastors Primus and Secundus, unaware of what was about to befall their corrupt radio ministry, were still at the studio arguing about the bundle of counterfeit rupees.

&&&

With only a few hours sleep Humboldt was surprised at how smoothly his next day moved along. For one thing, it was sunny and cooler, and he enjoyed driving his old Buick to the office, taking another unnecessary detour simply to prolong the trip. At Prior Leather, he found more positive developments. The office manager, Orlo Prior, informed him at once that his cousin, the president Malice Prior, was taking an unplanned and lengthy vacation out of the country. His cousin Moribund was ill, and his cousin Dorset was playing in a golf tournament. The personnel manager, his vile cousin Ribald Prior, seemed fully occupied in preparing the paperwork for another of his attempts at adding a fictitious employee to the payroll, this time named William McKinley. All in all, with his accounts in balance and his troublesome relatives either away or distracted, it looked like and was, a decent day.

More relaxed, he unconsciously slipped back into his former routine of working a full eight hours. In the mid-afternoon, his desk nearly empty, he read a nasty and inflammatory letter from a former employee, complaining about his retirement pay and full of foolish threats of writing his congressperson. The writer was a long-retired Prior and Cousins sales manager, one Legume Prior. As a consequence, Humboldt then spent nearly an hour finding and correcting the error made by the Trust in calculating Legume's pension. The error, if not fixed, seemed likely to impoverish the poor old man.

Thus, Humboldt found himself thinking of retirement income along with tonight's TV exposé and all that might follow. Safe from further forced espionage activities and back in his routine, a belief emerged. It was that suddenly impoverished old men didn't necessarily always say the right things if interviewed under stress, and that other interests could be harmed.

Deciding he had to protect the all-important Prior Trust, necessary for the survival of most of his relatives, he did his best to estimate the minimum time required just for the steps he wanted the Trust's lawyers to take, without any further time to change their minds. Then, allowing only that amount of time, he placed one of his quiet warning calls to the chief accountant. He explained what needed to be done and when. At the end of their conversation, the older man thanked him profusely, saying, "Of course you are right, Humboldt, as you always are. That's the only thing to do. Thank you for saving us again." Humboldt added another quiet suggestion. The chief accountant concurred. "Yes, I agree with that, too. If we're paying them, they'll have to keep quiet. I'll have our attorney write up the letter and the pension agreements and sign them all on your cousins' behalf."

After that, Humboldt drove home, stopping only at the grocery store, cooked himself a simple but ample supper, and sat down in his library to read and wait for the ten o'clock news. He made sure the television was already tuned to Channel Seven.

&&&

Epilog

All in all, as Humboldt considered it afterwards, Penny's special report had been quite satisfactory. She looked tired, but was gorgeously arrayed in a sparkling light blue summer dress. Her sandy hair was newly done, and her charming freckles and stylish legs were on full display. Exhibiting one of the ceramic Bluebirds, supposedly vital for communication with deceased loved ones, Penny's explanation of his cousins' exploitation of vulnerable nursing home residents took the viewers right to the heart of their villainy. Her brief but succinct interview with a certified public accountant concerning their tax reports was most revealing. Most persuasive of all, of course, was the dramatic 'sting' video and audio footage of their effort to defraud the hapless Indian businessman, Chandra Nomorpour, taking advantage of his credulous susceptibility to spiritualism. Thankfully, Mr. Nomorpour appeared in the live video only as a vague indistinct shape, caught as he was positioning the briefcase and hidden camera. The accompanying still photograph of him, apparently taken by the evil Miss Benson while Mr. Nomorpour was gazing down in horror at his gold and green slippers, was totally unrecognizable.

Humboldt watched Penny's expression carefully, as she read the letter of response from the authorities at the Second Church of the Revealed Truth, typed on its old-fashioned letterhead with the address on Emma Woodhouse Avenue. She said it had been only just received, and he guessed she was reading it for the first time. Over the signature of the senior trustee, one Mr. Malice Prior, the letter gratefully acknowledged the valuable information uncovered by the television reporter and her great service to the church. It went on to say that the Revealed Truth Radio Ministry had been terminated effective at once, and that the current ministerial staff of the church would immediately be retired and replaced. Complete refunds would be offered for figurine purchases and donations. Penny Rote paused and a slight frown flashed over her pretty face. Then she continued reading and then said that apparently no interviews would be granted.

Humboldt knew the Trust had signed the letter of behalf of his cousin Malice, who he imagined was now reposing on whatever Caribbean island lacked an extradition treaty with the United States. This fortunate circumstance was a result of the FBI visit, and had greatly assisted in another of his "small victories."

&&&

Now, for the first time, the scene shifts geographically. Heretofore, either for reasons of geographical ignorance or mere local boosterism, this history has been limited to events taking place in City-by-the-River, at various locations not too far from Woodhouse Avenue. Now, however, we move to an internationally prominent and beautifully designed larger city or district in the eastern part of the country. The visitor to this storied location finds on every hand, wide boulevards, majestic monuments, impressive marble and granite buildings, political wisdom, and money.

There, for the past few days, in the great gray building of one of the country's national security agencies, a very powerful computer had been especially busy. Not content with merely receiving and recording investigation reports from all of the special agents, it also had the task of correlating, associating, and linking each of these reports with all possible sources of matching information, internet and otherwise. Some of this so-called 'matching' information was highly accurate and secret, but some was highly public and often erroneous or even fictional, including the works of well-known and little-known writers, foreign and domestic. For the computer, it was sometimes difficult to tell which was which. Therefore, suspected correlations, associations, and links were printed and distributed for their all-important reassessment and validation by trained officials working for various other national security agencies in some of the other aforementioned buildings. One of these was the Central Intelligence Agency. There, upon review of one particular report, a surprising congruence of unusual names was noted, and therefore immediate and decisive action was indicated.

Later, on the day in question, in one particular very famous light-colored columned structure, surrounded by spacious grounds, it was time for the First Trusted Advisor to awaken the Central Figure from his afternoon nap. These naps had become longer of late and the First Trusted Advisor blamed this on certain adverse political trends. There had been few successes to keep the Central Figure awake and enthusiastic.

After a minute or two of gentle reminders of his place in history, the Central Figure stirred. The First Trusted Advisor confirmed certain basic facts, repeating the current time, date, and place, as well as their schedule for the rest of the day. With these basics behind them, the two men moved to an oval shaped seating area, and the Central Figure inquired in his well-known regional twang, "What else is new, Chief Guy."

The First Trusted Advisor despised the use of that nickname, partly because it raised the possibility that the Central Figure didn't recall his real one. However, he simply took the question as permission to invite a third person into the room.

Characteristically, while representing in the Central Figure's mind, one of his most important national security functions, this third person, the Fifth Trusted Advisor, known to the Central Figure as "Buddy Boy," had no long-standing connection with national security. He had been recruited just after the election as a key staff aide to the Central Figure. His hiring had been based primarily on his loyalty and his views on certain social matters of importance to the Central Figure's political party.

The Central Figure boomed, "Hi there, Buddy Boy, you old son-of-a-gun, how ya doin'?"

The Fifth Trusted Advisor respectfully acknowledged this welcome, sat down, and greeted the other man. Then, after some pointless small talk, he continued, speaking in a half-whisper. "There are rumors of a new crisis."

The First Trusted Advisor already knew about this and had summoned the Fifth Trusted Advisor to brief the Central Figure on it.

The Fifth Trusted Advisor continued. "I'm hearing that, as it sometimes does, the Bureau (by 'Bureau' he referred to the FBI or Federal Bureau of Investigation) has busted out of the corral and is trying to lasso and hog-tie a key guy from the Agency." (By 'Agency,' he was referring to the Central Intelligence Agency or CIA.) This type of rumor-mongering was an important part of his job.

Even when just recovering from a nap, the Central Figure could successfully grapple with basic communications such as this. Indeed, he asked for more information. "Damn it, Buddy Boy. What the hell are they doin' it for?"

"Well," the Fifth Trusted Advisor continued, "we're not certain about that. For some reason, they're trying to trump up charges against one of the CIA's senior guys. He's a long service fellow, a real veteran from the black side. Now he's semi-retired somewhere in the Midwest. He really knows where the bodies are buried."

The First Trusted Advisor nodded supportively.

Now confused, the Central Figure hesitated. He wasn't yet fully awake from his afternoon nap and the specifics of inside-the-beltway slang had never been his strong suit. From 'Buddy Boy,' he had received the impression that a distinguished CIA veteran, who had also once been a champion of civil rights, was now the victim of FBI persecution, and was being accused of complicity with murder. That was so typical of this place and so different from when he'd been governor.

Anyway, it was time for a decision. He asked, "Chief Guy, what's our old boy's name?"

The First Trusted Advisor (also known as Chief Guy) looked at the Fifth Trusted Advisor (also known as Buddy Boy).

The Fifth Trusted Advisor consulted a hand-written note that he'd received that morning from someone in a downtown coffee shop. "My confidential source says our man's name is Humboldt Prior. He has quite a record of achievement, a real American hero. He must be protected. We dare not lose him. There are grave national security implications."

An American hero? The Central Figure didn't hesitate. He grinned, and in a more emphatic version of the regional twang, said firmly, "Give our old boy a full damn pardon, one of them real complete pardons. Have it on my desk for signature in half an hour." Smirking, he turned to glance out the window. Decisions like this were fun.

The First and Fifth Trusted Advisors stood up respectfully. The First Trusted Advisor said, "Right away, sir." Because of the ever-increasing volume of their use, he always kept a supply of preprinted pardons close at hand. Once he had selected the correct version and had typed 'Humboldt Prior' into the appropriate blank, the deed was as good as done.

&&&

Humboldt received his copy of the pardon about two weeks later. As he'd never been charged with any crime, he was mildly surprised, but with the eccentricities of the then-current administration, he supposed it probably had something to do with terminating that decades-old Prior Trust tax matter. He therefore consulted his valued old friend, the chief accountant of the Trust. This wise man, in turn, showed the presidential pardon to the Trust's attorney.

The attorney confirmed the pardon, saying, "This document is legitimate, retroactive, current, prospective, and all encompassing. It's as complete a pardon as I've ever heard of. I wonder what in the world it's for?"

The chief accountant nodded. "It's application to Humboldt, of all people, is simply inconceivable." However, when he called Humboldt, he merely said, not wanting to worry his valued associate, "It must be something they're doing to clear their old tax files. Probably it was given to hundreds of other innocent people. I'm sending it back to you. Just keep it with your other old papers."

With this advice, Humboldt had to let the matter drop. That it might relate only to his recent encounter with those misguided FBI agents seemed impossible to believe.

FBI Special Agent William Boat was also extremely puzzled by the pardon. On receiving an information copy, he remarked to Probationary Agents Michael Dinsbury and Clarence Omsworth that he had never seen a more comprehensive pardon, particularly of a person who was only a potential witness. As Humboldt had been the only seemingly believable person they had encountered during the Second Church of the Revealed Truth investigation, he had naturally come under some additional suspicion. Now, however, there was nothing they could do and the case was soon closed.

Humboldt Prior, of course, knew nothing of this action, but the whole matter of the FBI visit was receding from his mind. Anyway, he spent less time brooding on it than might have been the case, because he was very interested in something he was writing. It had occurred to him that between his personal observations, the old papers stored on the third floor of Prior Leather, and the extreme detail of "Building for Truth, Osgood Prior and the Construction of the Second Church," he might be able to write a brief article on the construction for the journal of his local historical society. He'd never tried this before, but now being semi-retired, he had ample time to write.

A few days later, at odd moments, he also considered telling Penny Rote about the pardon. She had called him two or three times since the newscast, once casually asking him, "Are you busy this evening?" Now, he'd be seeing her tomorrow at a private luncheon, hosted by her news director, an individual with the absurd name, as Humboldt recalled it, of Sidebotham. The purpose was to privately commemorate the success of the sting and the resulting television news broadcast of award-winning potential. It would be good to see her again.

However, after more consideration, he thought better of the idea of mentioning the pardon. She still didn't know he had been willing and ready to take sole responsibility for their intrusion of the Second Church of the Revealed Truth. No, the pardon had better remain just another of his "small victories."

End

Made in the USA
Lexington, KY
19 July 2011